Blood and Circuses

Books by Kerry Greenwood

The Phryne Fisher Series

Cocaine Blues

Flying Too High

Murder on the Ballarat Train

Death at Victoria Dock

The Green Mill Murder

Blood and Circuses

Ruddy Gore

Urn Burial

Raisins and Almonds

Death Before Wicket

Away With the Fairies

Murder in Montparnasse

The Castlemaine Murders

Queen of the Flowers

Death by Water

Murder in the Dark

Murder on a Midsummer Night

Dead Man's Chest

The Corinna Chapman Series

Earthly Delights

Heavenly Pleasures

Devil's Food

Trick or Treat

Forbidden Fruit

Short Story Anthology

A Question of Death:
An Illustrated Phryne Fisher Anthology

Blood and Circuses

A Phryne Fisher Mystery

Kerry Greenwood

Poisoned Pen Press

First U.S. Trade Paperback Edition 2008

10 9 8 7 6 5 4 3 2

Library of Congress Catalog Card Number: 2006940850

ISBN: 978-1-59058-520-7 Trade Paperback

Poisoned Pen Press
6962 E. First Ave., Ste. 103
Scottsdale, AZ 85251
www.poisonedpenpress.com
info@poisonedpenpress.com

Printed in the United States of America

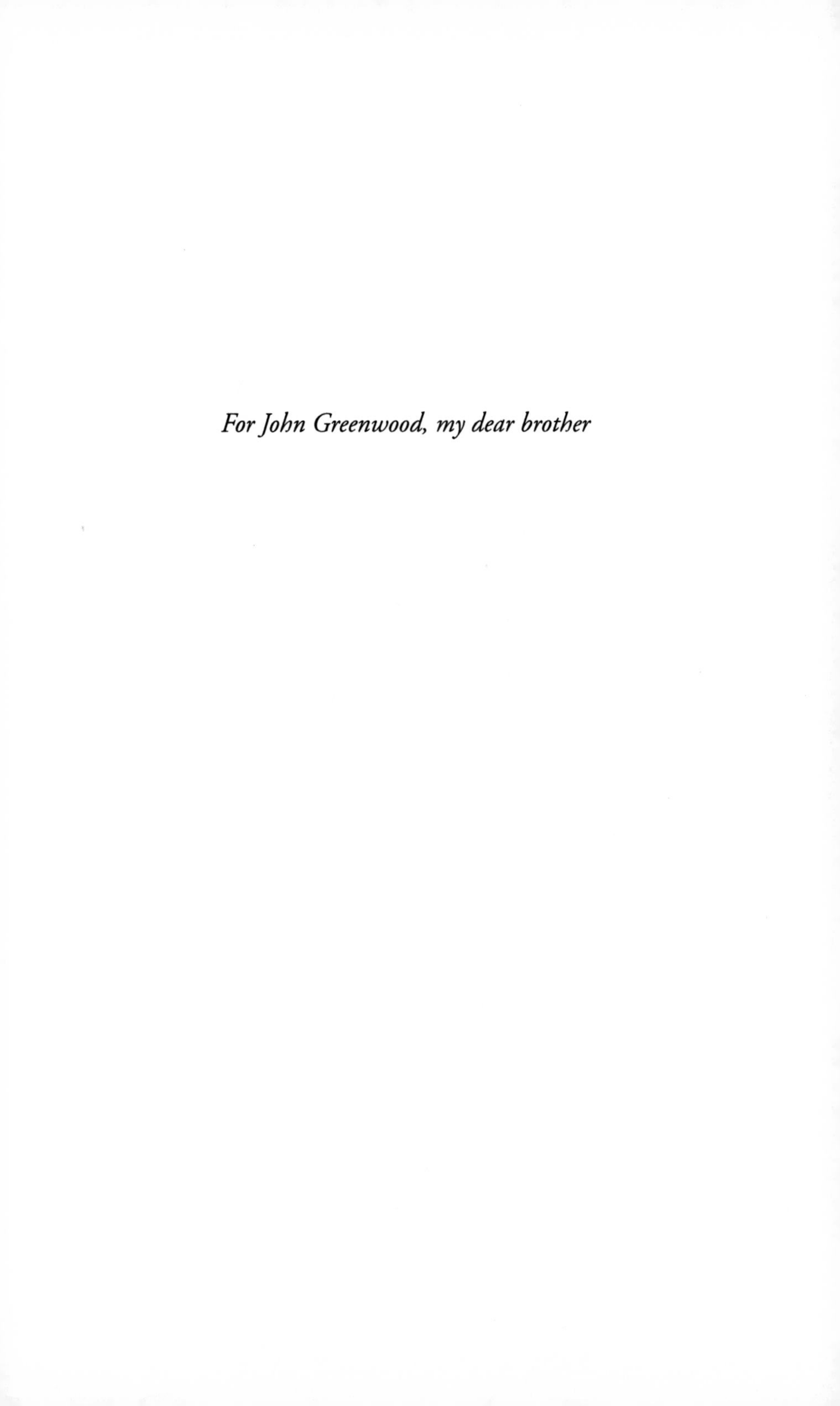

For John Greenwood, my dear brother

'People must be amused, Squire...
they can't always be a-working, nor yet
they can't always be a-learning. Make
the best of us, not the worst.'

—*Hard Times*, Charles Dickens

Acknowledgments

Fervent thanks to David Greagg, Jean Greenwood, Nick Engleman the juggler, Gregory Carter the clown, Jenny Pausacker, Richard Revill, Keryn D'Arcy, Stephen D'Arcy, Roz Greenwood, Ann Dwyer, Meredith Rose, Sophie Cunningham, Simon Barfoot the diva, Judith Rodriguez, Jude Bourguignon, the staff at Footscray Library, the Performing Arts Museum, the Moscow Circus, Circus Oz, Bullen's Circus, and all circuses, carnivals and fairs.

Chapter One

These were a part of a playing I heard
Once, ere my love and my heart were at strife
Love that sings and hath wings as a bird
Balm of the wound and heft of the knife.

The Triumph of Time,
Algernon Swinburne

Mrs. Witherspoon, widow of uncertain years and theatrical background, was taking tea in her refined house for paying gentlefolk in Brunswick Street, Fitzroy. It was four o'clock on a warmish Friday afternoon. The month was October and the year was 1928 and she had no idea, as she reached for the last slice of fruitcake, that the worst moment of her life was a mere minute away.

A drop fell from the ceiling and plopped into her cup. She asked.

'Oh, dear, that Mr. Christopher has let his bath run over again. I've told him and told him about that.'

Mr. Sheridan leapt to his feet, and Mrs. Witherspoon glared at him. 'Not you, Mr. Sheridan, if you please.'

'I'll run up, shall I?' offered Miss Minton, who was behind with her rent until another show should manifest itself and was consequently disposed to be helpful.

'Yes, dear, you do that, but don't open the door, will you? Mr. Christopher is so careless with doors and I won't have no immodesty in my house.' The voice was full, rich as the fruit-cake and perfectly pitched to carry to the back row of the stalls. Miss Minton, who had been a showgirl and dancer since she was seventeen, grinned and went out. They heard her feet clatter on the uncarpeted stairs.

The company consisted of Mrs. Witherspoon, a magician called Robert Sheridan, a character actress whose stage name was Parkes and whose past, it was darkly hinted, would not bear examination, as well as the Miss Minton who had just departed on her mission.

The others were paying close attention to what they could hear of her progress along the corridor to the bathroom.

'I say, Mr. Christopher,' the girl called. 'Hey!' she added. They heard the bathroom door open with its characteristic creak. Mrs. Witherspoon tutted at the behaviour of modern girls and finished her cup of tea, brushing idly at another drop which had fallen on her hair. Miss Parkes hid a smile. Mr. Christopher was slim, moved like a dancer and had dark Valentino hair and finely cut features. Miss Parkes had watched Miss Minton chasing him for weeks; she would not miss an opportunity to corner him in the bath. And there would be a surprise in store for her when she did: a life in the chorus line, thought Miss Parkes, injured the modesty.

The sounds of emptying water that they were expecting never came. Instead, Miss Minton ran back exclaiming, 'He's not there, Mrs. Witherspoon, and he hasn't been there. The bath's as dry as a chip.'

It was only then that they all looked at the ceiling.

A large red stain, like the ace of hearts, was spreading and dripping. No one even thought that it might be red wine. Mrs. Witherspoon put up a shaking hand and wiped her cheek, where another drop had fallen.

Her palm came away stained with blood.

She recalled, with dreadful inner turmoil, that she had finished her cup of tea.

◇◇◇

The arrival of the police was not enough to drag Mrs. Witherspoon out of her place of concealment, so a very discomfited Constable Tommy Harris held a conversation with her through the door.

'Whose room is just overhead?' he asked desperately. A gasping retch was all his reply. Miss Parkes nodded at him and he left the door.

'I can tell you about it. The poor old dear has realized that she's drunk blood in her tea and that's upsetting, wouldn't you agree? The bathroom is upstairs and the adjoining room is Mr. Christopher's. He is a circus performer and he is usually asleep until tea every day, because he performs at night. I've been up and tried his door but it's locked.'

'And who are you, Miss?'

'My name is Amelia Parkes. I'm an actress and I live here.'

The constable eyed her narrowly. She was a middle-aged woman, with cropped brown hair, brown eyes, and the beautiful complexion of those who use greasepaint and seldom see the sun. The constable was new to the area; he was sure that he had seen that face before but he could not remember where. She did not assist him but smiled slightly. The constable thought that she had a really lovely smile.

'Well, Miss, we'd better see about it,' he said. 'Where are the keys?'

'Just wait over there, will you,' Miss Parkes requested politely. 'I'll see if I can get them.'

The constable withdrew to the back doorstep and left Miss Parkes to tap on the door and whisper to the wretched inmate. After a few moments, the door opened a crack and a bunch of keys was thrust out. Miss Parkes took them, murmuring something that the constable did not catch, and then bore them to the back step.

'Here we are. I think we'd better leave her alone. She'll feel better when she's thrown up everything in her stomach, poor old chook.'

The rest of the inhabitants were gathered in a palpitating group in the front hall. None of them liked to go back into the dining room, where a succession of gory drops now defiled the white linen tea-cloth. Constable Harris walked past them and up the stairs, unlocked the relevant door and tried to open it.

It would not budge.

'What's wrong?' Miss Parkes called up and he shouted, 'It's bolted on the inside! Can I get in through a window?'

'Only if you've got a long ladder. There's no balcony on the back.'

'Open up!' yelled Constable Harris in a voice calculated to pierce an alcoholic fog. 'Come on, you in there! This is the police!'

Dead silence was the only reply. Miss Minton whimpered and the magician put an arm around her. She leaned against him gratefully, only to recoil with a little shriek as something moved in his breast-pocket.

'Sorry,' he said, removing a dove with an automatic flourish. Miss Parkes bit her lip. This did not seem to be the moment to laugh. Sheridan's dove fluttered up to perch on the lintel, something Mrs. Witherspoon would never have allowed had she been present. 'There,' said the magician, holding out his arms. Miss Minton replaced herself in his now dove-free embrace and Mr. Sheridan held her close, congratulating himself that his luck was holding, with all the women who did not matter, at least.

'There, there, little girl,' he soothed. 'We're all upset.'

Constable Harris appeared at the head of the stairs and called down to Miss Parkes, 'Can you show me how to get onto the roof?' Miss Parkes left Miss Minton to the wiles of the magician without a qualm and led the way up to the skylight.

'Do be careful,' she urged, as the young man stepped out onto the slate roof.

'It's not safe, you know. Mrs. W was always meaning to have it fixed.'

Constable Harris had the sun-kissed, blue-eyed, milk-fed country look which Miss Parkes had always found most attractive. He grinned at her, showing white teeth.

'I'll be all right, Miss. I'm fit, I do a lot of sport. Can you go down and look after the old lady? I'll need her in shape to answer questions if there's dirty work afoot.'

'And do you think there is?'

Miss Parkes had a direct gaze and Constable Harris liked her, although he was still pestered by her resemblance to someone he had seen. A long while ago. In a paper, perhaps? He said soberly, 'I reckon he's done himself in, Miss. The door's not only locked, it's bolted on the inside. And I don't reckon anyone tried the roof. You'd have heard.'

'Yes. Just the same, Constable, I think I'd rather stay here, in case you need some help.'

'All right, Miss.'

He grinned again and walked carefully down the steep leads to the gutter and along towards Mr. Christopher's room. Lying down on the sun-warmed surface he leaned as far over as he dared. The window was uncurtained and the sun was bright. Moreover the light was on.

What he saw so surprised Constable Harris that he gave a loud yell, lost his grip and began to slither over the edge. He flailed wildly. Just in the nick of time, he was braked and suspended in space by a firm hand gripping the back of his tunic.

Miss Parkes had leapt the ledge and run down the roof with the lightness of a bird. As the constable hung over the edge, gasping, she threw all her weight back to balance him but she was not heavy or strong enough to drag him back.

'Well, this is a pickle, isn't it?' she remarked in the same voice she would have used to a child who had come in dripping with mud. 'What's your name?'

'Tommy.' Harris tried not to look down to the flagstones of the yard, where Mrs. Witherspoon was even now emerging from the water-closet. They were hard stones, unyielding. He tried not to think of what he would look like after he had met them from this height. Head first. The grip which was holding him did not slacken and the voice was as smooth as milk.

'Tommy, you will have to save yourself. I'm not strong enough to drag you up by main force. And if you struggle you'll send us both over. Do you understand?'

'Yes!'

'Now, you will reach back with your right hand. Like that—yes, slowly, don't make a sudden move. Don't look down. Look straight ahead. Another six inches and you will do it. Good. That's the gutter. Have you got a good grip?'

Tommy Harris had a grip on the gutter which would deform steel. The rim cut into his hand and he clutched tighter.

'Right-ho.'

'Good. Now, reach back with the other hand, *slowly*. I'm trying to support your whole weight, you know! You're touching the gutter now. Have you got it?'

His left hand found the metal and clung with simian strength.

'Good. Now I am going to let go and get back into the skylight.'

He made an inarticulate cry which might have been, 'No,' choked and called, 'Don't let go of me!'

'I am going to let go and you are going to lie still and cling. Keep your arms straight and you can't fall. I will get your feet and drag you inside.' The voice was cool and held great authority. Some of her calm was creeping into his mind. He took a deep breath.

'Good. You're brave, Tommy my lad. I'll count three, then all you have to do is hang on like fury and I can bring you safely inside. All right?'

He nodded. His mouth had dried to the consistency of coal.

'One, two, three.' Her grip relaxed, very carefully, and he heard her scramble back inside. For what seemed like endless ages he clung to the gutter. Then two hands closed on his ankles like pincers and he was dragged slowly and inexorably up the roof.

'Let go now, Tommy. I've got half of you and I'm not going to let the rest fall,' he heard her say and he struggled to believe in her enough to be able to let go. The drag on his knees and thighs grew stronger.

'Let go, Tommy,' she coaxed. He tried to unlatch his hands and couldn't.

Above and behind him, he heard Miss Parkes sigh.

'Let go at once!' she yelled and hauled with all her force. Constable Harris was inside the window and collapsing into Miss Parkes' arms before he knew what had happened.

'There,' she said, setting him on his feet and dusting down his tunic. 'That was very brave. You don't have any head for heights, do you?'

'And you do.' He gazed at her, open-mouthed and rumpled. 'You're…I know where I've seen you before!'

Miss Parkes stepped away from his touch as though she might contaminate him, her face blank with what looked like pain.

'Yes, you must have seen me at the trial,' she said sadly. 'I thought that you were too young.'

'When did they let you out, Miss Parkes?' he asked, suddenly awkward and faltering. 'I mean, yes, I remember the papers. They had a field day with the murder of your…'

'My husband,' she said in a remote, cold voice. The brown eyes which had looked on him almost with love, certainly with regard and compassion, were now as cold and hard as pebbles. 'I was released from prison last year and I have been acting in some small roles. I am presently understudying Juliet's nurse.'

'But you were a trapeze artiste; the Flying Fantoccini, that was the name.'

Constable Harris, suddenly aware that he had hurt his rescuer deeply and unfairly, was dissolved in confusion. He took her hand, feeling the callouses, noticing now her light, easy stance and the strength of her arms.

'I don't care about that old case,' he said, blushing pink. 'Thank you, Miss Parkes. You saved my life.'

She returned the pressure of the hand slightly and then released herself. 'What did you see through the window that sent you off the roof?' she asked to change the subject. 'Is Mr. Christopher there?'

'He's there,' said Constable Harris, recalled to duty. 'Oh, he's there all right. Excuse me, Miss Parkes. I gotta call the station. There's a nasty mess in there and it's gotta be cleared away.'

Detective Inspector John—'Call me Jack, everyone does'—Robinson arrived at the boarding house in Brunswick Street in a police vehicle which had seen better years, thus dead-heating the small and fussy police surgeon. Doctor Johnson had been called out from a golf game at the eleventh hole. He had been playing for the captain's medal and exhibited the expected chagrin of a man who had been forced to abandon a two-stroke lead and a chance of being stood drinks by the club's most notorious miser.

'Well, what have you got for me?' he snapped.

Jack Robinson shrugged. 'I know as much about it as you do, Doctor. Sergeant Grossmith is in charge. Ah, here he is,' said Robinson with relief, as the small doctor swelled with wrath. 'Hello, Terry, what's afoot?'

Sergeant Terence Grossmith was huge. His expanse of blue tunic was as wide as a tent. He had thinning brown hair and large, limpid brown eyes, which seemed to hold an expression of such placid benevolence that hardened criminals had occasionally found themselves confessing to him out of a sense of sheer incongruity. His local knowledge was legendary. He had been born and raised in Brunswick Street and he knew every respectable tradesman, greengrocer, tinsmith, landlady and thief; every small-time crim and shill and lady of light repute in the place; every corner, hidey-hole, sly-grog shop and repository for stolen goods in the length of that notorious street. He loved the place. He had never sought promotion, because it would take him away from it.

Robinson liked Grossmith. Usually he knew not only who had done the crime but where they lived and whose brother they were by the time the detective inspector arrived. Now, however, this paragon among sergeants seemed puzzled. He was rubbing a hamlike hand through his sparse hair and frowning.

'Funny case, sir, and funny people,' he said dubiously. 'I don't know what to think.'

'But it's murder?'

'Oh, yes, sir, it's murder all right. Sure as eggs. This way, Doctor. The boys will have had the door down by now.'

'Why your benighted department can't wait to call me out until they've got a real corpse I don't know.' The doctor's voice sizzled with outrage. 'If you can't open the door how do you know there's a murder? Have you dragged me away on a Sunday from a very good golf match because of something that someone saw through a keyhole?'

The sergeant looked down on the tubby doctor from his six-foot height and said calmly, 'No, sir, my man looked through the window and perishingly near fell off the roof. The door's bolted on the inside, but it's murder all right. There's blood leaking through the ceiling of the room below. And the constable said that the room is a mess. Ah,' he added, as a crash and splinter from above offended the Sunday quiet. 'There we are. This way, Doctor. Sir.'

Doctor Johnson stalked up the steps and into a hallway festooned with theatrical posters, then took the stairs beyond, following the large figure of Sergeant Grossmith. Robinson walked behind. As always at the start of a case, he felt downhearted and tired. There was so much evil in the world. 'O cursed spite! That ever I was born to set it right,' he quoted to himself. The Mechanics' Institute English literature classes which his wife had taken him to, much against his will, had been very useful. A man could always rely on Shakespeare to hit the nail on the head. Robinson wondered how he had done without him.

He came into a clean corridor lined with coconut matting. The door of the third room on the left was broken and two panting constables were pulling the wreckage away. It had been a good stout door, Robinson observed as he paused at the threshold. Not this modern flimsy stuff, but the solid carpentry of last century, which held that a door was not a door unless it weighed half a ton and was wood all through. He observed the shattered remains of an iron bolt, which had resisted the efforts of two constables and a crowbar for ten minutes. Evidently the murdered man had valued his privacy.

The room was lofty, though small. It had been calcimined light blue, the ceiling a dingy shade of cream. There were water spots where the roof had leaked and stained the plaster, but otherwise the fabric seemed in good condition. The floor was uncarpeted except for a square in the middle. Blood had spurted onto the walls but most of it was pooled on the floor beside the bed, whence it had dripped down through the cracks to spill into Mrs. Witherspoon's tea. Robinson hated the smell of blood. 'Who would have thought the old man had so much blood in him?' thought Robinson, with Shakespeare.

There was a wardrobe, a dressing-table laden with cosmetics, a chair with a gentleman's dressing-gown laid over it, and a large trunk with CHRIS/CROSS painted on it in gold and black. The walls were decorated with two small prints of English landscapes and an oil sketch of a beautiful girl riding a white horse.

Jack Robinson became aware that he was surveying the room so as to avoid looking at the body. He had never been able to cultivate a taste for corpses.

'Hi!' the police surgeon summoned him. 'Come and look here, Robinson! This is supposed to be a man's room, isn't it? And the occupant a man? Well, I can tell you one thing. The person in this bed is certainly dead. Stabbed through the heart, I'd say. But this corpse isn't a male.'

He peeled back a blood-soaked blanket and revealed the chest of the corpse. Under gentlemen's pyjamas were small but perfectly formed breasts.

Chapter Two

There is a tide in the affairs of women
That, taken at the flood, leads—God knows
where.

Don Juan, Canto 6,
George Gordon, Lord Byron

Phryne Fisher was lazily contemplating Sunday from a horizontal position. She thought about rising from her green sheets and doing something energetic, like swimming or a brisk walk along the foreshore at St. Kilda. She thought about it again and snuggled back into her pillow.

She was bored. Her favourite, Lindsay, was doing law exams which he really should pass this year and was locked in his own rooms with a torts textbook, subsisting on black coffee and panic. Her adopted daughters were still at school. Her communist friends Bert and Cec were involved in the strike on the waterfront. Bunji Ross the aeroplane pilot was away with a flying circus and there was no pretty young man in the offing. There seemed to be no reason to get up and go through the process of being dressed when there was no one she wanted to see and nothing she wanted to do.

It was five o'clock and she had done nothing whatsoever all day; however, she was hungry. She sat up, smoothed her perfectly black, perfectly straight hair and went to take a cold shower.

'Dot!' she called. 'Drat!' she added, remembering that Dot would be in church.

Thoroughly put out, Phryne showered, dressed in a light cotton dress and sandals and went downstairs to find out if there was any chance of a late lunch or an early dinner. Awaiting her was a table laid with a cold collation and a note pinned to the muslin netting which protected the food from flies.

Dear Miss Fisher,

Mr. B and I have gone to my niece's wedding, as we arranged last week. We'll be home before midnight.

Mrs. Butler

Phryne whisked off the cloth and a wineglass, caught by the edge, toppled and crashed to the floor. It was one of a set which she had brought from Venice, with a delicate green twisted stem. Irreplaceable.

Phryne swore, which made her feel better. She went to the broom cupboard, found a pan and brush and flung the fragments into the rubbish bin. She fetched a kitchen glass.

'I shall sit down and have some salad and then I shall go for a walk,' she said aloud. 'I am completely out of sorts today and not fit for human company, even if there was some. Which there isn't.'

A touch on her knee made her jump. On inspection it proved to be the black cat, Ember, politely intimating that he would like some ham too.

Phryne was glad to see him and offered him ham in strips, so that he had to take it from her hand. He did, with a delicacy which enchanted Phryne, allowing her to stroke his smooth black back and to lift his chin to look into his leaf-green eyes. After tolerating her handling for a while, he turned away to begin washing. Phryne watched him as she ate the rest of the ham and some cheese. He polished each paw with precise licks, then rubbed them alternately over the opposite ear.

Phryne had poured herself a glass of dry white wine and was engrossed in watching Ember's ablutions when he stood up, pricked his ears and gave the hallway a sharp glance. Then he rose and walked to the kitchen door. The audience was over.

The doorbell rang.

Phryne waited for a moment before she remembered that there was no one else in the house. She put down her glass and went into the hall. It was evidently going to be a trying day.

When she swung the door back, she was confronted with a mountain of clothed flesh. Peering around it was a woman with red hair and a snake about her neck; behind her was a dark and beautiful male face. Phryne sighted upwards and said joyfully, 'Samson! Come in, but look out for that lintel, it's a bit low. And Doreen and Alan Lee. My dears, how very lovely to see you.'

Samson came into Phryne's hall, which had never seemed tiny before. Alan Lee and the woman with the snake followed. They stood in a huddle, overawed by luxury, until Phryne drove them into the parlour like a farm-wife mustering chickens and sat them down. Only the sofa was big enough for Samson and it creaked as he settled himself.

'This is a lovely house,' sighed Doreen, unwinding her snake and allowing him to drop to the carpet. 'Look at all them soft curtains and the paintings and all that blue and green. Feels like it's under the sea.' She stared at a painting, a full-length nude called *La Source*, and then glanced at Phryne. There was no doubt about the model.

'What would you like to drink?' asked Phryne. 'I've got beer and wine.'

'I'll make a cuppa,' said Doreen. 'What about you fellers?'

'Wine,' said Alan Lee. 'If you please.'

'I'll have a drop of beer,' said the strong man.

Doreen went off to the kitchen, where Phryne heard the kettle clang onto the stove and the pop of the gas. She supplied Samson with a bottle of beer and gave Alan Lee her own glass of wine. She had once spent the night with him, in a caravan when the carnival had camped on Williamstown Road, and she had pleasant memories of the encounter. She had also solved a small problem in detection for him, foiling an attempt to frame his sister for theft. She smiled at him and Samson impartially, pleased to see some people. Phryne did not like to be alone.

'Well,' she said, when Doreen had returned with her tea. 'What brings you here, friends?'

'We been following Farrell's,' said Alan Lee in his husky voice. 'I've still got the carousel and Anna has the shooting gallery. Anna'd be here but she's sick. Everyone else gets morning sickness. Anna gets sick in the afternoons.'

'Oh?' Phryne did not want to comment. Anna Lee had been unmarried when they had last met.

'She's my wife,' said Samson proudly. 'And she's expecting.'

'Congratulations, Samson dear.'

'Anyway. We've been trailing Farrell's for six months. Good show, usually. You might have seen the ads in the paper—it's Farrell's Circus and Wild Beast Show. Old man Farrell runs it, he got it from his dad and his dad's dad before him. Farrells have always been circus people. And the carnival, it goes along with the circus, sets up outside, with the booths and the sideshows. We don't take any custom away from the big top, we just share the audience. We need the circus and the circus needs us.'

Alan Lee drained his glass and set it down and Phryne refilled it. The dark face was shadowed, the mobile mouth tight. He's worried, Phryne thought.

'But something's wrong,' he said, confirming her guess. 'Things are going very wrong for Farrell's.'

'What sort of things?'

'Lots of 'em. Bad luck happens, you know, and you can have a run of it. But Farrell's is like it's under a curse.'

Alan Lee passed one long hand over his brow. Half-gypsy as he was, a belief in curses was just under the rational surface of his mind. Phryne took his hand. It was calloused and hard and the fingers gripped with surprising strength.

'Listen,' he said. 'They had a real bonzer trick pony, Socks was his name. Could do everything but talk. I never seen a neddie like him. He could dance and leap and Miss Younger could do anything with him. Well, two months ago Socks is found dead in his spot in the horse lines. No one seen near him. All the others chipper. But Socks dead; poisoned, they say, with eating some weed. Maybe yew, that's enough to kill a grown beast.'

'Unlucky,' said Phryne. The hand squeezed hers hard enough to hurt.

'No. That's just the beginning. We been following Farrell's all the time. They came into town last week and it's been bad luck all along. Socks dying was just the first thing. Then the tightrope broke. Luckily it was under a newie and they had him on a governor.'

'What's a governor?'

'A kind of harness with a line rigged up to the flies so that he can't fall. To the ground, I mean. They say that the line was old and it frayed against a block. But I know that Sam Farrell had all them lines renewed before we started travelling in August. It's been like that all along the coast. It was Geelong, wasn't it, Doreen, that we had the fire?'

Doreen shook her head, flicking back her startling red hair. Her snake reposed in comfortable loops around her, with its flat scaly head on her feet.

'No, the first one was at Little River. That was in the men's tent; they said it was someone's fag end. Geelong was the second, started in some cotton waste near the carousel.'

'And if I hadn't been on the lookout, I would've lost my living,' said Alan. 'It was only a small fire but it made a lot of smoke. Scared off a lot of punters. I didn't see who started it but it was done on purpose. I don't leave fuel anywhere near the merry-go-round. It's stored under my caravan. And I could smell it. Petrol.'

'What then?' Phryne got up and handed Samson another bottle of beer. The first had vanished without touching the sides.

'Then there was me,' said Samson. 'I'm strong, I am.' He rippled a few muscles in his massive forearms complacently. 'So

I don't have much trouble from the boys in them small towns. They sorta stay away from me. But five of 'em set on me in the street, after dark. And they had knives. Hayseeds don't carry shivs. I never seen such a thing. If Al hadn't seen 'em and come running, they woulda killed me.' He opened his shirt to reveal a long, healed gash which sliced up from his chest to his upper arm. It had been aimed at his heart. 'And they cut Al up, too. They weren't no hayseeds out to pick me. They was,' he pronounced the word carefully, 'assassins.'

Alan Lee turned over the hand which was holding Phryne's and she traced the slash on the back. It had left a white scar three inches long, having been done with a very sharp knife.

'A souvenir of Colac,' he said with a mirthless smile. 'That same night a gang attacked Farrell's head rigger and sank the boot into him. He had eight broken ribs and he's still in hospital. And riggers are the most important men in a circus. Everyone depends on 'em.'

'It's been niggle, niggle, all the way,' observed Doreen. 'Sit still, Joe, you silly snake. Little things—like bookings cancelled and animals taking sick and audiences falling off. One of them things, or two, you could expect. But not all of them. So Farrell's is in trouble. Old man Farrell is worried. It's not a big show, like Wirths, that can work over the winter in the Olympia. Farrell has to clear enough in the season to pay for the winter camp, and there's the vet's bills and the food for the stock and all that. We thought that we'd get back to Melbourne and then hook up to another show—a lot of carnies have done that already, they say it's jinxed. But I like Farrell's. So I went to Mama Rosa.'

Alan Lee stared at Doreen. 'You went to the gypsies?' he asked incredulously. 'But you don't believe all that fortune-telling stuff, Doreen? It's all made up.' He turned Phryne's hand over and intoned in a falsetto, 'You will take a long journey over water and meet a dark-haired man and you will marry and have ten children and be very happy. It's all rubbish, Doreen! It's superstition.'

Phryne recovered her hand, while Doreen blushed with rage.

'Well, I just thought I would. She's been right for me before. She told me that Mum was going to marry and leave me the snakes and the Princess of the Amazon lark. She told me I'd be a princess. You just put a sock in it, Alan. You ain't never forgiven your mum for being a gypsy. And if I want to go to the fortune-teller, what's it to you?'

Joe, the massive python whom she had named after Stalin, lifted his head off Doreen's feet and raised his body three feet into the air, flicking his tongue. Alan Lee did not pursue the matter. Phryne reflected that it was never wise to quarrel with a woman with that shade of hair and ten feet of well-trained constricting snake at her disposal.

Doreen stroked the snake and continued, 'She did a reading of the cards for me—the real cards, not the patter about the King of Spades being a tall dark man. I know the difference! She was worried, too, or she'd never have let me see 'em. They're real old, with pictures on 'em. She drew the Eight of Wands, reversed...'

'So?' Alan Lee poured a third glass of wine and Phryne noticed that his hands were trembling. He evidently knew what that card meant.

'So she said it wasn't a curse or fate or anything, but a secret and malicious enemy. She said that the gypsies were worried about Farrell's as well and were thinking of leaving but there wasn't another show to trail. She told me that this enemy was a man, tall and with white hair, and that I'd see him within three days. She also said that there would be more blood within two weeks but not at the circus. So, two days later, I meet the new partner of Sam Farrell's show. His name is Mr. Jones and he's tall and has white hair. And just now we went to see Mr. Christopher and he's dead. Stabbed to death in his boarding house in Brunswick Street. So we come to you.'

'But why me?' asked Phryne, confused. Samson snorted.

'Women always get things hind-end before. That old woman, Miss, she said that the problems would all be solved if we went to see a woman with black hair and green eyes whose name began with an F. You're the only lady we know who matches.' He sat back and beamed at her with perfect faith.

'I think,' said Phryne, at a loss, 'I think that we had better all have something to eat.'

Detective Inspector Robinson surveyed the corpse. The woman was lying on her back with her head on a rolled pillow, staring straight up. He saw that the eyes were blue and he closed them. They sprang wide again.

'Rigor is not present,' said the surgeon, feeling the neck and well-turned jaw, which were as soft as putty. 'Cause of death is exsanguination from a massive stab-wound.' He probed gently. 'Yes, right through the heart, I would say, and it might have cut the rib. Corpse must have been pulled about a bit while dying, or just after death, probably to get the knife out. That's why there's so much blood. Arteries spurt, you know.' Robinson gulped. 'You are looking for a big, heavy knife, Robinson, at least seven inches long, double edged and about an inch wide. I'll be able to tell you more later.'

'Time of death?'

'Can't tell, it's warm in here. Maybe two hours. Could be longer, perhaps as long as ten. Considering the weather, you know. This morning, after dawn, I'd guess. It's six o'clock now.'

Robinson scanned the face, trying to avoid the gaze of the eyes. She had been quite tall, slim, with manicured hands. Her hair was cropped short and there was an odd, oily glaze on the skin. He touched the cold cheek and sniffed. Cold cream. At least the beautifully formed face bore no expression but faint surprise. The faces that had died hard still grimaced in Robinson's sleep.

Constable Harris, who had searched the floor, carefully avoiding the pool of drying blood, produced his findings. A small bottle which had contained a proprietary sleeping drug, now empty, two crumpled handkerchiefs, a sleeve link, two buttons, a torn strip of flimsy paper with a little blood on the edge, a stick of kohl, and a small notebook covered in red suede.

'That paper might have been used to wrap the knife,' observed Robinson. 'Nothing else? No? In that case, Sergeant Grossmith, you'll want to start searching for the murder weapon. You heard the description, Terry?'

Sergeant Grossmith nodded. He left, taking the second constable with him. Robinson returned to the corpse. The wound which had killed her was terrible. The little doctor was rendered almost pleasant in the face of such sudden death. 'She can't have felt a thing,' he murmured. The blue eyes in the wax doll's face stared Robinson out of countenance.

Constable Tommy Harris had opened the wardrobe and was examining the garments. He called to Robinson, who left the dead woman thankfully.

'Yes, what is it?'

'There must have been two people living in this room, sir. Look. Gents' trousers and suits and ties and shoes. And ladies' clothes and er...garments and shoes, too.'

The constable blushed a little and Robinson grinned. He laid a pair of trousers over his arm and measured them against a close-fitting dress.

'I think it's stranger than that, son. I haven't seen you before. What's your name?'

'Constable Harris, sir.'

'Who lives in the house and where are they?'

'Sir, the landlady Mrs. Witherspoon, she was took sick and she's lying down. A showgirl called Miss Minton, she's with the old lady. A bloke who's a stage magician—Sheridan is his real name—he's downstairs in the parlour. And a lady called Miss Parkes who's an actress is there too, and my partner's with them. Sir.'

'Good. And what's all this about the roof?'

'Er...I wanted to make sure that it wasn't just someone oversleeping, sir, so I climbed out on the roof and it was steeper than I thought and real slippery. When I saw him—I mean her—lying all bloody, I lost balance and Miss Parkes ran out onto the roof and got me back. She's as light as a cat on them glassy leads.'

'I see. Unusual skill for an actress.'

Robinson eyed the uncomfortable Harris. There was something that he was not telling his superior in rank. Finally Tommy Harris said reluctantly, 'I recognized her, sir. She's the woman who killed her husband in the circus, ten years ago. Her name was…'

'Oh, indeed. Mrs. Fantoccini. So they let her out, did they? I remember that case. Her husband beat her and was unfaithful and stole her earnings and gambled them. Nasty. Then he suggested that she supplement their income in an unacceptable way. No wonder she greased his trapeze. I went to see her when the kids were young. She was as graceful as a bird, used to do somersaults in the air. Hmm. And she had no difficulty walking that very dangerous roof?'

'No, sir.'

Robinson replaced the garments and went to examine the window. It was open.

'Was the window open when you looked in?' he asked.

'Yes, sir.'

'No dust on the sill. Mrs. W keeps a clean house. Pity. Not a smear. No sign that something has come in. Or someone. Doctor?'

'Yes, what is it?'

'Could a woman have struck that blow?'

The little doctor pushed his glasses up onto his forehead and stared. 'She'd have to be a pretty unusual woman. That blow would have felled an ox.'

'Ah, but the woman I have in mind is unusual,' said Detective Inspector Robinson. 'Come on, Constable. I want to meet Miss Parkes.'

He left the police surgeon filling out his certificate and walked down the corridor, with Constable Harris plucking at his sleeve. At the head of the stairs he turned.

'Well, Constable?'

'Sir…Miss Parkes…'

'Yes, what about her?'

'Sir, she saved my life.'

'Yes,' said Detective Inspector Robinson and went down the stairs. 'So she did.'

In the drinking pit called the Blue Diamond, further down Brunswick Street, Mr. Albert Ellis was taking a dim view of certain political developments. His employees were nervous. Hell's foundations were prone to quiver when the boss of the Fitzroy Boys took a dim view of a situation.

Mr. Ellis was small, dark and dressed in a navy suit. His distinguishing feature, according to the criminal history sheet kept by Sergeant Grossmith, was teeth like a rat. He was acutely aware of these intrusive dental adornments, so he never smiled.

Wholesale Louis, the trader in dubious goods, looked at the Mad Pole, whose name was Janucz and who could bend sheet metal in his hands. The Mad Pole looked at Mr. Ellis, as it was no use expecting sense from his bench mate Cyclone Freddy. It was well known that since Freddy had wound up his career as a tent fighter by king-hitting the local constable into next week, he had not been as acute as formerly, which was not very acute anyway. He was also prone to take offence if anyone looked at him. No sensible man wanted to cause Cyclone Freddy to take offence.

'What's the problem, Boss?' asked Louis.

'It's like this. The Brunnies have been moving into our territory. They pulled that payroll robbery at the shoe factory. I just got word from a dog about it. It was Jack Black Blake's boys. They got inside information from that bitch Pretty Iris.' Wholesale Louis nodded. The others sat waiting to be told what to do. Albert Ellis aimed and fired at his men like a sniper. 'We can't have that. Can we?' He raised his eyes. 'Well, can we?'

'No, Boss,' said Wholesale Louis, and the others echoed him. 'But,' added Louis, 'we're short-handed with Jonesy gone into the bush on that job. When you expecting him back, Boss?'

'When the job's done. Might be a couple of months. That don't matter, Louis. We can handle the Brunnies one-handed. Something will have to be done,' said Mr. Ellis slowly. 'I got an idea. Is Lizard Elsie still in the front room?'

Chapter Three

And I the aged, where go I
A winter-frozen bee, a slave
Death-shapen as the stones that lie
Hewn on a dead man's grave:

The Trojan Women, Euripides
(translated by Gilbert Murray)

Miss Amelia Parkes and Mr. Robert Sheridan were sitting uncomfortably on the edge of the horsehair sofa in Mrs. Witherspoon's plush parlour. The magician was practising passes. The constable left to watch the pair was fascinated by the way an ordinary coin flickered and vanished in his long fingers. The room smelt of fatigue. Miss Parkes had composed herself, feet together, back straight, eyes fixed on the door. Mr. Sheridan muttered, 'Oops-a-daisy,' and produced an egg from the constable's ear.

The magician was suitably tall and dark, with an oval face and the beginnings of a double chin. His hair was as black as stove-polish and he had dark brown eyes. His skin was pale, his hands long and fine, and his whole person neat and stylish. Even with the stress of murder and his own apparent grief, he was, Miss Parkes reflected disagreeably, as crisp as though he were straight out of his box. She herself was conscious that her sojourn on the roof had not improved her stockings and that her hair was standing on end. She was also cringingly afraid to her soul of the law and the police. Even the cool, official tone of the detective inspector's voice outside the door flooded her system with terror, so that she thought she might faint. She shivered.

'I say, Miss Parkes, are you all right?' asked Mr. Sheridan.

'No, I'm not all right,' she snapped. 'There's been a murder in the house. That can really ruin a nice peaceful Sunday. And I liked Mr. Christopher.'

'No need to bite a chap's head off,' he said, hurt. 'You know how long I have loved her. I'm all jittery with the thought that she's dead…my beautiful Christine. I even muffed that simple pass. My hands are shaking. I wonder how long they're going to keep us here?'

'Until they are ready to talk to us.'

'You look white as a sheet. Would you like to lie down?'

'No. I'm quite all right, Mr. Sheridan.'

'You don't look it,' he said. 'You sure that you…?'

'For God's sake, man, leave me alone!' Her voice rose to a dangerous pitch and Mr. Sheridan moved from beside her to a chair near the door. He was frightened of hysterical women. Miss Parkes' eyes were glittering and her hands were clutching at the arms of the sofa.

The constable standing by the door said soothingly, 'Not long now, Miss, I can hear them coming down the stairs. Then I can get that half-witted girl to make you some tea.'

'Who is the officer in charge?'

'Detective Inspector Robinson, Miss.'

The name evidently meant nothing to Miss Parkes. She clutched even harder at the sofa and said, 'What are they doing, Constable?'

'Searching the house, Miss. Looking for the murder weapon.'

'Weapon?' she asked through lips that seemed to be numb.

'Yes, Miss. The knife.'

'I see.'

Footsteps sounded in the hall and the door opened. Tommy Harris looked in.

'Mr. Sheridan, the detective inspector would like to see you now,' he said. 'Hello, Miss Parkes. I've brought you a cuppa.'

The attending constable accompanied Mr. Sheridan out of the room. Constable Harris gave Miss Parkes a cup of strong, sweet tea and said, 'You drink that, Miss, and you'll feel better.'

Miss Parkes, who had learned to be obedient to authority, drank the scalding tea and began to feel better, as ordered.

The magician was ushered into the presence of an affable policeman. He had brown hair, brown eyes and utterly undistinguished features, but his voice was deep and pleasant.

'Mr. Robert Sheridan, is it? Sit down, sir, we won't keep you long. Now, you're the only man in the house and so we have to ask you to do something unpleasant. I hope you'll help us.'

'Yes?' asked Sheridan.

'We understood that the occupant of the room was a male person but it seems that the corpse is a woman. We want an identification. Can you do that for us?'

'Yes,' said Sheridan, 'but…'

'But?'

'I don't think that you understand about Christine,' said Sheridan slowly. 'She was…he was…one of them that is born wrong. Born both, if you see what I mean. Christine and Christopher as well. Nothing for her to do but join the circus.'

'You mean that the woman was a man?' asked Grossmith incredulously. Robinson smiled.

Mr. Sheridan protested. 'She was so beautiful, I can't believe she's dead. She wouldn't ever look at me, of course. She had the best attributes of both sexes. But she was a freak,' he said flatly.

'And Mrs. Witherspoon knew about him? I mean, her?'

'Of course. Christine worked for Farrell's Circus. She had a turn, half-man and half-woman, you know.'

'Androgyne,' said Robinson. 'I've heard of it.'

'She wasn't an "it",' protested the magician. 'She was the most beautiful woman I have ever seen. I loved her and I don't care who knows it and you can keep your sneers to yourself, you stupid cop!'

Terence Grossmith snorted. 'He was a freak, as you said. Someone did him a favour, killing him.'

Mr. Sheridan howled and lunged for Grossmith's throat, who subdued him without difficulty and sat him down on the chair. The magician muffled his face in a silk handkerchief out of which another dove fluttered. Detective Inspector Robinson turned on his colleague a glare of such actinic brilliance that he subsided with a muttered apology.

'Calm down, Mr. Sheridan,' said Robinson. 'Now, tell me about yourself. You work for Farrell's Circus?'

'I am a stage magician,' said Mr. Sheridan loftily, putting his handkerchief back in his sleeve with an automatic flourish. 'I have worked for all the big circuses. Sole Brothers. Wirths. But they were unappreciative of my talents. So I condescended to join Farrell's. Farrell's is not what I am used to, but some experience in these smaller shows can give a magician a new freshness.'

Robinson knew overmuch protestation when he heard it. Mr. Sheridan was evidently not the best of circus magicians, and his affectations of speech were beginning to grate on the policeman.

'Come along, Mr. Sheridan, let's have a look at the deceased.'

'I can't stand the sight of blood,' said Sheridan edgily. 'Especially not hers, not Christine's.' He began to sob again. 'Couldn't you ask Miss Parkes? Cool as a cucumber in emergencies, she is. Blood never bothered her. I remember when Tillie cut off half her finger with a chopper. Miss Parkes was the only one who kept her head. She held the cut together, got the silly minx to a doctor and saved the finger too. And she hauled your constable off the roof—and that's thirty feet high. I would have been terrified.'

'That's very interesting,' observed the sergeant. 'Not afraid of the sight of blood, eh? And her with a...sorry, sir.'

Detective Inspector Robinson reflected that only Providence knew how he was tried by his colleagues. He switched off the glare and escorted Mr. Sheridan upstairs.

The pool of blood was drying. The police photographer had hauled his apparatus up the stairs and down again. The police surgeon had made a discovery.

'I say, Robinson, look at this,' he said, revealing the lower part of the corpse. 'I was wrong about her being female. This is an hermaphrodite. Perfect blend of male and female—oh, I do beg your pardon,' he added as he sighted Mr. Sheridan. He drew the blankets up and stood aside to allow Sheridan sight of the face.

Mr. Sheridan paled and leaned on his attendant constable.

'That's Christine. Oh, Lord, Christine, my Christine!' he gasped. 'My hat, look at all that blood…' and he fainted into a tidy heap in the doorway.

◇◇◇

Detective Inspector Robinson was admitted into Mrs. Witherspoon's room. It was dark, reeked of roses, and was the most cluttered room he had ever seen. The walls were hung with theatrical posters. Every available space was filled with tables which supported vases and knick-knacks and souvenirs and framed photographs, most of them depicting a buxom young Mrs. Witherspoon beaming at the camera. On the wall was a large oil painting of the same subject, dressed in flowing draperies and contemplating a sheaf of lilies. Miss Minton, subdued and scared, was sitting beside a large bed heaped with pillows, in the depths of which Mrs. Witherspoon lay, retching weakly and crying like a torrent.

'Come now, Mrs. Witherspoon, pull yourself together,' urged Miss Minton in her high voice. 'Here's a policeman come to see you.'

This brought a fresh outbreak of lamentations. 'Oh, oh, the police in my house!' Detective Inspector Robinson was reminded of his Mechanics' Institute Shakespeare. 'Oh, woe, Alas! What, in my house?' he quoted to himself, and Terence Grossmith at his side said, 'Sir?'

'Nothing. You wait outside, Miss Minton, if you please. Sergeant Grossmith has a few questions. Now, Mrs. Witherspoon, just give me a moment and then you can rest again.'

He drew the curtain and the cool evening light came streaming in. Mrs. Witherspoon sat up against her pillows and sniffed.

'I just need to know what you have been doing today,' said Robinson, 'and something about your paying guests.'

'We rose late, because it's Sunday,' said Mrs. Witherspoon in a whisper, 'and we had breakfast at ten. Not a large breakfast, because we have tea at four. It's what we always do on Sundays, a high tea. Mr. Witherspoon used to like it.' She started to cry again and Robinson patted the plump, veined hand.

'Of course. And you are being very brave. Now who was at tea?'

'All of us, except Mr. Christopher. Oh, poor Mr. Christopher!'

'Did you know about Mr. Christopher's profession?'

Mrs. Witherspoon bridled. 'Of course. He was a perfectly respectable person and a nice fellow. He couldn't help the way he was born. And Farrell's is a very well conducted show. I was in the theatrical profession myself, you know.' Her eyes strayed to the photographs. 'I like theatrical people. Miss Minton is a dancer and Mr. Sheridan a stage magician and Miss Parkes is an actress. Perfectly respectable.'

'Yes, yes,' soothed Robinson. 'And was everyone at breakfast?'

'Yes. And then we went off to our own rooms. I believe that Miss Minton went to church. Mr. Christopher usually went too but this morning he seemed worried and said that he had letters to write. His people...well, they didn't meet, you know, that was not to be expected but they did correspond. They're in Ballarat; very well to do, I understand. Being what he was, he couldn't stay in the country. People are so cruel. He used to say he was only happy since he joined Farrell's.'

'So everyone was here for breakfast. And tea. And they all went out in between. Good. You're doing well, Mrs. Witherspoon.'

'Thank you.' Mrs. Witherspoon sat up a little higher in her bed. 'Now, sir, is there anything else?'

'Your guests. What can you tell me about them?'

'Miss Minton has been here almost a year. She's between shows, so she's a waitress down at the Blue Diamond. Just while she's resting. She's a bit modern but a good girl. I don't have any carrying on in my house. Mr. Sheridan, now he's a real gentleman. Mind you, I think his father was a grocer. But a well-spoken man and the words he knows! Good as an education. He's been here three months and it's nice to have a man in the house. Houses with all women get, well, quarrelsome. Miss Parkes has only been here a couple of weeks. I don't know much about her but she's a quiet body. I've had Mr. Christopher for three years. He always stays with me when he's in Melbourne,' she said proudly and then burst into fresh tears. 'Oh, a murder in my house! Poor Mr. Christopher! Who could have done such a dreadful thing?'

As Robinson had no answer to that, he patted the landlady on the shoulder and regained the hallway with some relief.

'Sir,' said Sergeant Grossmith proudly, 'we found this.' He held out a long, heavy knife, stained with a gummy brown substance.

'Good. Where was it?'

'Miss Parkes' room, sir.'

'Was her door locked?'

'Yes, sir. It was in the wastepaper basket, wrapped up in this.' The knife was bedded in crumpled pale paper.

Robinson looked at the weapon. 'I've never seen one like that before. Have you, Sergeant?'

'No, sir. I've seen a blade that long but it's a very heavy hilt. Weighted with lead, I think.' He turned the knife to exhibit the cross-hilt, made of brass and set with large glass stones. 'Very theatrical, you might say. But it did the job all right and it's as sharp as a razor.'

'Very good, Sergeant. Get it down to the laboratory and see if there are any fingerprints on it. I doubt it; the murderer obviously wrapped all that paper around it to avoid that very thing. Everyone knows about fingerprints these days.' He sighed.

'Well, Miss Minton next. Where is she?'

'I sent her down to the parlour, sir, with the rest of them. That magician chap came out of his swoon pretty fast. Are you thinking the same as me, sir?'

'Oh, yes, Terry, I expect so. Door bolted on the inside, window open. Unusual strength in the blow. Unusual agility required to get in through that window. The weapon found in her room. And a proven track record. I'll leave her till last.'

Jack Robinson went heavily down the stairs. He met very few female murderers, because there were very few of them in existence. Usually they had good reason for killing. Miss Parkes certainly had had good reason to remove her husband. But he liked competent women and admired courage. He quite liked Miss Parkes, who had rescued the hapless Constable Harris off the roof with speed and dispatch. He did not like to think of her returning to prison. No, he corrected himself, she would not go to prison again. For Miss Parkes there was the madhouse or the gallows; no other choices were possible. Robinson sighed again, hoping that she was insane. Hanging women was abominable. He went back to the parlour.

Miss Minton had replaced herself in the magician's arms and was shrill and excited. 'We saw the blood come through the ceiling. Oh, it was horrible!' She gave a small sob and Mr. Sheridan echoed it. 'Then I went up to see if it was the bath and Mr. Christopher wasn't there and then your constable went out on the roof and he said...he said...'

She sobbed again. Miss Parkes had not moved. Her hands were clasped together so tightly that her knuckles were as white as pearls.

Robinson said, 'Miss Parkes, what did you do today?'

'I got up for breakfast and then I went back to my room. I took a nap, if you must know.' Her voice was toneless. Robinson had heard the like before, in prisoners. 'I fell asleep and I didn't wake until after three. Then I got dressed again and came down to tea.'

'Did you see Mr. Christopher this morning?'

'No.'

'But you knocked on his door,' said Miss Minton shrilly. 'I saw you.'

Robinson looked at her. She had pulled out of the magician's embrace and was pointing a finger at Miss Parkes. 'I saw you! When I came home from…from church.'

There was a hesitation in her voice, which Robinson marked. He asked Miss Parkes, 'Did you knock at the door then, Miss Parkes?'

'No,' said Miss Parkes. Her eyes avoided the detective's gaze.

Miss Minton was offended. 'I tell you, I saw her! I had just come to the head of the stairs and I saw her!'

'Very well, Miss Minton. Miss Parkes, can you explain this?'

Grossmith, on cue, produced the knife in its wrappings. Miss Parkes stared at it.

'No,' she said again. 'I can't explain it. Where did you find it?'

'In the wastepaper basket in your room.'

'It's her!' screamed Miss Minton. 'She did it! She killed Mr. Christopher!'

The magician moved away from Miss Minton. She leapt to her feet. 'Why?' she demanded. 'Why did you kill him? You must have crept through his window and stabbed him. I liked him. He was nice. Why did you kill Mr. Christopher?'

She collapsed in tears and burrowed into Mr. Sheridan's chest. He appeared to be shocked and levelled the second accusing finger of the morning at Miss Parkes. 'You bitch,' he said in a low, intense voice. 'You stole her from me. My Christine. You stole her. You always disliked her, didn't you? Why were you knocking on her door? You utter bitch.'

Robinson intervened.

'Miss Parkes, I have no alternative but to ask you to come down to the station to answer questions in relation to the murder of…er…Mr. Christopher,' began Robinson heavily. 'You do not have to say anything, but anything you do say will be taken down by this constable and may be given in evidence. Have you anything to say?'

'I didn't do it,' said Miss Parkes through stiff lips. 'I did not kill Mr. Christopher.'

◇◇◇

Doreen had ransacked the kitchen and found sufficient salad for all of them. The argument continued around the table. Phryne had opened another bottle of wine and was beginning to feel embattled.

'Think about it,' urged Alan Lee. 'We need you. We're going to be ruined if Farrell's goes bust. There's no circus going on the road before Christmas, and the Agricultural Show is over. We'll be skint and starving if we can't get out of town before the end of the month.'

'Yes, I understand, but what do you expect me to do?' asked Phryne.

'Why, come with us,' said Alan Lee. 'Come with us and watch and you'll be able to tell what's going on. Then we can stop it.'

'Oh, yes? And how do you expect to stop it?'

'We have Samson. He can stop a train with one hand.'

Samson smiled modestly and took some more bread.

'Please,' urged Alan Lee.

'No,' said Phryne. 'What could I do? Besides, I'd stick out in your carnival like a sore thumb.'

'You'd be in disguise. We'd have to get you into the circus itself, not just down among the carnies. You can ride, can't you?'

'Yes, but…'

'Won't take you long to pick up a few tricks. You can sell tickets and maybe do a little acrobatic riding. Anna could teach you. She did a sharp-shooting cavalry act before she got so big. Or Molly.'

'Who's Molly?'

'Molly Younger. She can teach a horse to do anything but talk. Oh, Lord, Doreen, I forgot about Molly. I wonder if she knows about Chris?'

Doreen swallowed an enormous mouthful and gasped. 'Gosh, I forgot about that! Someone ought to go and tell her, Alan. I'll do it.'

'What about Molly and Chris?'

'She was...well, they were close. They were going to get married. Poor Molly. First Socks and then Mr. Christopher. You see, Phryne? Something has got to be done. We can't go on like this.'

'So you want to smuggle me into the circus, where I don't know anyone, in order to find out who is sabotaging it? It's insane, Alan. I like you all very much but I don't see that I can help you.'

'Leave her alone, Alan. If you were this rich and had a lovely house like this and all that money and nothing to do, would you leave it all to go haring off on a wild-goose chase with people like us?' Doreen's voice was scornful. 'You'd be mad. I could work all my life and never be as comfortable as this. Look at this house—she's got a car and a staff of servants and everything to make her happy. Our problems ain't her concern. We're only carnies, you know.'

'Don't say that, Doreen. I didn't say I wouldn't help. I just don't see how I can.' Phryne was slightly hurt. 'I haven't lived like this all my life. I was poor enough when I was a child.' She began to sound self-justifying in her own ears and held her tongue.

Alan Lee took her hand and stood her up, then surveyed her. He saw a slim young woman in a skimpy cotton dress. Her black hair swung as she turned her small head to look at him. He ran hard hands down her body with the impersonal touch of a farrier.

'You're soft, living like this,' he said insinuatingly. 'Look at that thigh and the buttock. There's been muscle there but not now. And these hands,' he laid Phryne's bare inner arm to his cheek, 'smooth as silk. Never done a tap's work in years. You're so beautiful I almost can't bear to look at you. You've got the build and the lightness and the hands to be an acrobat or a rope-walker or a rider, yet you're wasting away in idleness. What's more, I'd bet good money that you're bored. Ain't you?' The dark eyes bored into Phryne's green ones. 'You are, ain't you, Phryne? You gotta remember that I know you.'

'And I know you,' said Phryne, taking a handful of his hair at the back of his neck and squeezing. 'I know you too, Alan. And you are right. I am bored. But that's all I am—bored. I shall be amused tomorrow.'

'Will you? As well as I can amuse you?' His hand lingered at her waist and the touch tingled.

'Not in the same way,' she said lightly. 'But amused none the less. Now, let us have some more lunch and talk about it. I'm not saying that I'll do it. I just want to know what you've got in mind.'

Alan Lee sat down. Doreen, who had continued eating during the conversation, remarked, 'He's right. You could've been a ropie or even a flyer but that takes too long to learn. I reckon you'd make up good as a rider. It's not too hard to learn. I can do it and so can Anna. Just a matter of sticking on and not panicking. There's a finale in the horse act where they have ten girls come in, standing up in the saddle. One of 'em fell last week and broke her leg. You could take her place, after a few lessons. You're too distinctive with that hair, though, and them green eyes. Can't do nothing about the eyes so you'd have to wear a wig, or a cap. Might only take a few days to put your finger on what's crook with Farrell's. I'll give you a name, too. Fern. That's close enough to Phryne.'

She pronounced the name correctly, with a long 'e': Fry-knee. It sounded even more Greek and alien in Doreen's flat Australian accent.

'Fern,' said Phryne, tasting the name. 'I have to think about this.'

'Don't think about it,' said Samson. 'Never does to think too much. Just do it.'

She looked at him.

'Please,' said Alan Lee.

Phryne wavered. She had indeed been very bored. The round of social engagements and parties stretching in front of her seemed suddenly tedious as a twice-told tale. The concerns of her own circle were narrow. Everyone she liked was busy elsewhere. Her household would get along even more smoothly without her.

'If you can teach me to stand up on a horse,' she said, 'I'll try it. But only for a while.'

Samson reached across the table and shook her hand, engulfing it to the wrist. Doreen grinned. Alan Lee swept Phryne into a close embrace.

And Ember, encountering his first snake when he sidled into the parlour in quest of more ham, shrieked and fled up the curtains, where he remained despite coaxing and bribery, hissing and clawing ferociously at every attempt to rescue him.

'I hope that this is not an omen,' said Phryne, wondering if she owned a stepladder. 'I do hope that I'm not going to regret this.'

Chapter Four

Panem et circenses (Bread and circuses)

The demand of the common people,
Imperial Rome

Jack Black Blake shot his immaculate cuffs and said crisply, 'Billy, what do you hear?' The boss of the Brunswick Boys was well dressed, dapper and good looking. He had dark hair, slicked back, and a large diamond on his hand, outside his glove. Today the gloves were lemon-yellow kid but they did not seem to be affording him any pleasure. He was smoking a fat cigar and scowling into his beer.

The Brunswick Boys, known to the police as the Brunnies, were having a council of war in the august confines of the Brunswick Arms hotel.

Billy the Dog, so named for carnal atrocities too awful to mention, muttered, 'Not much, Jack. They say the 'Roys are out to get us.'

'What about it, Snake?' Snake, a tall man with reptilian eyes, nodded, as did Reffo, his mate. They were of a height and stood shoulder to shoulder as though expecting attack.

Little Georgie, who combined the knife-wielding abilities of his Italian mother with the ability to run amok of his Malay pirate father, ventured, 'We gotta do something, Boss. They're saying on the street that we got no balls.'

Jack Black Blake wore gloves, it was said, because he could not bear the touch of human flesh. He tapped on the bar.

'They'll find out if we have balls,' he said quietly.

Miss Amelia Parkes, once Mrs. Fantoccini, was escorted into Russell Street Police Station by Constable Tommy Harris, who kept a hand on her arm. He did not think that she would escape. He was afraid that she might collapse.

Tommy was shocked. Miss Parkes had saved his life. She had rescued him with bravery and dispatch. The scene which had ensued as she was taken out of the boarding house still stung his ears. Mr. Sheridan had moaned, 'How could you, how could you rob me of Christine?' Miss Minton had screamed, 'I knew it!' loud enough to bring the landlady to the head of the stairs. When old Mrs. Witherspoon had caught the drift of the conversation, she had denounced, 'Out of my house, hussy! I gave you a chance. I was sorry for you. But out of my house you go, bag and baggage! How could you do it? How could you kill poor Mr. Christopher?'

Mrs. Witherspoon had then broken down, and Tommy Harris' last sight of the household was Miss Minton hurrying up the stairs to mingle her tears with those of the old woman crumpled on the top step.

And Miss Parkes had said nothing, beyond mumbling, 'I didn't do it.' She now moved at his side with the even pace of a sleepwalker.

Tommy Harris didn't like it. There was something wrong. And yet, there was enough evidence to convict Miss Parkes. The knife. Her dexterity on roofs. And the locked and bolted door.

They paused at the entrance to the station and he said, 'All right, Miss Parkes?' and she croaked, 'Fantoccini. My name is Fantoccini. Prisoner number 145387. Sir.' Tommy Harris was very uneasy. He delivered Miss Parkes to the detention officer and she answered his questions in the same toneless voice.

Constable Harris went to find his sergeant. 'Sir,' he saluted. 'Sir, can I say something?'

Sergeant Grossmith looked up from a pile of papers. 'Yes, Harris, what is it?'

'I...sir, I don't think she did it.'

'Oh, I see. How long have you been in the force, Harris?'

'Eight months, sir.'

'All of eight months, eh? Well, Constable Harris, I am always interested in the views of younger officers. But I don't find "I don't think she did it" convincing. She had the knife and the skill and she's killed before. I expect she had a reason. Anyone else in that house strike you as a suspect?'

'Sir, no, sir.'

'Well, then. Cheer up, son. Jack Robinson's in charge of the case. He won't make no errors. He's brought her in. He must think she did it. Now take that knife down to the lab and pull yourself together. Or I'll tell the lads about how you had to be rescued from your roof by a murderer. A female murderer.'

Tommy Harris took the knife. 'I still don't think she did it, sir. She didn't have to rescue me and reveal that she was good with heights. She could have let me fall.'

'You're green, Harris. Some of the nicest people I know have been murderers. I remember old Charley Peace now, he could play the violin like an angel and was very kind to dogs. He just didn't like people. Go on, Constable. Trust Robinson. He knows what he's doing.'

Tommy saluted and went out. Sergeant Grossmith snorted. What namby-pamby recruits they were getting these days. In his day no mere constable would have questioned the actions of a superior officer.

Meanwhile, Jack Robinson was facing Miss Parkes in the little interview room which was the antechamber to the cells. Howls and wails came through the wall. Evidently the drunks were noisier than usual.

'Now, Miss Parkes, tell me, what did you know about Mr. Christopher?'

Miss Parkes was moving through a maze of unbelieving horror. The police station and the official voices had slotted her straight back into her prison persona. She had been a good prisoner, diligent and meek, and she had thought that she had escaped. Now the prison smell, unwashed humanity and urine and despair, reeked in her nostrils again. She grasped at her mind, which was slipping.

'I did not know him well. He worked for Farrell's Circus, as a freak. He was happy there. He said that he could not have been happy anywhere else. In the circus, he was valued. He made a good living, I believe. He was very good looking. He lived like a man. Mr. Sheridan was convinced that he was a woman and pestered him all the time, bought him flowers, that sort of thing, but Mr. Christopher never gave him the slightest encouragement. Miss Minton thought he *was* a man. We used to giggle about it, Mrs. W and I, because she was going to get a shock if she managed...you know what I mean. But Mr. Christopher was a real gentleman. He said that he had a fiancée, anyway, a trick rider in the circus. Her name was...was...'

The name had gone. She shook her head.

'Molly Younger. Her picture was on his wall.' Jack Robinson had done some research. 'So you did not know him well?'

'No. No one did. He was a very private person. Kept himself to himself, as Miss Minton would say. I never saw him perform. I...I would not be welcome at the circus, especially not that circus.'

'It was Farrell's where...'

'Yes. My husband and I and the others worked for Farrell's and it was at Farrell's that...that he died.'

'I see.' Robinson referred to his notes. 'Now, as to the day of the murder. Sunday, that's today. What did you do today?'

'I got up for breakfast at ten, then I went back to my room for a nap,' she said wearily, rubbing her eyes.

'Do you usually sleep on a Sunday afternoon?'

'No but I was so sleepy after breakfast that I went to lie down and I dropped off. I woke at three-thirty and had a wash and then I went down to tea. Mrs. W's teas are very good and I don't have to watch my figure any more. Then blood dripped through the ceiling and your constable came and got stuck on the roof. After that you came and all of this happened.'

'Miss Parkes, did you kill Mr. Christopher?'

'No.'

'Did you climb out on the roof and get in through his window and stab him in the heart?'

'No...no, I don't think so. But I killed before. I killed my husband. I hated him. I know how to kill. The ultimate crime. I might have killed him. Oh, God, how do I know? I can't remember. I might have done it in my sleep.'

'But you had nothing against Mr. Christopher?'

'No, nothing.'

Miss Parkes began to laugh. The laughter stretched, became unbalanced. Then she began to scream, silencing the drunks in the cells just beyond the room.

'Better lock her up,' observed Robinson. 'Send in a doctor.'

'No, no!' shrieked Miss Parkes. 'No, don't lock me up, don't, please. Not again. I can't bear it. I can't. I can't.'

Two policemen carried her to a small cell. When she heard the thud of the latch and the rattle of keys, she fell silent.

Robinson was unhappy. He sought out Sergeant Grossmith. 'Terry, I don't like this,' he began.

'Did she confess?' Sergeant Grossmith asked.

'In a way. She said she might have done it while she was asleep. She's gone off her rocker.'

'Well then, a guilty but insane verdict. She'll spend the rest of her life in a nice cozy loony-bin, out of harm's way.'

'Hmm.'

'If it's any consolation, my Constable Harris came and told me she didn't do it. Want to hear his reasoning? Because she rescued him from the roof. Said if she was a real murderer she wouldn't have revealed her skill with heights. She would have let him fall. I don't know. In my day I would never have dared to speak to my sergeant like that. These young blokes…'

Sergeant Grossmith continued to talk for some time but Detective Inspector Robinson was not listening.

Early in the morning, Phryne was transported to Farrell's Circus and Wild Beast Show in Alan Lee's old truck. Samson had also come, presumably as a chaperone. As instructed, she was wearing a scarf over her hair, a leotard, soft shoes and an old cotton dress.

The day was going to be hot. Williamstown Road was empty. The scents of summer reached her; baking earth, melting tar, sweaty humans, and the circus smells of dung and engine grease and drying shirts.

Alan Lee parked the truck in the carnies' camp. Some tents had been erected but most of the personnel seemed to live in caravans. Horses grazed in lines. Children ran on the urgent errands of childhood, threading their way through stalls and booths.

'I'll go and get old Bell,' Alan Lee said. 'She's safe enough. Samson, you ask Mr. Farrell if we can use the ring and get someone to rig up a governor. If he ain't there, ask the Bevans if they'd mind us using their rig.' He looked at Doreen, who had come up to meet them. 'I reckon you'd better go and see Molly, Doreen. She mightn't have heard. About Chris. We'd better tell the old man, too.'

'I reckon,' agreed Doreen reluctantly. Then she added with relief, 'No, I don't need to. Look.'

Two men were crossing the encampment. One was tall and stout, in a blue uniform. The other was smaller, in plain clothes, with a face and stance which was hard to remember.

'They're cops,' said Doreen. 'I seen enough cops to know a Jack when I see one.'

'And a Jack it is, too,' said Phryne. 'I have to intercept him and quietly. If he greets me publicly I won't be any use to you.'

'Easy enough. He's going to pass through our camp, so I'll scrag him when he comes past my van. Come on.'

Alan Lee and Doreen, with Phryne between them, sauntered toward the caravan, built on the ruins of a truck. Phryne slipped inside and as the policemen walked past, Doreen said quietly, 'This way.'

Jack Robinson caught sight of Phryne's face over the half-door and turned smoothly. He sat down on the caravan step, facing the camp and said, 'My feet are killing me. I haven't been a flat foot for too long. How do you feel, Terry?'

'You're getting soft, Jack,' said Terence Grossmith, who knew that his chief was fond of twenty-mile walks. 'Well, I could do with a spell, too. Any more room on that step?'

The two officers sat down and Phryne whispered, 'Hello, Jack dear, what are you doing here?'

'I'm trying to find out about Mr. Christopher,' he replied evenly. 'What about you?'

'I want to find out who's trying to ruin Farrell's Circus. Your murder is just a part of a long line of very bad luck.'

'Is it? But we've got our killer.'

'Who?'

'A woman who was with this circus ten years ago.'

'Mrs. Fantoccini?' Alan Lee asked, bewildered. 'She's out of jail?'

'Ten months ago and she's done it again,' said Sergeant Grossmith complacently. 'Made the arrest within the hour.'

'Oh. Why?' asked Phryne.

'That's what I'm trying to find out,' said Robinson.

'You've got your doubts about her, haven't you?' said Phryne, who had known Jack Robinson for some time.

'Not to say doubts. Questions, maybe. Well, keep your eyes open, Miss, and be careful. Bad luck can be catching. I take it you don't want me to recognize you?'

'No. And my name is Fern.'

'Then I haven't seen you, Fern. Come on, Terry, I reckon these poor old plates'll bear me a while longer. What was the name we wanted?'

'Younger,' said Grossmith aloud, consulting his notebook ostentatiously. 'Miss Molly Younger.'

'You're in the wrong camp,' said Samson, coming up, with perfect innocence. 'She's over with the circus folk. Go toward the big top and turn right at the elephants.'

'Thank you,' said Jack Robinson, heaving himself off the caravan step and collecting his offsider. 'Come along, Sergeant.'

'The Bevans say we can use their rig,' Samson told the others. 'Mr. Farrell seems real put about. But he said we could use the ring. What were those cops doing here?'

'Lost their way,' said Phryne. 'All right, Alan. Let's go and get Bell and see if I can learn to stand up on a horse.'

Bell was a placid, smooth-paced horse with a broad back and an accommodating disposition. She stood about fifteen hands and was a soothing chestnut colour. She had a delicate mouth and intelligent eyes.

Alan Lee strapped Phryne into a canvas jacket, which had stout lines attached to it at the waist. He cast the line to Samson, who attached it to a hanging rope slung over a block and hauled until Phryne rose a foot off the ground.

Doreen took charge. 'All right, mount up, Fern.' Phryne vaulted onto Bell's broad back. The horse stood like a rock. 'Off you go, Bell,' ordered Doreen, and Bell began to walk. Phryne had no difficulty maintaining her seat. Doreen grunted. 'You can ride, then. Good. Come up, Bell.' Bell increased her pace imperceptibly, so that she was soon cantering. 'Now, Fern, put both hands on her neck and swing your legs over to the right, so that you're sitting side-saddle.'

Phryne put both hands on the patient neck and made the movement, slid off, was brought up short and replaced on the horse. She tried it again, nettled that a physical skill should elude her so completely.

'Now the other side,' ordered Doreen, and Phryne found herself facing the outside of the ring, as Bell continued her smooth canter. 'Again,' ordered Doreen, and Phryne slid from one side to the other without falling. She grinned.

The scent of horse and sweat brought back the struggles which the young Phryne had endured learning to ride a cross-grained pony in the cool Shires. It had taken months before she had managed to get onto April the pony's back, and stay there. April had not been patient with novices. By now, April would have taken Phryne over to the nearest gorse bush and flung her into it.

'Back astride,' Doreen commanded and Phryne regained her seat. 'Now. You've got to trust me. Bell is moving fast enough to hold you in the saddle if you kneel. Just like swinging a billy round your head. Same thing. Put both hands flat either side of her neck and push your knees up onto her back. As long as you stay with your spine over the horse's spine you can't fall. One movement, make it smooth. Now.'

Phryne found the movement easy, though odd. She reflected that being educated by April had made her a good rider. Anyone who could stick onto April could ride anything and in any conditions. She was kneeling on Bell's back, on all fours. She was just about to say, 'How simple!' when she found that it wasn't. The horse slid out from beneath her and Samson hauled her up and onto Bell's back again. The harness cut into her ribs. She concentrated. It was a matter of balance and trusting that Bell would not swerve or change pace. The rough horse hair chafed her inner thighs. She bit her lip.

The trick was to keep up a constant pressure with the knees. Four more circuits and she could kneel and not fall off. Doreen said, 'All right. Now slowly lift your hands and straighten your back. You can't fall. Try it.' Phryne suppressed an unworthy urge to clutch at Bell's mane and straightened her back. She balanced herself as she once had on a beam at school. Bell's movements were as smooth as machinery. Phryne was kneeling up and the empty tent was flying past. She laughed aloud and wobbled perilously, then regained her balance. This was clearly no laughing manner.

'Stay like that for a while,' said Doreen, and Phryne and Bell completed two circuits. Phryne found that she could balance better with her arms outstretched. Alan Lee watched the slim figure with a private smile. Samson anchored the governing rope with careless strength. 'Now you're going to stand,' said Doreen. 'Put your hands down again, bring up your feet. Come up, Bell.'

This was going against every instinct of self-preservation and all Phryne had ever learned about horses. She fought an inner reluctance to do anything so foolish, pulled her knees in toward her chest and straightened her back. It did not want to straighten.

'Feet further apart and flat. Good, you're supple enough. Now, when I tell you, push down with your hands and stand up. Do it in one movement. You gotta flow, not jerk. You can do it. Come on.'

Phryne attempted to convince herself that it could be done and failed. Bell completed another circuit. Phryne began to sweat and her hands slipped on the chestnut hide. She lifted them, one by one, to wipe on her cotton dress.

'You can do it,' called Alan Lee.

'I don't think I can,' wailed Phryne from her upside down position. Her thigh muscles twinged, presaging cramp.

'Don't think,' said Samson. 'I've got you. Hup!' he roared, taking Phryne entirely by surprise, so that she had released her grip on Bell and was standing up, arms out, actually standing up on Bell's back, with the ring fleeting past and some force holding her on.

Every rider is familiar with the drag of gravity as a horse jumps a fence. But this force did not pull her down. It appeared to be encouraging her to stay mounted. She noted from her perspective of the watchers that she must be leaning in towards the centre of the ring.

'Good. Stick on,' encouraged Doreen. 'See? I told you anyone could do it. Try a handstand.'

Phryne, elated, bent again and laid her hands on the horse's neck.

'Not there—you'll strain her neck. In the middle.'

Attempting to move back, Phryne lost her balance and fell. The governing rope brought her up short of the sawdust. Doreen brought Bell to a halt and stood caressing the soft nose.

'Here's your carrot, Bell. Fern? You all right?'

Phryne was sweaty, bruised by the canvas jacket and completely above herself.

'Fine. I'm fine. Can we do it again?'

'Yes,' said Alan Lee. 'And again every day. I reckon you'll be able to stick on good-o by the time we get on the road again. See? I told you. And now you're coming with us. You promised,' he reminded her.

'Yes, I promised. And I'll come. Oh, that was lovely.'

'Come back tomorrow,' said Doreen. 'Meanwhile, you need to practise handstands and balance. Alan can take you home and he'll come and get you again. Now we gotta take Bell back to the lines and groom her. She did bonzer for you, Fern. But she's the best. There ain't many neddies with a pace like hers. Molly trained her up from a filly.'

Phryne led Bell out of the big top. Samson, having removed the governor, carefully detached it and undid his line, returning the hanging rope to exactly the same length and position.

'Never meddle with a rope and never move it,' said Alan Lee. 'Someone's life might depend on it. If you watch the flyers, you'll see what I mean. But the Bevans don't like an audience when they're rehearsing. You'll have to sneak into the show. You'll see 'em put out a hand for a line, knowing that it's there. If it ain't there...' He left a significant pause and Phryne nodded.

'Quite. Who was Mrs. Fantoccini?'

'Why do you ask?' Alan Lee seemed taken aback.

'Jack Robinson said he arrested her for murdering Mr. Christopher.'

'Oh, yes. Well, she was one of the Flying Fantoccini. The husband and two brothers and Amelia Parkes and her sister Ella. They was good, too. Eh, Doreen?'

'Good? They was great,' said Doreen. 'She never oughta married that bastard George, though. He treated her like a dog.'

'And what happened?'

'Look, this was ten years ago, I wasn't here,' said Doreen sharply. 'I knew Amelia when we was kids together. I'da said she wouldn't hurt a flea. But he knocked her about. Stole her money. They say…' She lowered her voice and looked sidelong at Alan Lee and Samson, who took the hint and shifted out of earshot. 'She told me that he made her have an illegal operation, you know, to get rid of a baby.'

'Why?' whispered Phryne. 'Wasn't she married?'

'You can't be a flyer if you're expecting.'

'That's terrible!'

Doreen's eyes glinted. Phryne noticed that her eyes were not green as she had thought, but a dark, almost charcoal grey.

'Yair. And she wanted that baby real bad. But she loved him so she did it, and after that she was so scarred up inside she couldn't never have another. She went strange then. Cold. You couldn't get close to her. But I was away when it happened. Alan might know.

'Alan?' she called him over. 'What about the murder?'

Alan Lee seemed uncomfortable. 'I was here, yes, but I didn't see it. Come along, we'd better get Bell back before her legs stiffen.' As they walked, he began to tell the story in brief, unwilling sentences.

'George had arranged a big finale. Six flyers all crossing each other, simple enough. But he insisted on his own trapeze; he had small hands and he needed a thinner bar. That night, they were all flying and he reached his bar and then he slipped. He fell. He fell outside the net, because he was at the top of his flight. Forty feet to the ground and he was dead. When they lowered his bar, they found it was smeared with engine grease. His wife, she had engine grease in her fingernails, and his brothers knew he'd been beating her. They knew about the baby, too.' He grinned at Doreen. 'You can't keep secrets in a circus. And that day, he had been heard to tell her that he was short of money and that she should go on the street to earn him some, because that's all she was worth. He called her a clumsy flyer and untrustworthy in the air. She killed him all right. She admitted it.'

'And I can see why,' observed Phryne.

They had traversed the carnies' camp and were entering the horse lines when a tall man with white hair roared up to them.

'You, what are you doing with my horse?' he bellowed.

'We had permission, sir,' explained Alan Lee. 'We are bringing her back now.'

'You carnies are all horse thieves!' yelled the tall man, face flushed with rage. 'You put her back right now!'

'Yes, sir,' said Alan Lee submissively. Phryne wondered why he did not yell back at this rude person. Then she understood. Alan Lee, though delightful, skilled and beautiful, was low down on the circus pecking order, so he could not reply with the cut direct. His humbleness annoyed Phryne. She stared at the interlocutor, wondering what was eating him. He seemed unnaturally angry.

'You stay in your own camp,' he snarled. 'I don't want any of you diddikoi coming into my circus and stealing my animals and upsetting my people.'

'I asked Mr. Farrell,' said Samson quietly. Samson was hard to overlook. He loomed over the man, broad as a door, and he was not smiling. 'Mr. Farrell said it was all right. We're training a new rider for the rush. Why don't you ask Mr. Farrell about it?' Samson asked with quiet menace.

The man cast a glance around the group, his eyes resting on Phryne.

'You the new rider?' Phryne remembered her place in the hierarchy of the circus and reined in her temper.

'Yes, sir,' she muttered, hanging her head.

'What's yer name?'

'Fern, sir.'

'You just remember who I am,' he said pompously. 'I'm Mr. Jones and I own Farrell's.' He pinched Phryne's cheek. 'Nice little girl. You treat me right and I'll treat you right.'

Phryne refrained from an answer but scuffed her soft shoe in the dust.

'You get that horse back to the lines,' Mr. Jones ordered brusquely. 'And mind you rub her down.'

'Yes, sir,' said Alan Lee again and they led Bell away.

'Whew!' said Phryne, as they were brushing Bell and feeding her more carrots. 'What a tartar! I thought you said Farrell owned the circus?'

Alan Lee looked aside. Broad and well-tended equine sides hid them from eavesdroppers.

'He did,' he whispered. 'Get over a bit, Bell, you're crowding me. But this Jones has a half-share, they say. He ain't popular.'

'He ain't,' agreed Phryne.

Miss Parkes was served dinner in her cell. By negligence, someone had allowed her a knife. It was blunt but it could be sharpened. When the constable came to take the tray of untouched food, he did not notice that it was missing.

Chapter Five

All the world's a stage
And all the men and women merely players;
They have their exits and their entrances
And one man in his time plays many parts.

As You Like It, Act II, Scene vii,
William Shakespeare

'A circus, Miss?' Dot surveyed her employer, who was stripping off a shabby cotton dress and a leotard and examining her bruises. 'Why?'

'You remember Alan Lee.'

'The gypsy, Miss?'

'Yes, the gypsy. Except that he isn't a gypsy, he's half-gypsy. I have a lot to learn about circuses, Dot. They're a lot more complicated than they look. They seem to have a class system. Circus folk at the top, carnival people in the middle, and gypsies at the bottom. Or that is how it seems at the present. Farrell's has had a lot of trouble and they asked me to help—and I'm at a loose end, Dot. Nothing in the offing but social events, the occasional ball and flirting with all those tedious young men. I want something new to do and today I stood up on a horse's back.'

'But, Miss, I can't come with you in a circus, can I?'

'No, Dot dear.' Phryne stepped into her bath and began lathering her rope burns with *Nuit d'amour* soap. 'The girls don't generally have a maid.'

'But Miss…'

'Oh dear, Dot, don't take on! I can look after myself.'

'But, Miss Phryne, who'll run your bath and take care of your clothes and…'

'I ought to be able to manage,' muttered Phryne, and Dot produced her trump card.

'Miss Phryne, it isn't ladylike.'

Phryne swore. 'Damn and blast all ladies to hell. No, I didn't mean that. Come and talk to me, Dot, and don't worry. I'll be all right, and if I'm not it will be all my own fault, and I shall limp home and you can look after me and tell me every morning that I did it all to myself against your express advice. Agreed?'

'I suppose so,' said Dot. She was a small, plain young woman with long hair firmly suppressed in a plait. She was wearing a beige linen dress, embroidered with a bunch of bronze roses. Phryne sat up in the bath and began to count off points in her argument on soapy fingers.

'All right, Dot. One, I agree that it is an escapade unworthy of my respected parent, the earl, and that my mother and sisters would have kittens if they knew. But they are all in England and with any luck no one will tell them. Two, it is very unlikely that anyone who knows me will see me. Three, if they do see me they are not going to recognize me because I shall have my hair covered and be made up and riding in a circus. Even if they notice it they won't believe it. "Phryne Fisher," they will say. "Doesn't that girl look like the respected Miss Fisher? But of course it can't be. It's just a chance resemblance."'

Phryne climbed out of the bath and Dot wrapped her in a moss-green velour towel.

'Four,' she continued, 'I will be living with the girls so my virtue will be safe, rather more safe than I would like it to be, and five, I promise to be careful. And that's all I am going to say about it, Dot. I will need some cheap clothes. Can you spare time this morning for a shopping trip?'

'Yes, Miss,' said Dot. 'I don't like it but if you promise to be careful...What do you like about circuses?' she added curiously, dropping a crisp linen morning dress over Phryne's sleek black head. 'Nasty dirty places, all smells and noise and them poor animals all locked up in cages. I feel real sorry for them poor lions.'

'I never thought about the lions,' said Phryne, whisking a powder puff over her nose and applying Extreme Rouge lipstick. 'I suppose it is tough on them. It's not the animals, anyway, though I made the acquaintance of a mare today who would run all stockhorses to a standstill. Bell is her name. What a sweet creature. I must take some carrots, Dot, remind me. And apples. And a few packets of those extra strong peppermints. Horses love them. No, what's fascinating about the circus is the people. And I don't expect you to like them, Dot. They aren't respectable.'

'That's why you like them,' commented Dot.

Phryne looked at her companion's reflection in the mirror and grinned.

Tommy Harris was drinking in the Provincial Hotel, as near to the centre of Brunswick Street as made no difference and the best place to pick up whispers. The Provincial occupied the middle ground of hotel culture. It was not so respectable that it discouraged the crims, or so low a place that the commercial travellers, the truck-drivers and the local tradesmen couldn't drink there. It was getting on for four o'clock and Tommy was well ensconced in his corner of the public bar, a schooner of Victoria Bitter in front of him and a cigarette alight in a tin ashtray beside him. Tommy Harris only smoked in pubs. It counted as protective colouration.

'Gidday,' muttered someone behind him. 'This seat taken?'

'No, mate, take the weight off,' said Tommy affably, without turning. A body slid into the seat beside him. A blocky body and a fair head, cropped close. Hands like shovels and pale blue eyes in a fighter's face. Tommy identified him at once. He had some unpronounceable Balkan name and his associates had decided to call him Reffo. He did not seem to mind. He was a member of the Brunswick Street Boys, otherwise known as the Brunnies. Tommy Harris knew that the Brunnies and Albert Ellis' 'Roy Boys were involved in a slight argument which had littered the suburb with damaged adherents, although they had not killed anyone yet. As long as they involved no innocent bystanders, Sergeant Grossmith had ordered that no official notice was to be taken of this difference of opinion.

'Want a drink, Reffo?'

Reffo nodded and Tommy signalled to the barmaid. She came over and leaned her elbows on the bar, confronting them with a vast expanse of pearly bosom which was always just on the point of bursting its bonds and spilling out of her black dress. Mary of the Provincial might have heard of the Mabel Normand bra, guaranteed to give that boyish look, but she wanted no truck with it. She grinned at them, patting her curly hennaed hair.

'H'lo boys, what can I get yer?'

'Pint for me mate,' Tommy grinned back. 'Looking beautiful today, Mary.'

'Sauce,' she commented, pleased, and drew the beer. It was chill and foaming.

'Well, Reffo, what brings you here?' said Tommy.

'I got something you might be interested in,' said Reffo through a moustache of foam. 'For a price.'

'Oh, yes? You tell me what it is and I'll decide about the price.'

'You're only a tiddler,' said Reffo scornfully. 'Where's your old man?'

'He authorized me to deal,' said Tommy easily. 'You talk to me or nobody.'

Reffo thought about this, never an easy process for someone who had been hit on the head as often as he had. The nostrils curled, the forehead corrugated. Tommy watched, fascinated. Finally Reffo seemed to come to a decision.

'A quid.'

'If it's worth it.'

'Tell the old man that the 'Roy Boys is mixed up with something big. Real big.'

Tommy Harris was amused. He stubbed out the cigarette which had been chugging away in the ashtray and lit another, trying not to breathe in the smoke. He offered one to Reffo, who took two and tucked one away behind his ear.

'Them?' scoffed Tommy. 'No one would trust 'em with anything big. What sort of big?'

'You know that Seddon what walked out of Pentridge?'

'He was dead, Reffo. You don't walk any more when you're dead.'

Reffo gave the constable a scornful look. He was about to speak, caught himself, and continued, 'That's all you know. And then there was Maguire the robber.'

'Yes?' Tommy was interested for the first time. Maguire had managed to cut himself out of a police van taking him to court. No one had seen him leave the van but when it arrived the robber had not been there. The constable left in the van with him had been found in a drugged sleep, with chloroform burns to his face and no memory of how the prisoner had got out of his handcuffs. The present whereabouts of Damien Maguire were unknown. Every cop in the state was looking for him.

'Go on, Reffo, this might be worth a quid. Do you know where Maguire is now?'

'Nah. But the 'Roy Boys do. Ask 'em. And there's the man that attacked them kids. You want him for three little girls, don't you?'

'Smythe? You know where he is?' said Tommy eagerly. Late one night, Ronald Smythe had slipped from his house, although it was being watched by four constables. He had never been seen since. The police wanted to renew their acquaintance with Mr. Smythe very badly.

''Roy Boys know. What's that?'

An argument had started in the front bar. It had increased in volume, and now became inescapable. Mr. Thomas the publican was discussing the reason why he should give another bottle of cheap ruby port to Lizard Elsie, the sailor's friend.

Lizard Elsie stood five feet high in her damaged canvas shoes. She was dressed in an assortment of carefully chosen rags, topped with what had once been a rather expensive ball-gown, to judge by the remains of the sequins, and a tatty feather boa wound three times around her neck. The ruby-port content of Lizard Elsie's blood was low. This always made her cross.

'No, Elsie, I already gave you a free bottle yesterday. Don't drink it all at once, I said. I'm not giving you any more of my port.'

Lizard Elsie pushed aside her tangled black hair with both dirty hands. She levelled black eyes at the publican and screamed in a shrill voice like a seagull, 'You mean bastard! You mongrel cur! Wouldn't give a poor girl the drippin's from your fucking nose! Bloody well gimme me port or you'll be fucking sorry!'

Tommy Harris reflected that they didn't call her Lizard Elsie for nothing. Her tongue was definitely blue. The respectable patrons of the Provincial were drawing away and remembering appointments and lunch and requirements to go back to work or the missus. Mr. Thomas saw this and lost his temper.

'You get out of my nice clean establishment, you and your foul tongue! Get out before I call the cops!'

Lizard Elsie did not reply in words. She seized a stool and flung it at the bar.

Bottles shattered. Mary the barmaid ducked and came up splashed in liqueur and picking glass out of her hair. Small specks of blood freckled her magnificent bosom. Three drinkers leapt to help her remove the splinters.

Tommy Harris glanced sideways and realized that Reffo had left him, without even waiting for his pound. He looked through the window and sighted the blond man standing on the corner of Johnson Street, waiting for the traffic to clear.

'Bloody well gimme me red biddy!' shrieked Lizard Elsie, pleased with the smash. 'Or I'll get another chair!'

At that moment, when all eyes but Tommy's were on the brawl, a car slid around the corner of Johnson Street. There was a shot, perhaps two shots. Tommy Harris found himself running. He came out of the pub and dropped to his knees to cradle Reffo in his arms, whose life spurted out of a dreadful hole that had been blasted in his chest and onto the unforgiving bitumen of Brunswick Street.

'They got me,' commented Reffo. He said something in his own language. Then he gasped, 'Exit,' and died.

His was the first death that Tommy Harris had seen. He knelt in a spreading pool of cooling blood, holding the dead man close and reminding himself sharply that constables do not cry.

The occasion was also notable for the fact that, for the first time in living memory, Lizard Elsie had slipped away from a fight without insisting on her bottle of ruby port.

Detective Inspector Robinson invited his visitors to be seated. Grossmith steered Tommy Harris into a chair beside his own. He was worried about the boy—one of his most promising constables. First he had nearly fallen off a roof and been rescued by a female murderer. The next day he had watched Reffo die. It might have been too much for the young man. He was a country lad, after all, came from Hamilton. He wasn't a kid who had lived in the streets like some. Grossmith himself had found his first corpse when he was ten, an old drunk who had died in a lane in Fitzroy. But Harris was shaking and his face had blanched so that his freckles stood out like ink-blots. Grossmith did not like the look of him.

Neither did his superior officer. Robinson said very gently, 'Tell me what happened, Constable. What did Reffo say?'

'"They got me," sir, he said. "They got me," and then he said something in Balkan. I didn't understand it. Then he said, "Exit" and then he died.'

'Both barrels of a shotgun at close range,' said Grossmith. 'It don't do you no good. Blasted out most of his guts.'

Tommy Harris made a sound like a sob and then shut his mouth hard. Robinson pressed a buzzer. His sergeant looked in.

'Get us some tea, will you? Lots of sweet tea.' The sergeant looked at Constable Harris, pursed his lips and nodded. Robinson said to Grossmith, 'What can you tell me about Reffo?'

'Real name Georgi Maria Garinic, thirty-five years old, native of Rumania. Came to Aussie after the War, naturalized, took his oath and all. Been living in 'Roy, making a crust as a carter and driver. Big, strong, blond bloke. Known associate of the Brunswick Street Boys, that's Jack Black Blake's mob, the Brunnies. Not nice citizens. You remember Blake. Record as long as me arm. He hangs around with the Judge, Little Georgie who's as mad as a cut snake, Billy the Dog, and Snake Eyes. Not nice citizens. Feuding with the 'Roy Boys at the moment. Crims. Petty stuff, mostly. Receiving stolen goods and the odd burglary. I'm sure as eggs that both the Brunnies and the 'Roys are standover merchants but I can't get no one to complain about them. You know what it's like. They're all terrified that if they stand up in court they'll get a petrol bomb through their front window. I reckon the Brunnies had something to do with the butcher's shop fire but I can't prove it. Lately we been thinking that they had something big on. That's why I sent Harris down to the Provincial. Reffo ain't what you could call truthful but them Brunnies hate the 'Roys. I thought we might pick up a useful word or two.'

'Perhaps we did. Ah, thanks, Sergeant. Here you are, Harris.' Robinson spooned sugar into the solid white cup and put it into Tommy's hands. 'Drink up. Help yourself, Terry. Now, I am going to tell you something confidential. Do I have your word not to disclose it?'

Grossmith nodded. Harris gulped tea and said, 'Yes, sir.' He was pleased that his voice did not shake.

'Good. The interesting thing that Garinic said was "Exit". We've heard that before. For the last six months we have been losing prisoners. There was Maguire and there was that rat Smythe. You know about them?' They nodded. Tea was putting colour back into Harris' white cheeks. Grossmith absently gave him his cup and Tommy drank, feeling more centred. 'But what you haven't heard about is Seddon.'

'He's dead, sir. Died in prison,' said Grossmith. As Robinson did not speak, the big man added, 'Didn't he?'

'Oh, yes. Certified dead by the prison doctor and carried out in a coffin. Given to his family to be buried—that won't happen again, I can tell you, not without a post-mortem. Because last week I got this.'

He handed them a card in a stiff white envelope. It showed dancing crowds of gaily dressed people. 'It's postmarked Rio de Janeiro.'

Terence Grossmith read the spiky, idiosyncratic handwriting with difficulty. 'It says, "Dear Jack, just to let you know I've arrived safely. If you are still doing that literature course, I refer you to *Romeo and Juliet*, Act IV, Scene i. Best regards as always, William Seddon." William Seddon? Is this his writing, sir?'

'Yes. They say it's identical. The Shakespeare reference is to the scene between Friar Lawrence and Juliet, where he gives her a drug to mimic death. It annoyed me at the time but we have been lucky. If that cheeky bugger hadn't needed to crow about getting away, then we wouldn't have had a clue. But there is an undercurrent in the underworld, if I may put it like that. They are all talking about Exit. If you have the money, Exit can get you out of the country. I don't know how to find them. No one will tell us anything else about it.'

'I never heard of it,' said Grossmith. 'None of my telltales have told me anything about it.' He was deeply ashamed. Robinson saw this and hurried into speech.

'It hasn't been mentioned in Brunswick Street, Terry, or it hadn't until Harris here got the office from Garinic. If it had been, you'd have heard about it. I think that the 'Roy Boys might know more. Clearly they thought it important enough to kill for, if they snuffed poor Garinic, though we still don't know that. He could have had a lot of enemies. But the smart money has to be on the 'Roys. Now. We have to stamp on this and stamp on it fast. You have read the papers, haven't you? You know what's happening in America. Gangs and bootleggers and machine-gun killings on the street. The police are helpless there and I regret to say that a lot of them have been bought and paid for. We aren't going to let that happen here. We have been put off balance by the War, the whole nation has. To an extent, we have lost our nerve and there are a lot of people out there that the police surgeon reckons are potential loonies. If this Exit thing gets established, then bang goes law and order and it will be every man for himself. You remember the police strike, Terry? All the damage done in that was a few shops looted and a smallish riot. Can you imagine what would happen now, in 1928, if there was a police strike?'

Terence Grossmith thought about it. The nerves of the people had been stretched to breaking point by the Great War, and the succeeding generation didn't seem to care about anything, or believe in anything. He shuddered. Robinson nodded.

'Exactly. We're on the edge of a knife all the time. Anything could push us over. So we aren't going to allow that to happen. Are we?'

Constable Harris, much recovered, said, 'How can we stop it, sir?'

Grossmith grunted and Robinson smiled. He had a peculiarly beautiful smile, which invited trust.

'We will find a way. First thing is for you to tell me everything that Garinic said. And when you've finished, Sergeant Grossmith will tell me all about Lizard Elsie.'

◇◇◇

Phryne Fisher was visiting Foy and Gibson's and had bought an armload of clothes. Cotton dresses, patterned with flowers which never grew in any garden. Underclothes of the respectable poor; one pair of washing silk for Sundays, and the rest of cheap Sea Island cotton in a distressing shade of pink. She had also purchased three pairs of sandals, two pairs of soft dancing shoes, a couple of Sylk-Arto nighties, a straw hat, a cheap fibre suitcase and a down quilt. It had an apricot cover emblazoned with white daisies. Dot thought it rather nice.

'I'll need a costume, too,' said Phryne. 'I presume that it will be provided. I can hardly ask any of the usual people to make it up for me. This is going to be exciting, Dot! I've got too reliant on things and people. It will do me good to manage on my own for a while.'

Dot hefted the parcel and led the way out of the shop.

'Have you ever managed on your own, Miss Phryne?' she asked as Mr. Butler piled the parcels into the car.

Chapter Six

He smelt of lamp-oil, straw, orange-peel, horses' provender and sawdust and he looked the most remarkable sort of centaur, compounded of the stable and the play-house.

Hard Times, Charles Dickens

Phryne ate well, Mrs. Butler having been invigorated by her niece's wedding. There she had put down the pretensions of three of her most irritating relations by referring, in passing, to her employer the Honourable Miss Fisher's rank as just below the relict of a duke and above the daughters of baronets. Mrs. Butler's relations had never seen a baronet, even at a distance, and had been properly silenced. Mrs. Butler's triumphs were always reflected in her cookery. Phryne finished the exalted form of shepherd's pie and pushed a piece of lettuce around her plate.

'Have you ever managed on your own?' Dot had asked, and Phryne was now wondering if she ever had. She had been surrounded with people since birth. First her sisters, her brother and her parents in that small set of rooms in Collingwood. There she had been poor. Hungry, sometimes, and always cold. There her younger sister had died of diphtheria one winter. Phryne had gone badly clad to Collingwood Primary School and learned the rudiments of literacy, and there had been people there, too, who could be charmed or coerced into helping the little girl with the strange name get what she wanted.

Then the great change had come and the family had been uprooted and dragged across the ocean to the counties and wealth, not because of any virtue in themselves but because the War had killed the younger sons of every family in Europe. Mr. Fisher had been translated into a lord and Phryne had been sent sullenly to boarding school to be made into a suitable daughter of the aristocracy. At school she had been unpopular because she was wild and did not care about the things the school cared about; standards of behaviour and learning and sport. People again, all around her, in the dorms and on the playing fields. Malleable, useful people. After that, Melbourne had been easy. She had money and position, beauty and style.

She had never been alone.

Phryne allowed Mr. Butler to take away the plate. What am I worrying about? she wondered. The circus was composed of people just as society was, just as school had been. There was always a man to be persuaded, bought, daunted or charmed.

'And I'm the woman to do it,' she said aloud.

'Miss?' asked Mr. Butler.

'Nothing to signify, Mr. B.' He hovered at her shoulder.

'Another glass of wine, Miss Fisher?'

'Thanks.'

He poured the wine, a rich red Burgundy, and retired to the kitchen.

Phryne looked around her dining room, which was hung with pale damask. The carpet, patterned with green leaves, had been specially woven for her. On the wall, opposite the big windows which opened onto her pocket-handkerchief front garden, hung seven oil sketches of dancing acrobats. They were freely drawn, light-hearted and perfect just as they were. Phryne had snatched them from the artist's hands as they were completed, despite Mrs. Raguzzi's protests that they were not finished. Usually they refreshed her spirit. Today they looked as animated as dolls.

'I shall do without luxury for a while,' she said aloud. 'Then it will all be lovely again. Alan is right. I am soft.' She flexed her hands, which had acquired rope burns from getting on and falling off Bell's patient back. 'Hello, Dot, how did you go with the second-hand rag trade?'

Dot exhibited a nightie washed almost transparent and two pairs of thin unmentionables. She hung a ratty cardigan over the chair and sat down.

'I hope you know what you're doing, Miss,' she said seriously. 'I heard nasty things about that circus.'

'Did you? Tell all.'

'I was in Brunswick Street, Miss—that's a good place for old clothes—and there were two women searching through the rags. Gypsies, Miss. You can't trust people like that. The old woman said, "We can't but go with Farrell's. It's not a long trip. But we need to get out to the sticks. The Jacks'll move us on in two days." The other one said, "They're cursed, Farrell's is got the evil eye," but the first one told her that she knew the evil eye when she saw it and it wasn't on Farrell's. Then they went out and I didn't hear no more. I wouldn't take the word of a gypsy for anything. But…'

'But?'

'They know about curses,' said Dot slowly, crossing herself. 'So I bought you this.'

Phryne took it. Dangling from a leather thong was a round silver medal. On it was depicted a man fording a river, with a child on his shoulders.

'St. Christopher, Miss. Patron saint of travellers. I didn't get a silver chain because maybe you won't want to have anything valuable on you in such a place, with all them thieves about.' Phryne was about to laugh, then caught sight of Dot's serious face and didn't. 'I'd feel happier about this if you'd promise to wear it, Miss Phryne.'

Phryne tied the bootlace around her neck, so that the medal hung just at the base of her throat. She didn't want anything to dangle when she stood on her hands, her balance on a horse being shaky at best.

Dot looked at her seriously. 'I'll be praying for you, Miss Phryne,' she said. Phryne put down her glass and hugged Dot and kissed her on the cheek.

'Thank you, Dot. I appreciate it. And I promise I'll wear it. I will need all the help I can get. What with the circus and the carnival and the gypsies, there must be a hundred and fifty people in that camp and I'm supposed to find out who is sabotaging the place. It sounds impossible. So if you can ask God to help me, it might assist. In any case, He's more likely to listen to you than me. Come on. Have a cuppa and I'll tell you how we are going to make me look like a daughter of the people, down on her luck and glad to get a place in Farrell's Circus and Wild Beast Show.'

Dot, comforted by Phryne's acceptance of the holy medal, drank her tea and listened.

'Lizard Elsie,' said Sergeant Grossmith indulgently. 'What a girl! I reckon she'd be getting on for fifty now. Been a beauty in her time. Portuguese, her dad, a sailor off a ship, they say, and her mum no better than she should be. Elsie was a pretty one. Her mum sold her to a gentleman when she was fourteen. But you can't treat Elsie like that. Bit off half of his ear and him a respectable man, too. Then she lighted out the window and took to...well, I don't quite know what you'd call it, sir. She's not a whore. Far as I know she ain't never been a whore. She lives with the sailors while they're ashore, till they both of 'em drink away his pay and he signs up for a new ship and Else finds a new partner. She don't thieve from 'em, that's why they call her the sailor's friend. But rough! She's as rough as bags. And swear! A man ain't never heard language like it. She'd make a bullocky blush, would Elsie. But she's getting on, the old Else. I don't reckon she'll last much longer, poor old tart. She's taken to the red biddy and that's cruel on women, red biddy is.'

'What's red biddy, sir?' asked Constable Harris.

'Ruby port and metho,' said Robinson shortly. 'Kill a brown dog. Go on, Terry. Who are her associates?'

'Well, sir, I wouldn't have said that she had any. She never used to. Time was, the first collar any young constable made in Brunswick Street was to haul Lizard Elsie in for Indecent Language. I did it myself, must be near thirty years ago. And the things she called me! That's when they named her Blue-tongue Lizard and the name stuck. Everyone calls her Lizard Elsie now. She's been standing over the publicans in the last year or so, threatening to break up their hotels if they don't fork out. Most of 'em don't mind, it's cheap enough muck, God knows. And it just ain't worth the mess to try and chuck her out. She can fight like a cat—all scratches and bites—she can throw a mean punch and she ain't afraid of nothing, Elsie ain't. But since she got on the plonk she's been going downhill. I'll put the word out. She used to lodge in Marian Hayes' guesthouse. I'll be able to tell you tomorrow, sir.'

'All right. And remember what I said about Exit. If you can find it, Sergeant, it will be a great feat, though I won't offer you promotion. Now, as to the other matter. I have detained Miss Parkes in custody. She says that she might have done it and she doesn't deny it, but I'm not happy about the case. The laboratory says there are no fingerprints on the knife. Here's the report. The knife is unusually heavy and well balanced, and the lab says that it might be a throwing knife. The stones on it are glass and they suggest that it belongs to a variety or a circus act. Then there is the post-mortem on Mr. Christopher.' He rummaged among the pile of papers on his desk. 'Yes. Here. The pathologist has had a lovely time with this one. He told me that he hasn't seen such an interesting cadaver since he was at medical school. "Body of an hermaphrodite aged approximately twenty-five with well-marked male and female features...might have had functioning male genitalia...blood supply to an intact womb with all structures present...unbroken membrane suggests that the subject was a virgin." Oh, he's having a high old time with this. Where was that...? Aha. "Cause of death, deep penetration injury to the upper chest. Heart pierced, overlaying rib cut through. Wound seven inches deep and approximately an inch wide. Massive insult to muscle and lung. Exsanguination. Vessels almost empty. Suggest a knife blow given with considerable skill and with great force." Now, I've seen Miss Parkes and although she's strong for a woman, I don't know if she's that strong. I think I might have jumped the gun a little with her. What do you think?'

'If she had killed that...that thing, I reckon she oughta get a medal for it,' said Grossmith. 'Sorry, sir, but them freaks turn me up. I never could abide 'em, the dwarves and the rubber men and all them. As to Miss Parkes, well, she mighta been angry. An angry woman is pretty strong. Look at Lizard Elsie.'

'She's not the angry type,' said Harris reflectively. 'Nor the panicky type, either. She wasn't strong enough to pull me up the roof on her own, sir. But she didn't fluster and she thought about what to do as though she had all the time in the world. I wasn't much help, either. I was scared to death.'

'Understandably,' commented Robinson. 'I know you don't think she did it. I think I might release Miss Parkes. I haven't formally charged her yet. What do you think, Terry?'

'No one else in the house had the time. She was out of reckoning for hours. She says that she was asleep but she was alone. I dunno, Jack. I reckon she killed it, all right.'

'And you, Constable?'

Constable Harris hesitated. His sergeant nudged him. 'Go on, boy, spit it out.'

'Well, sir, she hasn't got anywhere to go. We came and got her and she can't go back to Mrs. W's house. She's been getting her life together and we came in and smashed it all to bits. I...I don't know what would happen to her if we let her go.' He was still powerfully affected by Miss Parkes' brown eyes and her courage and the strength of her warm hands.

'Well, we gotta either charge her or let her go. I reckon we charge her,' said Grossmith. 'Even though I think she did a good day's work.'

'There is the notebook,' said Robinson. 'Mr. Christopher's little red book. It seems to have lists of names and places in it. It's stained, so I've sent it to the lab to see what they can make of it. They can photograph through filters and so on, it seems. Modern science. Also, we've had a look at the ashes in the fireplace. Love letters, they seem to be. Addressed to Christine. The sender's name is burned away. Well, let's have Miss Parkes charged, then, and we can keep her in custody for a while and see what else happens. By the way, Sergeant Grossmith, what did you get from the carnies about Mr. Christopher?'

'Not much, sir. Didn't seem to have no enemies. Did two shows a day, dressed half-man, half-woman. Always lived out of the camp when the circus was in town. Kept himself to himself, like Miss Parkes said.' He opened his notebook and referred to his meticulous notes. 'The owner of the circus, Samuel Farrell, aged forty-eight, says that it'd been working with his show for some years and it seemed very happy and was a good performer. The really disgusting thing was Miss Molly Younger, thirty-two, trick rider, who told me that she was going to marry it. Pretty girl too, blonde. Wizard with horses, they say. She was real cut up about Mr. Christopher being dead, when she ought to have been down on her knees thanking God for a merciful release.'

'Sergeant Grossmith,' said Robinson, 'you will refer to Mr. Christopher as "the deceased", "the victim", or "him". Is that clear?'

'Yes, sir. If you say so, sir. No one noticed anyone being missing but them carnies only pay attention if someone's late into the ring. Their show was at eight o'clock and went on until eleven. After that everyone went to their own tent or caravan or whatever and no one noticed anything odd. They hadn't heard about the death of...of the victim until I told 'em the next day. The three that called at the house, sir, they was Alan Lee, thirty, carousel proprietor; Doreen Hughes, wouldn't tell me her age but about thirty-five, snake handler; and Samson, real name John Little, twenty-eight, occupation strongman. And, Jeez, he looks it, too. They said they was looking for...the deceased...to give him a message from Miss Younger. They ain't got no alibis for the night before, except that Samson was performing and Lee and Hughes were in the sideshows until midnight. No one in the whole show can really vouch for any of the others.'

'Hmm. Not helpful, is it?' Robinson looked at Harris.

'No, sir,' the young constable replied.

'Tell you what. We'll hang on to Miss Parkes a little longer. If your sergeant can spare you...?' Grossmith grunted agreement and Robinson went on, 'You make some enquiries about the other people in the house. Find out about the stage magician, Sheridan. See if he's got a record. And Miss Minton, she's working at the Blue Diamond. I seem to recall that as something of a dive. Nightclubbing has never been my idea of relaxation,' said Robinson, who preferred the undemanding company of his wife, his children and his orchids. 'That make you feel better, Harris?'

'Yes, sir. Thank you, sir.'

'And wherever you go keep your ears open for a whisper about Exit.'

The next morning Phryne Fisher awoke, threw on the shabby clothes and was transported to the circus by Alan Lee.

'I'll take you to meet Molly,' he said, sparing one hand from the wheel of the old Austin to lay on Phryne's shoulder. 'She'll take over training you, Fern. The circus folk, they don't like diddikoi. As you heard from Mr. Jones.'

'What is a diddikoi?'

His dark face creased in a grimace that might have been laughter or pain.

'I am. Half-gypsy, half-Gorgio—Gorgios are what the gypsies call everyone else. My mum was seduced by a Gorgio when she was sixteen and her own people threw her out. Luckily the man married her later but she had to leave the road and she lives in Prahran now. I haven't seen her since I ran away when I was twelve to go with Farrell's. The man said it was in my blood and hers too and called me a gypsy. And the gypsies won't have me because I'm the son of Marie who left the road and betrayed her people. So I'm a betwixt and between, neither fish nor flesh. I wasn't born on straw but I can't stay in one place. Like them, I'm a traveller. Like the man my father, I'm a good businessman, so I make a decent living out of the merry-go-round. It's uncomfortable, though. I only half believe in curses, for instance. If I really believed in them, I could go to Mama Rosa and get the curse taken off. If I didn't believe at all I could forget about it. But I'm in the middle.'

He shrugged and Phryne patted the hand on her shoulder.

'That's why I came and got you, lady. I don't think Mama Rosa got your name and description from the spirits. However, I know she's a shrewd old biddy with a finger on the pulse of the circus. And there are things Mama Rosa knows that she couldn't have got anywhere else. So I came and got you and now…'

'Now?' Phryne pulled the scarf further down over her eyes.

'Now you can find out what's happening and I don't need to decide my own future for a while. I don't want to leave Farrell's but I gotta make a living. If this tour don't clear a profit, I'll take off on my own. Carousels are popular. But I like Farrell's and I don't want to leave my mates. That make it clear?'

'Yes.'

'Also, once you're with the circus, you shouldn't have anything to do with us—with Doreen and Samson and me. Doreen's off today, anyway, to see her mum in Tumbarumba. She said to say goodbye. I hope she don't try and take Joe on the bus again. Now, listen. The circus folk don't mix with the carnies. You'll have to slip into their way of doing things, become one of them, if you want to find out anything. And to their way of thinking the carnies ain't no more important than the fleas on a dog. See?'

'Yes. I see.'

He stopped the truck on the outskirts of the camp. 'It's not what I want,' he said, staring past her through the dusty windshield. 'Not what I woulda chosen, Fern.'

'Not what I would have chosen, either.'

Phryne ran a considering hand down the perfect dark profile, the set mouth, the firm chin, until her fingers curled in the hollow of his collarbone and he shivered.

'Tonight,' she mouthed into his ear. 'Tonight is my farewell to luxury. Come and share it with me?'

The shadowed face inclined. The smooth cheek turned a little into her caressing palm.

'Tonight,' said Alan Lee.

◇◇◇

The horse lines were busy. Performers were grooming, trimming hooves, and plaiting manes and tails. The hot sun ripened the scent of dung and sweat and hay. Alan Lee led Phryne through the lines and presented her to a small woman who was applying sulphur and lard to a pony's back. Molly Younger was shorter, stockier and plainer than her image on the posters. She was dressed in riding breeches and a workman's shirt, with her long blonde hair dragged back under a peaked fisherman's cap. Alan Lee introduced Phryne.

'Fern, eh?' She looked at Alan Lee. 'All right, Lee, you can leave her with me.'

Alan Lee said, 'Good luck, Fern,' and turned away without another word.

'So. You can stand up on Bell?' Molly's voice was cracked and her eyes were red but she was brisk and her regard was as straight as a lance. She surveyed Phryne and ran a hardened hand down over her body. 'Some muscle there. But your hands are soft. You haven't done any trick work for a while, have you? Where have you been?'

'Dancing,' said Phryne in her hesitant Australian accent. 'I been dancing.'

'In one of the dancehalls, I suppose, shilling a dance? You'll have a harder life here. Now, anyone could stand up on Bell. Bell's my darling.' Bell, hearing her name, nosed into Miss Younger's hand and was fed a carrot. 'She's as steady as a rock and as good as gold. Some of the others are not so good. We'll take Missy here and see what you can do. I don't like taking my replacement riders off the chorus line,' she added, detaching a grey from the lines, 'but that silly bitch Alison has broken her leg good and proper and I'm missing a girl for the horse-rush.'

Phryne trailed Missy into a clear space. The grass had been beaten down and dried and the ground looked uncommonly hard. Phryne reflected that this was going to be a painful test if she failed.

'A circus ring is forty-two feet across,' said Miss Younger, reeling out a long rein and taking a bamboo pole with a few ribbons tied to the end, 'because that is the width that brings centrifugal force into action. A horse cantering around a 42-foot ring generates the force and allows the rider to stand up. I don't suppose you are interested in any of this, Miss Tea-dancer, but that is why you will stay on, if you stay on. Mount.'

Phryne leapt onto Missy's back. The creature did not flinch and began to walk in a circle. Phryne pressed her knees into the grey sides and urged her into a canter.

'No. Don't try and control your mount. That's why you haven't got any reins. Leave it to me. That is the horsemaster's job. Sit quiet and let me tell Missy what to do. You have to trust me, Fern.'

Phryne relaxed her grip and Missy completed two circuits. She was keeping in a precise circle even though there was nothing to guide her, not even a chalked outline on the grass. Molly Younger flicked the bamboo pole and Missy increased her pace, lengthening her stride into a smooth canter. Her pace was not as even as Bell's.

'Side to the left,' ordered Miss Younger. Phryne managed the movement and sat sidesaddle on the bare back, hands braced.

'Side to the right.'

Phryne was getting the hang of Missy's pace, which was slightly faster than Bell's because of her shorter legs. She slid and balanced, facing the outside of the ring. Caravans and tents flashed past. She did not look down but fixed her gaze on the flag flying from the big top.

Miss Younger flicked her whip again. 'Come up, Missy.' Her voice when addressing the horse was clear and gentle. 'Kneel up, rider,' she ordered Phryne.

Hands on the neck, Phryne thought, feet flat and apart. She brought up both knees in a smooth sliding motion and was kneeling, putting out both arms to balance. Two circuits flashed past.

'Hands and feet,' ordered Molly Younger, and Phryne managed to convince her back to straighten. She was getting dizzy from the passing scene and closed her eyes briefly. The St. Christopher medal flicked over at her throat.

'Stand up, Tea-dancer.'

Phryne was stung. She pushed away from Missy's neck and found herself standing, feet placed either side of the horse's spine, high off the ground and held up by that strange force. Missy moved sweetly beneath her feet. Phryne began to experiment with what she could do. She stretched out her arms, curved them above her head and then hastily replaced them in position.

'Arms by your sides!'

Phryne slowly lowered her arms until she was standing like a pole, leaning inward, perfectly balanced.

For a moment. Then Missy moved out from beneath her and she wavered, lost her balance and flung herself forward, landing astride with her legs around Missy's neck.

'Stop!' Missy slowed to a walk and halted. Phryne slid off her back and embraced the horse while the world went round and round.

'You say you've never done acrobatics before?' Miss Younger's voice was sharp. Phryne blinked as the world did an eightsome reel.

'Never,' she gasped. 'Not on a horse.'

'If Allie had been able to do that, she never would have broke her leg. You fall quite well. Tumbling, then?'

'Yes, a little.' Gymnastics at an English girls' school, Phryne felt, could probably be called tumbling. She smiled briefly at the idea of what her games mistress would say if she saw her pupil now.

'Good. We will practise every day and by the time we go on the road you may be good enough to be in the rush. Now take Missy back to the lines and let me see you groom her.'

Phryne gathered up the long rein and returned it to Miss Younger, then led Missy back to the lines with an arm over her neck, whispering endearments to the patient beast all the way.

Miss Younger supervised the grooming, feeding and watering of Missy with a closed mouth. When Missy nosed up to investigate the contents of Phryne's cardigan pocket, Miss Younger was at her side in a flash.

'What are you feeding her?' she demanded. Phryne held out a flat palm.

'Carrots,' she said meekly.

'Eat one,' Miss Younger ordered.

Phryne, remembering the untimely death of Socks, bit into a carrot and fed the rest to Missy. She waited until Miss Younger had turned away before she spat the mouthful out.

Phryne hated carrots.

Chapter Seven

Tell us the showman's tale, you say. And why not? The very thought of it brings back to my ears the jingle of bells.

Seventy Years a Showman,
'Lord' George Sanger

Tommy Harris returned to Mrs. Witherspoon's refined house for paying gentlefolk with a warrant to search everywhere for anything. He was determined to be thorough.

He had nothing to rely upon but the conviction that the woman who had drawn him away from the brink of that roof was not guilty of murdering Mr. Christopher.

He reached the house to find that the only person home was Tillie, the girl described as half-witted. She answered the door timidly and would only allow him inside after he had exhibited the impressive warrant, blazoned with the seal of the Magistrates' Court at Melbourne.

'Ooh,' she commented, handing it back. 'Well, you'd better come in, bettern't you? Missus is out. What do you want?'

'I've got a warrant to search everywhere,' said Tommy Harris, smiling at Tillie. 'I'm Constable Harris. Do you remember me?'

She wiped her hands on the greasy tea-towel she was carrying. 'Yair. You was here when they took Miss Parkes away.' Tears filled Tillie's eyes. 'I liked her. I don't reckon she killed Mr. Christopher.'

'I don't reckon so, either.'

'You don't?'

'No. So that's why I'm searching. But that's a dead secret, Tillie. You won't give me away?'

Tillie mopped her eyes with the tea-towel. She was a faded girl, with pale blue eyes and scraped-back blonde hair. She smiled slowly at Constable Harris. 'I won't give you away.'

'Good, now you tell me about the lodgers, while I have a look at each room.'

'The keys is in the scullery. I'll get 'em.' Tillie scurried away and was back in no time.

Tommy Harris began with the bedrooms. Miss Parkes' room was tidy, sparsely furnished and anonymous. The bed was neatly made. Harris lifted the mattress and felt down behind the pictures and the back of each drawer in the chest of drawers. Clothes, plain and well kept. Her stockings were darned with the correct thread. This was always an index, Tommy had been told, to the state of a woman's mind. There were no reminders of her circus past. Her prison-release document was the only personal item in the room. Her ashtray was full of pins and one loose button.

'All right, Tillie, who's next?'

'This is Miss Minton's room.'

'Do you like her?' asked Tommy, reeling back under a cloud of cheap scent. Tillie looked around to make sure that no one was listening.

'She's all right. Makes a lot of work. Lots of washing and ironing, with all them costumes. I don't know what sort of an actress she is, though. And,' Tillie lowered her voice further, 'I don't think she goes to church when she goes out on Sundays.'

'Why do you think that?'

'I asked her what church she was, cos I thought she might be a Catholic. I can't abide them Micks. She said she went to St. Paul's. But she don't.'

'How do you know?' The overpowering femininity of Miss Minton's belongings was stifling Harris. The window had evidently not been opened for some time. He pulled at a drawer, dreading that he might see something which would cause him to blush.

'She leaves at the wrong time. Service at the cathedral is eight and ten. She often don't leave until ten. I don't know where she's going but it ain't church. But she's got some pretty things.' Tillie gazed admiringly at a gown figured with gold dragons. 'And she smells nice.'

Love letters and cards and cheap novels with chocolate wrappers marking her place comprised most of Miss Minton's reading matter. Tommy glanced through them. The terms in which Miss Minton's person was described by one ardent suitor were too much for him. He felt his cheeks begin to burn.

He replaced the letters, felt along the mattress and under the bed. There he found three unmatched stockings and an earring. The walls of her room were hung with posters for various plays, and the small table was covered by a fringed shawl. Her wastepaper basket contained more chocolate wrappers and two types of cigarette butt—one long and lipstick stained; the other short, gold-ringed and brown.

'Oh! They're the ones that Mr. Sheridan smokes!' squeaked Tillie. Tommy Harris selected a representative collection of butts and put them into an envelope.

'Come on, Tillie, I'm stifled in here,' he said. 'Who's next?'

'This is Mr. Christopher's room,' breathed Tillie. 'All his stuff is still there. Ooh, this is creepy!'

Constable Harris had been taught how to search a room. He got down and crawled. His first effort had been thorough; at the end of half an hour his harvest was scant. The only things which he could not definitely state were Mr. Christopher's possessions were another strip of flimsy paper, which he discovered caught behind the picture of Miss Molly Younger, a length of twisted fishing line and a small white feather. The collection meant nothing whatever to him but he packed it all up in another envelope.

'What's the next, Tillie?'

'Mr. Sheridan's room.'

But no matter how Constable Harris turned the key, the door would not open.

'Missus'll be mad,' said Tillie. 'They ain't s'posed to muck about with the locks. In case of fire, she says.'

'Well, it won't open. Tell me about the house. Can you get into the roof? What about under the floors?'

'They fixed the ceilings where the roof used to leak but the painter ain't been yet. And now I expect she'll have to have the downstairs ceiling fixed. Ooh, to think of poor Mr. Christopher lying there bleeding like a tap! It's awful.'

'How did you feel about him, then?' asked Tommy, trying not to think of Mr. Christopher bleeding like a tap. Tillie screwed the tea-towel in her water-sodden hands.

'He was a gent,' she said sadly. 'Never any trouble and as nice-spoken as you please. Not like Mr. Sheridan. He's not nice.'

'What sort of not nice?' asked Tommy.

Tillie grimaced. 'He pinches,' she said, rubbing her bony hindquarters as though an old wound still ached. 'And he grabs. But now he's taken advantage of Miss Minton, I'll reckon he'll leave me alone.'

'Why do you think he's done that?'

Tillie looked up at the ceiling, scratched her nose and refused to comment further. Tommy Harris went downstairs to wait for Mr. Sheridan to return home.

◇◇◇

Phryne Fisher completed the grooming of Missy and said to Miss Younger, 'Are you hiring me?'

Miss Younger inspected Missy. She ran a hand through the soft mane and lifted a hoof to check that it had been properly cleaned.

'You can stay. If you aren't good enough to go in the ring, you can mend, wash, make yourself useful. Thirty shillings a week, five more if you go on. You sleep in the girls' tent, that's on the left of the big top. We go on tour on Friday. You'll need fleshings and a costume but we can look at that when we see how you progress. All right?'

'Yes.'

'Call me Miss Younger. You came with some carnies. Don't have much to do with them once we're on the road. Not if you want to be accepted by the circus.'

'No, Miss Younger,' said Phryne.

'Go over to Mr. Farrell's van and get a contract. Tell him to talk to me if there's a problem. And Fern…'

'Yes, Miss Younger?'

The horsemaster came closer, lifted Phryne's chin with a finger and looked into her face. Phryne looked back. The older woman's face was blotched with shed tears which powder did not entirely conceal. Phryne was sorry for her.

'I don't know what things have been like for you, being a dancer, but circuses are very moral. If you play at being a tart, you'll be taken for one.'

'Yes, Miss Younger.'

'And look out for Mr. Jones. He has an eye for a pretty face. You aren't precisely pretty but you're graceful and you're young and that's how he likes 'em. Don't be alone with him.'

'No, Miss Younger.' Phryne pulled her chin out of the horsemaster's hold. 'I can take care of myself,' she said. 'But thanks for the warning.'

Phryne walked across the circus toward the largest and most gaily decorated van. It had 'Farrell's Circus and Wild Beast Show' emblazoned along both sides in red and tarnished gold. She paused at the bottom of the steps. The half-door was open.

'Mr. Farrell?'

A grunt, and someone croaked, 'Come in.'

Phryne mounted the steps and walked into a cluttered little room, with a table full of papers and a typewriter. There were two chairs and two gentlemen occupied them. One was the tall man with white hair, whom she knew to be Mr. Jones. The other was a smaller man with a stockman's hat and weary blue eyes set in a nest of wrinkles.

'Well, well, what have we here?' asked Jones. 'The little rider.'

'Sir, Miss Younger sent me for a contract,' parroted Phryne, poised for flight. She recognized the look in Mr. Jones' eye and did not like it.

'Oh, yes. My name's Farrell.' Mr. Farrell stood up and reached out a hand crooked with arthritis but nonetheless strong. 'Hello. Welcome to the circus. What's your name?'

'Fern,' said Phryne. She realized that Doreen had neglected to provide her with a surname and added, 'Fern Williams,' fervently hoping that Dot would never find out that she had borrowed her name for such an unrespectable purpose.

'And you can stand up on a horse, Fern? That's good. Been a dancer? Thought so. Way you stand. Sit down, Fern. Before you sign you get the lecture on circuses. Want you to know that this is an Imperial tradition, one to be proud of, no matter what they say about us. Rogues and vagabonds, they call us. But the crowds in ancient Rome wanted bread and circuses and they got them. And ever since we have been travelling, bringing innocent amusement to the people. We cross the boundaries of what is possible. We fly higher, leap further. We defy natural laws. My old dad could balance with one foot on each of a pair of horses. They bet him once that he couldn't run the pair across a bridge and he laid the bet, then found when he was in motion that the bridge had a toll gate across it.'

He paused. Phryne asked breathlessly, 'What happened?'

'He called to the horses and they jumped it, with him aloft. He won his bet. He was a great rider, my old dad. And his father before him and me too, in my time. Perhaps you, Fern, if you practise enough. Which mount did Molly give you?'

'Missy, sir. She's lovely. Not so smooth paced as Bell, though.'

'She must like you. Missy's her second string. Good. Now, you get thirty shillings a week, five more if you are good enough to ride in the rush. We give you accommodation and food. You sleep in the girls' tent, left of the big top. That's where you leave your stuff and change before the show. If you aren't riding you can help the other girls with changing and mending and washing, you help wherever you're needed. This is a circus. We all help each other. When we strike camp you'll see all the principals helping as well. Always something to do in a circus.' He chuckled. 'You'll have to be ready to leave early Friday morning. I'll hire you for the tour. That's six weeks. If you don't practise or if you get into any hanky-panky I can fire you on the spot. Thieving or disobedience, the same. Is that clear?'

Farrell's face seemed to have been carved out of mahogany. Phryne nodded.

'Good. Be a good girl and you'll be happy with us, Fern. Sign here.'

Fern signed, crabbing her ordinarily free script down into a scribble. Mr. Farrell signed after her. His hand shook.

'Wait a bit,' said Mr. Jones. 'Stand up.'

The caravan was just lofty enough to allow him to stand. He reached out for Phryne, seized her shoulder and ran his hand down her side and buttock. His touch was not impersonal, like Alan Lee's and Miss Younger's, and Phryne squirmed. In her present persona she could not hand this mongrel the clip on the ear which he evidently required. She had to suffer his touch, turning imploring eyes on Mr. Farrell, who seemed uncomfortable but said nothing. Phryne stumbled and kicked Mr. Jones in the shin by what appeared to be accident. It was a sharp kick. He let go of her and swore.

'I'm so sorry,' she said tonelessly. As she turned to leave the caravan, she caught a glow of pure pleasure in Mr. Farrell's eyes.

'Now, I wonder what that means?' she asked herself aloud as she walked away. 'Mr. Farrell and Mr. Jones are not at one, it seems. Ooh, how I would like to boil that Jones in engine oil. How dare he touch me like that!'

'You had trouble with Jones?' asked a plump girl who was sitting on an upturned bucket mending tights. 'He's a cur. Felt me all over as though I was livestock.'

'I kicked him in the shin,' said Phryne with simple pride. The plump girl laughed.

'Good for you! What's your name? Can you darn?'

'Fern. I can't darn, sorry.'

'Can't be helped. Kicked 'im in the shins, eh?' She laughed again. 'I'm Dulcie. What's your line?'

'Horses.'

'Oh, you must be replacing Allie. Hope you have better luck.'

'What do you do?'

'Juggler,' said Dulcie laconically. 'Magician's assistant, wardrobe, costumes, and I'm one of the elephant girls. You doing anything special?'

'No, I was just going to have a look around.'

'I'll take yer, if you like. Your reward for kicking that mongrel Jones.' She stuffed the tights and thread into a canvas bag. 'I could darn tights all day and never get to the end of 'em. You'd better learn to sew, though. You want me to introduce you?'

'Thanks, I'd like that. It's big, isn't it?'

Dulcie stood up and stretched. She was the same size as Phryne but plump, with small hands and feet, brown eyes and hair, and a round cheerful face like a doll's.

'Biggest thing there is. The circus has magic. Changes people's lives. Look at me. I was working in a shop when I was fourteen. Came to the circus and got put on a horse on a governor in the clown's act. I stuck on good-o and Mr. Farrell asked me if I'd like to join. Never went back. Couldn't go back, p'raps. It's a hard life but most of 'em are. This way you get to travel and...well, you'll see. If it gets you, you'll never be happy staying in one place again.'

They had reached the Williamstown Road boundary. The circus camp was spread out before them, bright with banners and humming with activity.

'Now, there are three camps. Because we have to set up in a hurry, sometimes in the dark or the rain, the tents and caravans are always in the same order. Next to the big top there's men on the right and women on the left. Then after that, all round the big top, there's the caravans. We can tie the guys to them and it steadies the tent. From the left there's the clowns, two of 'em, Matt and Toby Shakespeare. Then there's the lion tamers, then three jugglers. After them there's the Cat'lans, they're balancers, you know, the Human Pyramid. They don't speak much English, you stay away from 'em.'

'Why?'

'Foreigners. They're,' her voice lowered to a whisper, 'almost gypsies. Mr. Farrell don't like to hear us say that but you just take the hint, Fern. Then, going round the big top, there's the three trucks that hold the seating and the canvas, then the two caravans of the flyers. The Bevans. You've heard of 'em. Famous trapeze artists. Lynn Bevan, that's the daughter, does the triple somersault, which is what all of them flyers aim for. She can do it two times out of three. Out from the big top to the left there's the booths of the carnies. Don't go near 'em alone. Not after dark. To the left of the carnies there's the big cats, the lions. We only got lions here, they're more reliable than tigers. Tigers is got a dirty temper. I wouldn't trust a tiger so far as I could spit. The other side, to the right, there's the horse lines, the camels and the elephants. You gotta put them as far away from the lions as you can. Our horses is well trained and won't spook, p'raps, but lions and horses don't get on. That's why we only feed our lions on beef or mutton. Not horse. We don't want 'em to get a taste for horse. Come on. We'll go take a look at the folk. Where do you want to start?'

'What are those other caravans over there, past the elephants?'

'Gypsies,' said Dulcie, spitting. 'That's the gypsies. You don't want to notice them. They don't like being noticed overmuch. Now, where shall we start?'

'At the left,' said Phryne. 'I've already been to the horse lines.'

'Oh, yair. Miss Molly talked to you? Be nice to her, Fern. Her fiancé's been murdered, so you can understand why she's a bit short with you. She's nice, or she was nice before someone killed Mr. Christopher.'

'Mr. Christopher?'

'Yair. Half-man, half-woman—Christopher and Christine as well. He had a turn in the show, just before interval. Some said that he ought to be in a booth in the carnival. But he was a nice bloke, or she was, you know what I mean. And Miss Molly, what wouldn't go near a man except in the way of business, she was real gone on him. He seemed to be fond of her, too. It's a real pity. I don't reckon they'll find who did it.'

'Why not?'

'No one cares about us,' said Dulcie matter-of-factly. 'We're rogues and tramps and vagabonds and the cops don't like us. They won't extend themselves catching him, whoever he is. Besides, Mr. Christopher wasn't just a circus performer, he was a freak as well.'

'Freak?' growled a voice from knee level. 'Freak? A glorious title.'

'Oh, hello, Mr. Burton,' said Dulcie, after she had looked to either side. 'This is the new rider, her name's Fern.'

Mr. Burton was a dwarf, dressed in cut-down overalls. Although he had the stature of a child, his face was wrinkled and his hair was grey. Phryne guessed that he might be forty-five. She knelt down and offered her hand.

'Pleased,' said Mr. Burton, kissing the hand with a courtly flourish. His voice was educated and crisp. 'Welcome. I'm Josiah Burton. Freaks, Dulcie?'

'Yair. I was telling Fern about Mr. Christopher and reckoning that the cops wouldn't bother much about finding who killed him.'

The dwarf tapped his front teeth with a forefinger. 'Hmm. All connected, I'd say, Dulcie. The fires and the lost beasts and the death of poor Mr. Christopher. How's Molly taking it?' He cocked a bright dark eye at Phryne.

'Not good,' said Phryne. 'She's been crying a lot. And she was very sharp with me.'

'You are a perceptive young woman, Miss Fern,' commented Mr. Burton. 'Someone doesn't like us and that's a fact. I'm talking to Wirth's. What about you, Dulcie?'

Dulcie seemed taken aback. 'You reckon it's that bad?'

'I do. You're taking her on the grand tour? Look out for the lions. Someone's been niggling them. Listen.'

Deep, angry roaring disrupted the camp and seemed to echo out of the ground. Horses neighed and camels bubbled and honked, made uneasy by the feral voices of the flesh eaters.

'Thanks for the warning. This way, Fern.'

Phryne followed Dulcie, stepping carefully over guys. A strong scent of cooking became apparent. Someone was having bubble and squeak for lunch.

'Hello, Mr. Shakespeare,' said Dulcie. 'Bit of bacon would go real well with that.' A blocky middle-sized man with a painted face looked up from stirring a pot over a small fire. His features were disguised but he had clear and beautiful grey eyes, and he smiled under his mask.

'Dulcie. Don't be cheeky. How nice to see you. You want some potato and cabbage?' He had a treacle-toffee voice, slightly accented. 'It's nearly ready.'

'No thanks, I'm showing a newie around. This is our new rider, her name's Fern. This is Mr. Matthias Shakespeare. Him and his brother are our main clowns.'

'Jo Jo and Toby, Musical Madness,' said the man, taking Phryne's hand with the one not occupied in stirring. 'Being myself and my brother Toby. Welcome to the Circus. Toby! Come and meet a new rider.'

A muffled assenting voice came from the caravan and Toby emerged. He was dishevelled and evidently had been interrupted, as one eye was outlined in white and the other was bare.

'Off with the motley, it's lunch time,' said Matthias. 'Meet Fern.'

Matthias looked at Phryne with appreciation and seemed to wish to further the acquaintance. Then he was distracted by his brother.

'I don't think much of that new greasepaint, it's dry and it flakes. I don't think I want any lunch, Matt. Hello, Dulcie.' Toby's voice was sad and dreary. He ignored Phryne.

'Oh, Toby, just a mouthful or so. You have to eat something. It's bubble and squeak. You like my bubble and squeak.' Matthias sounded worried.

Toby groaned. 'Again?' He slumped down into a canvas chair and put his head in his hands. Matthias patted Toby's shoulder and the man looked up. It was hard to discern his features under the heavy makeup but his mouth curved down, in opposition to the elevation of his painted smile.

'Cheer up, Toby,' said Matthias. 'Try a bit of lunch. You have to keep up your strength. Here, let me just dish up, then I have to clean my face. And you're right about the new paint. I think we'll go back to Max Factor. Come on, Tobias, give me a smile, eh?' They had forgotten all about the visitors.

Dulcie led Phryne on, through a maze of washing lines and parked vans.

'One of the rules is that you never look in a caravan window,' she instructed. 'If you have to go out at night, you don't talk to people you see and you don't say where you seen 'em. You don't go into anyone's tent unless they invite you. All right?'

'All right,' agreed Phryne.

The circus was vast and bewildering. The number of people who might want to destroy it was unknown and it seemed impossible to keep tabs on everyone. Phryne was conscious of being alone, in shabby clothes and completely ignorant. You've bitten off more than you can chew, this time, Phryne, she thought. You'll never make any sense out of this.

'To understand a circus,' she added aloud, stepping sideways to avoid a passing camel, 'you obviously have to be born in a trunk.'

'Too right,' agreed Dulcie.

Chapter Eight

Tread lightly, lest you wake a sleeping bear

Oliver Goldsmith's epitaph
on Samuel Johnson

Mr. Robert Sheridan, on his return home, was all apologies that the constable had not been able to get into his room, which he unlocked immediately.

'Oh, I see. You're moving out, then?' said Tommy. The room was bare, the bed had been made up and all the pictures and memorabilia were gone.

'I move back into my caravan tomorrow, so I took all my things down to Farrell's this morning.' Mr. Sheridan smiled at Tommy. 'I hope that is not too inconvenient?'

'No, Mr. Sheridan. When does the circus leave?'

'Friday. After that, it will be hard for you to find me.'

'Leave me an itinerary, please,' said Tommy, taking out his notebook and licking his pencil. Mr. Sheridan seemed a little put out but began, 'Rockbank on Saturday, we will be there four days. I expect to hear the Melbourne Cup there. Then Melton, four days, then Bacchus Marsh, only a couple of days. Myrniong after that, I don't think we're stopping there. Ballan for four days. Through Gordon to Wallace, four days, and then Bungareek—quaint, these rustic names, are they not? From

Bungareek to Ballarat. We expect to stay there a week. Or longer, if there is a good attendance. There usually is, say two weeks' audiences at Ballarat. Then to Sebastopol or Smythesdale. After that we do Linton, four days, and the run of little towns: Skipton, Carranballac, Glenelg, Lake Bolac—we swam the elephants there last year—Wickliffe, although we won't be stopping there because some idiot accused me of witchcraft there last season. Witchcraft, in 1928! Glenthompson, Dunkeld, and we finish that road at Hamilton. From there we take a different road back, along the coast. I'm not precisely sure of the route.'

'That will do, thank you,' said Tommy Harris, sure that if he didn't solve this murder by the time the circus got to Hamilton, he would never solve it. 'Can messages be left?'

'Just address a letter to the next town. Nothing travels slower than us. Of course, when I was with Wirth's, we travelled in style, on the train. On the road, Farrell's goes at elephant pace, four miles an hour. And slower, sometimes, depending on the weather, though that looks set fair. Is there anything more, Constable?'

'Not at the moment, sir.' Harris tried to look stern and official. 'But I may be seeing you again.'

'Always at your service,' said the magician and drew a string of flags from the constable's pocket. 'Well, well. How did they get there?'

Straight-faced, Constable Harris returned the flags to Mr. Sheridan and left the house.

◇◇◇

Miss Parkes was formally charged with murder. From the dock she said, 'I don't know if I did it.' The magistrate took this as a plea of not guilty and set her down for a committal hearing in ten weeks' time. Bail was not applied for and was formally refused. The magistrate remanded her in custody to await her trial.

Because there was no room in Pentridge for female prisoners, she was taken back to the watch-house. Such as remained of her sanity was applied to sharpening her stolen knife on the stone wall of her cell.

◇◇◇

Phryne was still following Dulcie around the circus. Scents arose and delighted her. Tar, sulphur, the reek of burning hoof and new-staunched metal in the horse lines. The strange thick odour of camel. The smell of drying hay. Canvas, toffee, engine oil. They were approaching a very grand large caravan. Outside it a slim blonde woman was sitting under an awning, rubbing liniment into the calf of one leg.

'Hello, Miss Bevan.'

'Damn! Can you reach around for me, Dulcie? I can't afford a cramp.' Dulcie nudged Phryne, who took the offered leg and began to smooth oil into the bunched muscle. Miss Bevan accepted her ministrations without bothering to acknowledge them. 'I can't ask Joseph for another massage so soon. He's very busy, you know.'

Phryne, rubbing assiduously, reflected that however busy the camp's horse doctor was, a lowly rider could be commandeered at any time. She wondered suddenly how Dot felt, attending on Phryne. Phryne, as employer and mistress, expected service, just as this flyer did. The tense muscle relaxed under her touch and Phryne got to her feet. Miss Bevan wiggled her toes. 'Thanks,' she said carelessly. She put her foot to the ground and stood up. 'Yes. That'll do. Is she new to the show?' she asked, looking at Dulcie. 'Better get her a practice tunic. I'll give her one of mine. Mum just made me three new ones. Falling off a horse knocks hell out of clothes, especially if you haven't got many.'

Phryne boiled with shame. Second-hand garments, hand-me-downs, had been an aspect of childhood poverty that had been hard to bear. She hated wearing clothes made for someone else. But she gulped her humiliation down and accepted a skimpy sky-blue tunic from Miss Bevan. It had been patched.

'Thank you,' whispered Phryne. 'It's very nice.'

'It's nothing,' said Miss Bevan. She lost interest in them and Dulcie drew Phryne on.

'That's the Flying Bevans. They're world-class flyers. Everyone wants to be a flyer.'

'Do they?' said Phryne, folding the tunic. Miss Bevan was right. It was nothing. Phryne was feeling angry and ashamed. She was being ignored. Miss Bevan had not even looked at her or spoken to her directly. 'Where now?'

'Round here are the sleeping tents. They double as changing tents.'

Phryne lifted a flap. A long row of beds lined one side of the tent. Each had a trunk or suitcase next to it. The other side was cluttered with costumes hanging over lines, properties, and what appeared to be an elephant saddle.

'Here's the kitchen,' said Dulcie. 'Hello, Mrs. T. What's for lunch?'

A bent crone scowled up from her covey of kettles. Steam had damped her hair and it hung in witch-locks around her nutcracker face.

'You take your fingers out of me pots, Dulcie,' she snarled. 'Lunch is over. You'll have to wait till dinner. And what are you trailing along with yer? Another mouth to feed?' She glared at Phryne. 'Ye're nothing but a nuisance, girl.'

Dulcie did not seem at all cast down. 'Stew again?' she asked. 'I dunno what you'd do if them sheep didn't keep on dying of old age.'

Mrs. T threw a tin mug with accuracy and venom. Dulcie ducked and caught the missile with effortless grace. Then she juggled it with a box of matches and a ladle. She tossed them back, one by one, to the old woman, who caught them easily. Dulcie backed away, taking Phryne with her.

'She's a good cook but she ain't half got a temper. You stay out of casting range when she loses her rag, Fern. Even chucked a chopper, once, and missed the old man's head by a whisker. He was complaining about having mutton stew ten days running. She told him to go kill a horse if he wanted a change of diet. She's married to a clown, though. That always sours the temper.'

'What, one of the Shakespeares?'

'No, they ain't married. They're Jews. They don't get married like us. No, Mrs. T married Thompson, the acrobatic clown.

He's a great performer and he loves his dog, but he's a real mean old cuss otherwise. Clowns are like that. They waste all their niceness on the audience. Then they ain't got none left for the rest of us. All right, now, that's the men's tent. Instant dismissal if you're caught inside it, no matter what the reason. Farrell told you that? This caravan belongs to Mr. Robert Sheridan, the magician, he ain't here yet. He don't lodge with us common folk when we're in town. Wait a bit. I have to deliver a message. Just wait for me here.'

Phryne felt in her pocket for a cigarette. There seemed to be no rule against smoking. She lit a gasper and drew in the smoke gratefully. She was feeling off balance. Deprived of her usual props and stays and allies, and having to speak with the accent of her childhood, she was losing confidence. No one seemed to like her, and she was used to being liked, or at least noticed. She closed her eyes.

A strong hand took hold of her scarf and pulled at it. She gasped, her eyes snapping open. The hand felt rapidly down her body until it reached her cardigan pocket. She let the scarf fall, grabbed for the hand and found she was holding an elephant's trunk.

The end was soft, pinkish, and as sure as the grasp of fingers. She sighted up along it to a grey mass of body, tethered by one foot to a picket. Bright eyes in the plane of the face winked at her. Sail-like ears flapped.

'Oh, you gave me such a shock,' said Phryne as the delicate trunk curled around her wrist with a warm noise like a kiss. 'My, you are big! What a huge creature you are.' The elephant gave an absurdly small squeak, the sort of noise that should have come from a mouse, Phryne thought. It rocked from foot to foot. 'What do you want?' asked Phryne as the trunk began to quest through her clothes. 'Oh, I see.'

There were three peppermints in her pocket, which she had brought to feed the horses. She was about to bring them out when the trunk curled back to the huge mouth and a noise like a concrete mixer offended her ears. The elephant had picked her pocket. 'I wonder who taught you that?' she asked aloud.

'Rajah, you're a bad girl,' said a sharp voice. 'You ain't been doing that pickpocket trick on our own folk, not after I told you it was a low mean act.'

A tiny man with hay in his hair ducked under Rajah's bulk and blinked into the sunlight.

'I'm Fern,' said Phryne. 'I'm the new rider in the rush.'

She waited for him to snub her, as Lyn Bevan had, but the small man was too busy apologizing for his elephant to concern himself with questions of status.

'Billy Thomas,' said the elephant keeper. 'I dunno where she picked that up. Did it herself, maybe. Queer creatures, elephants. Sorry about that. I keep moving her picket back and she keeps movin' it forward again. What did she get?'

'Three peppermints.'

'That's all right. I gotta be careful. She'll eat herself sick on fairy lollies, and what that does to her digestion don't bear thinking about. An elephant with a bellyache ain't no laughing matter. You watch her from now on. Elephants don't forget. Well, they don't forget someone who has peppermints in their pockets.' He ducked back under the canvas shade, pulling Rajah with him. Phryne could hear him hammering in the picket, to the accompaniment of a lot of cursing.

Dulcie returned and Phryne called excitedly, 'Dulcie, an elephant just picked my pocket!'

'Oh, yair, that Rajah. Nice old cow, otherwise. But she dearly loves lollies and Billy won't give her more than a few. So she steals 'em. Come along. There's the jugglers' caravans. I live there with my partner Tom. Next to us is the Cat'lans. I wish they were further away.'

Phryne caught the eye of a slim, dark man. He was sitting in the sun mending a pair of much-worn sequined trunks. He did not smile but scanned her with black eyes. She did not know what language he spoke, so she ventured on French.

'*Bonjour, M'sieur.*'

Dulcie dragged at her sleeve. 'I told you not to have nothing to do with them foreigners!'

Phryne pulled away. She had been pushed around more than she was accustomed to lately.

'*Jour*,' said the man, smiling a brilliant smile. '*Mademoiselle Àgata*!' he called into the tent. '*Quelqu'un qui parle français*! Someone who speaks French!'

Àgata emerged, a thin woman holding a suckling baby. She beamed.

'*Aaró? Si? I tant*!' She addressed Phryne directly. '*Vous parlez français? Et voila—ca me fait plaisir*. Do you speak French? What a pleasant surprise!'

'*Vous faiter partie du cirque*? Are you with the circus?' asked the man.

'*Oui, je suis écuyère…Et vous?* Yes, I am a rider,' said Phryne. 'What do you do?'

'*Nous sommes des équilibristes. Nous avons perfectionné le castell—la pyramide humaine*. We are balancers. We have perfected the human pyramid,' Àgata broke in eagerly. '*Vous devez venir vous voir. Nous sommes en troisième lieu à là liste, Mare de Déu*. You must come and see us. We have third billing.' Phryne found the woman hard to follow. She seemed to be thinking in another language. The accent was harsh and definite and she had never heard it before.

'*Bien sûr. Mais d'ou venez-vous?* But where do you come from?' One thing she was sure of. '*Vous n'êtes pas Français*. You aren't French.'

Àgata laid the baby over her shoulder and patted its back. It was small and dark and it burped resoundingly.

'*Non, senyoreta, nous sommes Catalans. Nousautres aimons mieux parler le français que le castillian*. We are Catalans. We would rather speak French than Spanish.'

Her husband interposed, seeing Phryne's difficulty. '*Je doute fort que vous parliez le catalan*. I doubt that you can speak Catalan.' He lowered his voice. '*Les autres nous appellent les étrangers*. The others call us foreign. *Il n'y a que le nain, M Burton, qui parle français*. No one else can speak French, except for Mr. Burton the dwarf.'

Àgata laughed. '*Un homenet bien enseigné.* An educated little man.'

Aaró agreed. '*Un petit bonhomme bien savant,*' he said. Phryne wondered if he was being ironic. *Savant* also described a performing flea. Then again, there was certainly something of the performing flea about the amazing Mr. Burton. '*Voudriez-vous nous faire le plaisir de souper avec nous?* Perhaps you will like to dine some time?'

'*Je veux bien. Je vous en remercie.* Thank you, I would be delighted,' said Phryne. '*Bon, je dois partir. Mon cavalier s'énerve.* I'd better go. My escort is becoming nervous. *Je suis bien contente d'avoir fait votre connaissance. A bientôt.* How delightful to meet you.'

'*Adéu,*' said Àgata. '*Petite cavalière.*'

'*A bientôt,*' echoed Aaró.

'*You* ain't foreign, are you, Fern?' asked Dulcie suspiciously. Phryne laughed.

'No. I learned—' Oops. She had to think fast. 'I lived in Collingwood when I was a kid. Went to school there. I picked up a bit of the lingo. Enough to get along. Come on. What's over there?' She pointed to a row of steel cages under a canvas awning.

'Lions. We gotta be careful. Mr. Burton said the lions was upset and an upset lion ain't nothing to fool about with. But all the newies want to see the lions. I'll go first.'

Phryne followed Dulcie into a narrow alley. There was a stench of raw meat and something more worrying, a reek of predator. The hair on the back of Phryne's neck bristled. An inheritance, she thought, from the days when lions hunted humans. Some small primitive Phryne had streaked across the grassland and up a tree just out of ripping distance of those terrible claws, those long sharp white teeth, that hot red gullet. That cave-dwelling Phryne was gibbering frantically in the back of 1928 Phryne's head.

Three men were discussing the racing news, seated on folding canvas chairs. The central figure was big and running to fat, with a crop of longish hair as white as wax. The other two were undistinguished, rather oily, in overalls. One had each finger and most of both palms strapped up in sticking plaster.

'Well, I'm putting my money on Strephon,' declared the man with the plaster. 'I like the name. And I reckon the weather'll suit him. Hello! What have we here?'

'Dulcie and a new girl,' said the big man languidly. 'Hello, Dulcie. Who is this?'

'Fern. I'm showing her around.' Dulcie sounded cautious.

'And of course you could not stay away from Amazing Hans and his equally amazing lions!'

Amazing Hans stood up. He had just a trace of German accent and was magnificent, his mane of white hair resembling that of the lions. He gestured to them to come under the awning. Iron bars made the occupants of the cages hard to see, but Phryne did not want to see them any clearer.

'Sarah,' he said. Something snarled in the half-dark and Phryne made out teeth and eyes. 'Sam, Boy, King, Albert and Prince. Presently of Farrell's Circus, soon to be...well.'

'You, too?' Dulcie eyed him disapprovingly. 'Ain't Farrell's a good show? And ain't Farrell been good to you? Bought you that new lion and all?'

'He has been good to me,' said Hans precisely. 'But he is no longer in charge. And too many things have been going wrong, Dulcie. These beasts need a lot of care, you know. There's the food and the vet's bills. It's costly.'

'Aren't they hard to handle? I thought that female lions were more fierce,' said Phryne. Amazing Hans scowled at her.

'What would you know? Amazing Hans does not need advice from a slip of a new girl. They recognize me as their master. Female and male.'

'They're just big cats,' sneered the man with the plastered hands. He ran a finger along the steel bars and whistled to the lion inside. It stood up and shook itself.

'You think so?' Hans laughed unpleasantly. 'Just cats, eh? I'd advise you not to take them for granted, Jack.'

Hans approached and Jack stepped back from him. Dulcie took Phryne's cardigan sleeve and drew her toward the sunlight.

'Not to be taken lightly,' advised Hans in a gentle voice. Jack took another pace away and snarled, 'What're you doing?' a split second before the air was wounded by a thunderous roar. A clawed paw shot out between the bars. Jack squealed. The claws had raked his skin, leaving thin parallel scratches as clean cut as a razor-blade. The stout cloth of the overall had been slit.

Amazing Hans laughed merrily. 'You'd better go and get Mrs. Thompson to put some lard on that,' he said. 'Don't come near my lions again. They've got a good memory,' he added, as Jack scuttled past him into the alley. 'And Prince has got your scent now.'

Phryne and Dulcie walked away. Phryne found that she was shaking.

'I don't like 'em either,' confessed Dulcie. 'Nothing that big ought to have teeth like daggers. Still, they're a draw.'

They had come to a small patch of grass outside a neat green caravan, where a shirtless, tanned man was plaiting leather boot-laces into what looked like a leash.

'Give me a hand with this,' he grunted. Phryne sat down and took the four ends from his hand and watched as the deft fingers moved like shuttles. After a few minutes, he tied off the end and looked up.

'Thanks. Who's this, Dulcie? I thought she was Andy. Want a cuppa?'

A kettle was singing on a small fire. Phryne was thirsty. So was Dulcie.

'Thanks, Bernie. Her name's Fern, she's a new rider. I'd kill for a cuppa, Bernie, thanks.' Dulcie flopped down onto the grass. 'I never realize how big Farrell's is until I take a newie around.'

Mr. Wallace made mugs of strong tea with milk and sugar and opened a tin of ginger biscuits. He accepted one of Phryne's cigarettes, without thanks, as though it were his due. Phryne had been bolstering her courage. Now it was leaking away like sand out of a sandbag. She sat down on the grass, ignored, and feeling utterly forlorn.

'This is the life,' said Bernard Wallace, smoking contentedly and blowing on his tea. 'Nice day, sun shining, no show tonight and Dulcie the juggler to talk to.'

A dog inserted its head under Phryne's elbow soliciting attention and biscuits. She managed not to spill her tea and stroked the smooth head absent-mindedly.

'Just Bruno, he's all right,' observed Mr. Wallace. 'What's new, then, Dulcie?'

'Nothing much. You heard about Mr. Christopher?' Bernard nodded. 'Lots of 'em are thinking of leaving. Even Mr. Burton. How about you?'

'Nah. Farrell's I started and Farrell's I'll end. Got a couple more years' work and then I'm off to the country with Bruno. I reckon Farrell's will last that long.'

'I hope so,' said Dulcie. 'Who would a couple of greasy fellers be, one with his hands all bandaged up?'

'A couple of fellers, I s'pose. There's a lot of newies this time round. And a couple of the worst roustabouts I ever saw trying to put up a pup-tent this morning. Talk about cack-handed! Give him a bit of your biscuit,' he advised, speaking directly to Phryne for the first time. 'He loves ginger biscuits.'

It was at this point that Phryne finished her tea and looked down. Instead of the dog she had expected, she found that she had been caressing the round furry head of a bear. He had black, twinkling eyes, almost buried in deep cinnamon fur. His ears looked to be insecurely gummed on and his nose was cold and wet at the end of a long snout.

Her hand fell from the domed forehead and the bear nudged her. She kept stroking and he rumbled blissfully and leaned on her. Phryne leaned back as hard as she could till they established an equilibrium.

'That's Bruno. He likes you,' commented Mr. Wallace with some surprise, as though the creature should have had better taste. 'Bears always take likes and dislikes at first sight. Some people they hate, some people they love. Some they just ignore.'

'He ignores me,' said Dulcie. 'Thankfully.'

'He likes me,' said Phryne, honoured but rather hot and squashed. 'Get off now, Bruno.'

She shoved hard and managed to scramble to her feet, still holding the ginger biscuit. As she came up off the ground, so did Bruno. He stood considerably taller than she and opened his mouth, begging. Phryne found that he had a remarkable array of what looked like very sharp teeth. His paws, resting on her shoulders, weighed her down. Phryne noticed that he was curling up the ends of his paws so as to keep his claws away from her skin. She was not afraid. She dropped the biscuit into the gaping mouth.

'There, good Bruno.'

The biscuit vanished instantly and Bruno sniffed at her for any others concealed about her person. When she opened both hands and he snuffled up a few crumbs, he dropped to all fours again and looked around hopefully for more.

'All right, you beggar, here's another biscuit,' said Mr. Wallace, getting up. 'But you gotta dance for it. Hup!' Before Phryne's enchanted gaze, Bruno lifted up onto his hind legs and solemnly circled three times. Then he sat down and waited for his reward.

'There you are, good bear. He's as good as a wife,' said Mr. Wallace, scratching Bruno behind the ear. 'Cruel to make him sleep in a cage next to the lions. But shire councils will be shire councils and they just don't understand about bears. Old Bruno fetches and carries and is as good as gold and he don't talk. What more could a man want? Have another cup, Dulcie?'

'No thanks,' said Dulcie. 'We'd better get on. Fern's got another lesson and I have to get back to the mending.'

'Come back and see Bruno again,' said Mr. Wallace to Phryne. 'He don't like many people. He'd like to see you again.'

Phryne walked back onto the path between the tents with an idiotic smile on her face. What have I come to? she chastised herself. I'm so dependent on approval, and this circus cares so little for me, that I am terribly grateful if a bear likes me. Still, he does like me.

Dulcie was saying something and Phryne wrenched her attention back to her companion. It seemed that Phryne had impressed Dulcie with her aplomb.

'Whew!' said Dulcie. 'I wonder you wasn't scared to death! He's supposed to keep that infernal animal chained up!'

'Bruno's all right,' said Phryne. 'Bruno is fine. But those lions are not. I do not like lions. What about those two men, then?'

'Oh, just that they didn't seem used to the lions. Everyone gets told not to go near 'em. They ain't safe. Even Hans knows that. Every wild animal trainer gets mauled sooner or later. And don't you go taking liberties with any of 'em, even if they look harmless, like Rajah or the bear. Rajah can pull up the big top on his own and Bruno nearly bit a kid's arm off down at Colac. Kid thought that he'd tease him with a toffee apple, pulling it out of reach. Bruno took the apple and bit the kid to teach him not to tease bears.'

'I'll be careful,' promised Phryne. 'But it worked, didn't it?'

'What?'

'I bet the little ratbag didn't tease any more bears.'

Dulcie laughed. 'Now, you know your way round, Fern? Are you staying here tonight?'

'No, I've still got a day on my lodging. I'll come in tomorrow.'

'And you all right for…I mean, you got somewhere to sleep and all?' said Dulcie. 'Cos I can lend you a few shillings if…'

'No, that's all right.' Phryne felt suddenly ashamed of her house and the exquisite dinner awaiting her. 'You're very kind, Dulcie.'

'I been broke before,' said Dulcie. 'That way to the horse lines and you better put on that tunic. And hurry. Miss Molly don't like to be kept waiting.'

◇◇◇

Phryne fell four times during her next lesson. Her knack seemed to have deserted her. Miss Younger scowled but said, 'You did all right this morning. We'll try again tomorrow.'

Phryne limped back to groom and water Missy, favouring a scraped knee. Then she walked out of the circus and caught a bus.

Once home, she telephoned her solicitor and ordered him to make urgent enquiries about the ownership of Farrell's Circus, authorizing him to make an offer to buy it if he could not find out any other way. She had to know why Farrell tolerated Mr. Jones.

When Alan Lee came to her front door, he was greeted by a woman in circus garb. Phryne had retained the scarf and the washed-out dress and she was limping.

'Come up,' she invited, leading him by the hand. He mounted the polished stairs to her boudoir. A sumptuous cold supper was laid out on the table. There were plates of smoked salmon, cheeses, caviar, olives, French bread and crisp salad. She locked the door behind him and led him into the bathroom.

'Tonight you shall share my luxury,' she said, pulling off the dress and the scarf and shedding battered undergarments, 'because tomorrow I shall share your poverty.'

Her fingers found the buttons of his shirt and she stripped him with automatic efficiency, dropping his stained garments to the floor. The bath was full of steaming water, scented with horse chestnut. It was a bewitching, delicate fragrance. Phryne stepped into it and brought Alan Lee with her. The marble tub was big enough for two. He moved like a sleepwalker, overwhelmed by her nakedness and the summer-forest scent.

His hands found the bruises of her falls onto hard ground. He stroked them as she slathered him with sweet-smelling foam, extinguishing the smell of engine grease and fairy lollies. He mouthed at the offered breasts, nuzzling and suckling and she embraced him close in the green water. His black hair was slicked against his head. He laughed, smooth as an otter, strong as an eel, and pulled her under.

Chapter Nine

Where have they cast me and to whom
A bondmaid?

The Trojan Women, Euripides
(translated by Gilbert Murray)

Joining the police force had supplied elements which had hitherto been missing in the life of Tommy Harris, who had led a blameless existence before he left his home in the country and came to the city in search of adventure. He had found excitement, suspense, more people than he had previously known to exist, and doses of carbon monoxide and alcohol that put a city patina on his over-healthy system.

He remained, however, a country boy and discovered that the methods he had previously used to subdue over-anxious horses worked perfectly well on his clientele. Now, taking his lead from his sergeant, he was trying to acquire subtlety. He was looking for Miss Minton, intending to observe her and draw deductions from her behaviour. He had heard that she was having an affair with a well-known theatrical producer, a point that could be checked. Tommy was in plain clothes and alone and was looking forward to an intellectual exercise in scientific police work.

But when he came into the Blue Diamond and found the owner's large friends beating Lizard Elsie, he felt that subtlety was out of place and that strong and immediate action was needed.

To simplify the situation he waded into the crowd, hauled off one man and threw him against the wall, fatally injuring the decor. He tripped another so that he slid across the room and collided with a pile of chairs. He pulled the old woman out from under a pile of bodies and saw that Elsie had her teeth fixed firmly in one attacker's ear.

'Let go, Elsie,' panted Tommy Harris. 'I've got him. Let go!'

Elsie muttered something and refused to unclench. Her victim was white and screaming.

'Get her off me!'

'Let go, Elsie!' commanded Constable Harris. The woman growled like a mastiff, her skinny hands clawing for the man's more delicate parts to complete her victory. The victim clutched at his groin and screamed again. He was a lot bigger than Elsie but this did not seem to be of much assistance to him.

The patrons of the Blue Diamond had all withdrawn out of reach and were watching, fascinated. Constable Harris noticed a party in theatre-going clothes. One of the men was smoking a fat cigar, and Tommy was put in mind of a ferret which had been his constant companion during his youth. It had been a good ferret, called Bandit, but it couldn't help biting. Once, when faced with the prospect of his sole offspring spending a lifetime with a ferret clamped to his finger, his father had found a novel solution. Deciding to apply it, Tommy leaned over, plucked the cigar from the man's lips and blew a cloud of strong Havana smoke into Elsie's face. Then he returned the cigar to the patron and dragged Lizard Elsie onto her feet as she sneezed and released her hold.

'There we are,' said Tommy in his butter-soft voice. 'That's better, Elsie girl.'

Her victim was sitting on the floor, holding his outraged ear with one hand and caressing his outraged genitals with the other.

'She's mad!' he yelled. 'She came in here asking for a drink and we was just showing her the door and—'

'Takes three of you to throw me out, you fucking bastards,' snarled Elsie. 'Three of you! It would have taken bloody four when I had me strength. I'm fifty years old and it took three of you to get me down.'

'Now, now, Elsie,' soothed Constable Harris. 'Let's you and me sit down and have a drink, eh?'

'That's what I was fucking trying to do.' Elsie was not pleased. 'When these curs jumped on me.'

'Well, well, these misunderstandings will happen,' said Tommy. 'Come on. You sit down here and have a drink and I'll have a word to the manager.' He took a bottle from a waitress' tray and put it down in front of the old woman. 'That's right. Want a glass?'

'A glass? What for?' asked Elsie scornfully, applying the bottle to her lips.

Tommy left her and went to intercept Mr. Albert Ellis, who was advancing across the ruined club with blood in his eye.

'Mr. Ellis, is it?' asked Tommy easily. 'Had a little trouble?' He surveyed the owner and did not approve of what he saw. Albert Ellis was overdressed, had teeth like a rat, and altogether too much pomade on his hair. He offended Tommy's taste in a way which Lizard Elsie did not.

'Constable Harris,' said Ellis, recognizing him. 'You going to arrest that bitch?'

'No, why should I?'

'She comes into my club, breaking my fittings, assaulting my staff…'

'If your staff can't deal with one old lady I reckon you should hire more,' said Tommy easily. 'And your decor ain't nothing to write home about, either.'

This was undeniable. The Blue Diamond was furnished with chairs and benches that seemed to have come from an old cinema. Its walls, what could be seen of them, were painted pink and covered with old posters of film stars. Small tables made of packing cases, and a bar constructed of an old ticket box completed the ambiance. People did not go the the Blue Diamond for luxury. It was licensed to serve drinks with food until midnight. A supper at the Blue Diamond consisted of one ham sandwich. The ham was transparent and local legend said that the same sandwich had been in use for as long as the club had been open. It was now fossilized. In future times, museums might bid for it.

The Blue Diamond would undoubtedly be closed down for violations of its liquor licence, to open a month later under a new name. Cigarette butts littered the floor and the hot air was heavy with smoke. A dance band was tootling away in one corner, and on the pocket-handkerchief dance floor people had been dancing before the fracas with Lizard Elsie had provided a more interesting show.

'I'm not having her in my club,' said Albert Ellis. 'Take her away.'

Lizard Elsie heard this and screeched, 'You pox-rotted mongrel! You promised me ten bottles of ruby port, you fucking cur!'

'Shut her up!' snapped Ellis, and two of the fallen rose groaning and closed on Lizard Elsie. Tommy recognized Wholesale Louis on the floor, and Cyclone Freddy and the Mad Pole rising from the half-dead. They were both big and dangerous and they seemed to be rather cross with Elsie. Tommy was alone. He reached for the old woman and gathered her into his arms.

'Come on, my girl,' he said. 'We're leaving.'

'Ooh, sailor,' crooned Elsie, nursing her bottle. 'Been a long time since anyone swept me off my feet.'

Tommy backed toward the door and it swung behind them. He was out in Brunswick Street before the boss could react.

Still, it wouldn't take them long. He hefted Elsie, who was surprisingly light, and began to run.

He had been so delighted with the idea of plain clothes work that he did not even have his whistle. However, he thought as he settled into a fast gallop, he must meet the beat policeman fairly soon. Then his colleague could summon assistance before Tommy and Elsie got the pummelling of a lifetime.

He heard voices behind them, and then feet. A shot pinged past him and buried itself in the door of the butcher's shop.

'They're shooting!' said Tommy with an astonished gasp. 'Else, they're shooting at us! We've gotta get off the street!'

Elsie, who had been hanging over his shoulder and watching behind, croaked, 'There's three of 'em, and that mongrel Louis's got a gun.'

'Elsie, what have you got yourself into?' wondered Tommy Harris aloud. 'It must be something big for them to risk shooting in the street—or shooting at all. It's like Robinson said. Gangsters.'

'Turn here!' shrieked Elsie uncomfortably close to his ear. Harris paused. At that moment some force slammed him back against the wall at the corner of the lane. He staggered and dropped his burden. Elsie landed lightly and pulled him around the corner by the arm.

'In here, sailor!'

She dropped to her knees and crawled under a fence. Tommy followed, feeling suddenly weak.

'Lie here and don't squeak,' she ordered and slid back. She reappeared with a soaked and muddy shirt, which she dropped beside him.

'Bit of shoosh,' she suggested.

Tommy Harris felt for his side and found that his hand came away warm and wet. I've been shot, he thought. He was in no pain and his principal emotion was amazement.

Feet clattered down the lane and past the fence and paused. A cigarette lighter clicked and yellow light flared over the corrugated iron fences. A dog began to bark. Tommy Harris held his breath, feeling Lizard Elsie's thin hand close on his shoulder. A voice said, 'Nah. No trace. And we winged him and there's no blood on these cobbles. Try the next lane, boys.'

The footsteps retreated.

'You're shot,' said Elsie calmly. 'I wiped up the blood with me second-best shirt. Crawl a bit back and we can have a light and I'll have a look at yer, sailor.'

Tommy, strangely weak, hauled himself back across what felt like razor-blades and lay back in a nest of musty rags.

A match scratched and a small kerosene lamp was lit. Tommy found he was in a galvanized iron lean-to, manufactured out of bits of an old water tank. Lizard Elsie had furnished her little humpy with two old mattresses and several tattered quilts. She had some cooking gear, an old Coolgardie safe, and a battered leather handbag stuffed with what looked like papers. She put the lamp on the safe and rummaged among her belongings for a sheet. When she found it, she began to tear it into strips.

'Let's get that coat off,' she said. 'Yer shirt's ruined.'

'I'm all right, Else. Just let me lie here for a while and I'll get up and call...'

He tried to sit up and found that he couldn't. His muscles refused to answer.

'No you ain't,' she said calmly. 'You're shot and if you don't let me bloody look after you, you'll fucking bleed to death all over me fucking bed.'

Tommy did not resist as she peeled off his coat and shirt and wadded old linen against his side. She sloshed some cold liquid into the wound. It stung. Her hands were sure and she seemed to know what she was doing.

'Is it bad?' he asked, hoping that his voice did not tremble.

'Nah. Just winged you and tore away a bit of yer skin. You'll be all right, sailor. Now, I'd brew you a cuppa but the fucking night-watchman'll be around in a tick and if he sees me he'll throw me out.'

'Is this where you live, Elsie?' The bandaging was tight and comforting and he still felt no pain. He was lazily interested in the pattern which the streetlights made through the holes in the galvanized iron. It couldn't be very weatherproof, he thought.

'Yair. This is me little nest. Between sailors, like. I'm gonna have to lie low. Who'da thought that bastard Albert Ellis'd have guns?'

'They shot Reffo,' Tommy pointed out. 'At least, I think it was them.'

'Yair.' Lizard Elsie was subdued. 'Yair. Outside the Provincial. They bloody shot Reffo all right.'

'Why did Albert Ellis owe you ten bottles?' asked Tommy hopefully.

'He fucking owes me more than fucking that,' said Lizard Elsie cryptically.

'What do you mean?'

'Enough fucking questions. Everyone's got a questions,' snapped Elsie. 'Now, we can either get out of here, through the factory gate once bloody old Smithy's made his bloody rounds, or we can stay out of sight and see what daylight'll do. Whaddaya think, sailor?'

Tommy Harris tried to sit up and found that his body had returned to his command. With this came a return of sensation. He clamped his mouth shut to stifle a groan. Red-hot wires seemed to have been run through his nerves and he could feel the throb of his own heart. Every beat hurt. Systole and diastole, they pounded on his senses until his eyes swam.

'Later,' he said and Elsie caught him as he fell back.

'Later,' she agreed. She shoved him a little aside and lay down beside him, suckling contentedly on the bottle which Tommy had grabbed at random. It was Napoleon brandy, kept in the Blue Diamond for the manager's own personal guests. Elsie was lulled and soothed. She wrapped her arms around the large form of Police Constable Harris, breathing in his fresh healthy scent of male human, tweed and shaving soap. Fevered and exhausted, he laid his head on her breast.

Such darkness as was to be found in Fitzroy echoed with the sound of leather-clad feet as the 'Roy Boys searched all the lanes and byways for Lizard Elsie, the sailor's friend, and her new protector.

Phryne Fisher rose from her green sheets, collected her lover and her circus gear, and faced her staff. They all looked worried.

'I don't know how long I'll be away,' she said, adjusting a turban over her black hair. 'It might be days or it might be weeks. If anyone comes looking for me you are to say that I am in the country for a rest-cure and I have left no forwarding address. Here is a list of towns where I'll call at the post offices for letters. Remember that I am called Fern Williams.' She glanced at Dot apologetically. 'Sorry, Dot dear, but I couldn't think of another name at short notice. If you really need me write to me, but use cheap stationery and a Coles envelope. If I need anything I'll write, or I'll telephone, supposing I can find a phone that isn't in the general store. If I need to be rescued, Mr. Butler can bring the Hispano-Suiza and just whisk me off home. This is Mr. Lee,' she added, presenting a sleek and glowing young man. 'Mr. Alan Lee. He'll know where to find me and his orders are mine.'

'Miss,' said Dot, 'what about Detective Inspector Robinson?'

'What about him?'

'Are you going to tell him where you are going and all?'

'That's a good idea, Dot. You ring him and tell him. If he wants me, then he can follow the same routine. If he really wants me, tell him to get someone to arrest me. I can't be seen to be on good terms with the cops.'

'Yes, Miss. Good luck, Miss Phryne.' Dot kissed Phryne on the cheek. 'You will be careful, won't you?'

'Yes, Dot, I will. I promise.'

Mrs. Butler stepped forward and offered Phryne a bottle.

'What's this?'

'Goanna oil,' said Mrs. Butler. 'If you're going to keep falling off a horse, Miss Fisher, then you'll need it.'

Phryne took a last look at the anxious faces and said, 'Thank you. I'll be off then.' No one moved.

She went out of her own back door, taking a last look at the solid, well-known and well-loved house.

'Right?' asked Alan Lee, running a caressing hand down her back. 'You want to leave all this and come to the circus, Fern?'

Phryne shivered pleasantly and kissed him very gently and lingeringly on the mouth. She would not be able to kiss Alan Lee again while she stayed with Farrell's Circus and Wild Beast Show.

'Right,' she said.

Half an hour later Alan Lee parked his truck near the carousel and Phryne leapt out, clutching the brown suitcase. Her dress was once-washed and a blinding pink. Her head was bound up in a closely fitting pink turban. Her only unusual attributes were hidden. Around her waist, in a custom-made webbing belt, was her card case, some coins and twenty pounds in notes. In a compartment in the cheap suitcase was her Beretta and a box of ammunition.

The circus was breaking up. Two trucks had been loaded with planks and seats. Phryne stowed her suitcase on the truck designated by a laconic rigger. He was dressed lightly in a blue singlet, army-issue shorts, boots, and a fixed hand-rolled cigarette.

'What are they doing?' she asked him nervously, expecting to be snubbed. He smiled indulgently down at the pink turban.

'You're the new rider, ain't you? Never seen this before? Well, first we take down the canvas,' he said, as gangs of sweating men passed him, unlacing and folding the sides of the tent. 'Then we take out the guys and dismast the king poles.'

'Which are they?'

'The two highest ones. They're jointed so we can carry them. But they gotta fall careful-like, 'cos they cost a fortune. So we slows the fall all the way with lines.'

'But what takes the strain?'

'Rajah,' he said, gesturing with a thumb. Rajah the elephant, in harness, was holding the lines which stretched up to the king poles without shifting her feet. Phryne noticed three men in a group, leaning against the guys and smoking.

The head rigger noticed them too. 'Hey, you blokes! Come and lend a hand.'

One of the group made a rude gesture and the rigger strode off into the collapsing tent. Lifting the man off his feet, the rigger swung him out from under the canvas. The man stood rubbing his arm with one sticking-plastered hand.

'You wanna work in a circus,' the rigger said calmly, the cigarette never moving from its position on his lower lip, 'then you work.'

'Mr. Jones said—'

'I don't give a...' The rigger noticed Phryne and did not finish the sentence. 'I don't care what Mr. Jones said. He ain't head rigger and I am. Now carry canvas or get out.'

Sulkily, the three men moved away. The rigger spat out his cigarette and ground it slowly into the dust with the heel of his boot.

'Now, you watch,' he said. The tent came down with a gusty sigh, ballooning gently, as the king poles toppled. Rajah trundled out as it fell and stood patiently waiting until someone undid her harness. An army of men fell on the flattened saucer-shaped mass and dissected it into laced sections of canvas, miles of line, poles, tent pegs, electrical equipment and wires.

'You've got electric lights, then,' commented Phryne.

'Yair, boss bought a generator. That's the generator truck. Much better than the old flares. Petrol vapour, they were, and bloody dangerous. The electric ones are beaut. But the flyers say that they're too bright and they get too hot up in the air. Flyers,' he chuckled, 'they don't come more temperamental than flyers.'

It struck Phryne that she was talking to the most important man in the circus. Without this tall and competent rigger, the temperamental flyers would have no trapeze, the circus would have no cover, no lights and no ring. He seemed to bear his responsibility lightly. His eyes, however, missed nothing.

Horses neighed, camels hooted and bubbled. Rajah was unharnessed and led through the crowd by one ear. The air was full of smoke as all manner of trucks revved and either started or did not start. The air was also filled with curses.

'Miss Fern,' said a voice at Phryne's hip. This time she did not look up and around but dropped to one knee immediately. The dwarf seemed nervous.

'Mr. Burton,' she said. 'Good morning.'

'Would you care to ride with me?' he asked diffidently. 'The Catalans and I travel in convoy. Or perhaps you have a companion already?'

Phryne's body ached suddenly with remembrance of Alan Lee's touch. She banished a treacherous thought of what it might be like to make love in a moving caravan.

'Am I supposed to travel with the rest of the girls?' she asked.

The rigger commented, 'Nah. The girls spread 'emselves wherever there's a place. You go with Mr. Burton, girl. You'll get a more comfortable ride with him.' He grinned. 'Safer, too.'

Since Mr. Burton had drawn himself up to his full four feet (advertised height, three foot, seven inches), Phryne interposed her body.

'Thank you for telling me about the tent,' she said hurriedly to the rigger. 'Most interesting.' He gave her a puzzled look and she realized belatedly that she had used the wrong voice.

'Gotta go,' she added and accompanied the dwarf across the disintegrating camp to his own caravan. It was drawn by a large and patient horse, who was being backed into the shafts by one of the Catalans.

'*Hola*,' he encouraged. '*Il vaut mieux aller seul qu'en mauvaise compagnie*. It is better to travel alone than in bad company,' he added, viewing the pink dress with disapproval. He recognized Phryne as she came closer and muttered an apology. Phryne grinned. The dwarf climbed the side of the caravan and took the reins.

'*Merci, Benet*,' said Mr. Burton. 'Will you sit beside me, Miss Fern?'

The solemn dark boy boosted Phryne up onto the wagon and she sat down beside Mr. Burton, clutching at her turban.

'It all vanishes so fast,' she said breathlessly.

The circus, which had looked so permanent, came apart and packed itself up with astounding speed. The horse lines were empty. Phryne caught sight of Miss Younger, sitting astride Bell with effortless ease, ordering the riders of the liberty horses into convoy. The lions' cages had been loaded onto two trucks, with Amazing Hans driving one. Phryne caught sight of his flowing mane of hair. The first trucks, carrying the tent and the seating, were already out of sight. Behind, in a straggling line which was nevertheless perfectly ordered, came the riders, the camels, Rajah and her friend Sultan, the flyers and tumblers and clowns. There followed the Catalans and Mr. Burton, then after them in a long line the riggers and the lions and the roustabouts, cooks and boys. After them, separated by a little space came the carnival and after them, also separated, the gypsies.

The wagon jolted onto the tarmac surface of Williamstown Road. 'Would you like to make some tea?' suggested Mr. Burton. 'There is a spirit stove inside.'

Phryne climbed back into an immaculate little room. Everything was dwarf-size, from the four-poster bed with the satin quilt to the tiny washstand and the miniature wardrobe. It was all decorated in English cottage style and must have been very expensive.

She managed to persuade the spirit stove to light. While she waited for the kettle to boil, she looked out of the chintz-curtained window at the passing scene. Children whooped and ran along the pavements. Adults stood and stared. Once she had watched a circus go past in this way. Now she was inside one.

A bubble of delight burst in her chest.

She called to Mr. Burton, 'How do you like your tea?'

'Two sugars. Black,' he said. 'I'll have to keep driving; can you bring it out here?'

Phryne managed to crawl back through the caravan hatch without spilling too much tea. Mr. Burton gave her the reins while he drank. The big horse plodded on after the others in perfect four-four time. *Clop*, clop clop clop. *Clop*, clop clop clop. Phryne felt suddenly very relaxed, almost sleepy. The creature needed no guidance from the reins. He knew where he was going.

'Thank you,' said Mr. Burton, putting down his empty cup in a niche evidently designed for it. 'Why not have your tea now and perhaps a cigarette? This is always my favourite part of the journey. The beginning. Who knows what lies ahead?'

As Phryne sipped her tea and lit a gasper, the small man continued without change of tone, 'And what are you doing in Farrell's Circus, Miss Phryne Fisher?'

Chapter Ten

Are summer songs for me and my Aunts
As we lie tumbling in the hay

The Winter's Tale, Act II, Scene iii,
William Shakespeare

'What's eating you?' demanded Detective Inspector Robinson, summoned out of his cubbyhole of an office by Sergeant Grossmith at eight o'clock in the morning. The sergeant seemed excited about something. 'Why are you tiptoeing like that?' Robinson did not get on well with mornings. 'Taken up ballet at your age?'

Sergeant Grossmith opened the door into the front office of Russell Street Police Station and motioned his chief to look.

There, offending the cleanliness of the mud-coloured lino, sat old Lizard Elsie the sailor's friend, clutching a bottle of what appeared to have been brandy. Her tattered dress was splashed with dark stains and her boa was balder than ever. She was fast asleep and smiling. This in itself was not unusual. What caused Robinson to step back a pace onto Grossmith's foot was the sight of Elsie's supporter. The ill-famed harpy was lying with her head on Constable Harris' tweed-clad shoulder. He was sitting with his arm around Elsie and his back against the wall and his eyes were closed.

'Well, well,' said Robinson. 'The Babes in the Wood. Just waiting for the birdies to come and cover them with leaves. How long have they been there, Duty Sergeant?'

'They came in, sir, about ten minutes ago and flopped down like that.'

'Thank you for this little comic interlude, Terry,' said Robinson. 'Now, hadn't you better wake your constable and ask him what in hell's name he thinks he's doing?'

Grossmith strode over to the pair and bellowed, 'Wakey, wakey!'

Lizard Elsie sprang to her feet, hands hooked into claws, and then identified the speaker. She grinned at him.

'H'lo, Terry,' she said. 'I brung your copper back.'

'Why, what's wrong with him?' Grossmith crouched down next to Harris. He shook him by the shoulder. The young man groaned and strove to focus. Grossmith roared, 'Harris! What's the matter with you?'

Robinson came out of the doorway and inspected the recumbent officer.

'Use your eyes, Terry. Look at his coat. And his shirt. That ain't booze. He's not drunk. That's blood. He's been hurt.'

'One of youse has got bloody eyes, then,' said Lizard Elsie sarcastically. 'Of course he's been hurt. He's been shot. It was that fucking mongrel Wholesale Louis. If you want to bloody know.'

'The 'Roy Boys,' said Grossmith. 'Call the police surgeon,' he shouted at the bemused duty officer. 'Don't stand there like an idiot! Jack, d'you reckon we can get him up onto the bench?'

Together they lifted Constable Harris. Lizard Elsie began to sidle toward the door and Robinson caught her arm.

'Stay with us, Else,' he said. 'I reckon we owe you a favour.'

'For a fucking change,' she told him. 'He's a good boy, he is,' she added. 'I was bloody getting the worst of it last night in the Blue Diamond and he piled in and rescued me. Then we ran away and fucking Louis shot 'im, so I hid 'im all night and we come 'ere on the first tram. He's not hurt bad. He's just tired and bloody shocked.'

'Elsie, you are a remarkable woman,' said Robinson.

'Too fucking right,' Elsie agreed.

In an hour, Constable Harris was recovered enough to be interviewed. The wound was revealed to be a long, shallow gash along his side, which hurt when he moved but was not serious. That he had not contracted tetanus the police surgeon attributed to Elsie's dressing of the wound with fine cognac.

'Best drink I ever had,' said Elsie wistfully. 'And I didn't like to waste it.'

'It wasn't wasted,' said the doctor. 'Keep the wound dry, lad, and get it dressed again tomorrow.' He took his leave.

'Now, Harris, tell me exactly what happened,' instructed Grossmith. 'Slowly.'

Constable Harris, who had been allowed to wash and change back into his uniform, felt clean and comfortable. He sat up straighter and ordered his thoughts. He then told, in minute detail, everything he could remember about the night before.

'Then I crawled into this humpy and I don't remember anything until Elsie dragged me onto the cobbles and we staggered out to the street and caught a tram. They almost didn't let us on. We must have looked a sight.'

'I wrapped him up and I stayed with him to keep him warm,' said Elsie slowly. 'You can bloody die of cold and shock if you ain't kept warm. Then I brung 'im back like he says. But what I wanna fucking know,' her voice rose in wrath, 'is where do them mongrel 'Roys get off, trying to snuff me what never did 'em any fucking harm? And why?'

'Ah. Yes. Now, you told Albert Ellis that he owed you ten bottles,' said Grossmith slowly. 'Why should he owe you ten bottles, eh, Else?'

Lizard Elsie looked past him at the wall. Her mouth shut tight.

'Come on, Elsie, you're in big trouble. Not from me. I'm not going to charge you with anything if all you did was go into the Provincial and start a fight with the publican so that the 'Roys could shoot poor old Reffo. Neither is my chief.' Elsie looked at

Robinson. He nodded. Grossmith continued, 'But you rescued Harris here, who seems to have a talent for being rescued by women, and the 'Roys'll be after you now. You've never done anything really wrong, Elsie, except swear the air blue. We got nothing against you. But I bet the 'Roys don't see it like that.'

'What can you bloody do?' asked Elsie. 'I spill my guts to you, then I go out on the street again and they're fucking waiting for me. Wholesale Louis with his bloody gun.'

'We can keep you in protective custody until we sort it out,' said Grossmith. 'You can walk out any time you like,' he added, as Elsie made a convulsive start for the door. He hung onto her. 'Wait a bit, Elsie. You and me, we've known each other a long time, eh? I always did the right thing by you, Else. I'd hate to see you dead.'

Elsie did not struggle. She allowed Grossmith to put her back in her chair.

'Yair. Well, you're bloody right. I did start that fight. Albert Ellis owes me ten fucking bottles of port, the mean bastard dog. And I s'pose I can trust you, Terry. I s'pose so,' she said reluctantly.

'And we could probably manage a bottle of beer a day,' he added. 'You know you've gotta get off the red biddy, Else, it'd kill a brown dog. A week on one bottle of beer a day and you'll be leaping like a spring lamb. But I'll give you a bottle of brandy out of the first-aid kit to start you off.'

'Whaddaya reckon, eh, sailor?' She nudged Constable Harris in his uninjured side. 'You're the one what swept me off me poor ole feet.'

'You stay for a while, Elsie,' said Constable Harris. 'While we have a little chat with Mr. Ellis and the boys. I'm anxious to meet them again.'

She sized him up in one sharp glance from her bright black eyes. Then she smiled a breathtaking smile from her wrinkled face, gentle and sensuous, which set Constable Harris back in his recovery.

'All right, sailor.' She patted his cheek. 'I'll do it. Come on then, Terry,' she laughed up at the big policeman, 'put the bloody cuffs on. I'll go quiet.'

Because there was no other accommodation available for females, the duty officer put Lizard Elsie in the same cell as Miss Parkes.

◇◇◇

Phryne Fisher managed not to spill her tea. She stared at the little man, who was driving the horse and preserving a perfectly blank face.

'Sorry?'

'I recognized you when Rajah pulled off your scarf,' he explained. 'No one else is likely to have heard of you.'

'And you have?' Phryne did not feel equal to denying it entirely and had now lost the initiative.

He smiled slightly at the tacit admission of identity. 'Oh yes. I read the fashionable papers.'

'Why?'

'Book reviews,' said the dwarf calmly. 'Since I graduated from Oxford I have kept up my reading. Literature is my field. Also, I like to see what the social set is doing. *Tempora mutantur, nos et mutamur in illis*. The times change, and we change with them. There has been a general failure of nerve since the War, would you not agree? No one believes now that there is a golden age ahead, not even Mr. Wells.'

'You were at Oxford University?' squeaked Phryne. 'Then what are you doing in Farrell's?'

'Where else could my...deformities be valuable? Everywhere else I am a freak. Here I am still a freak but I am a performer. Circuses are the only places where dwarves can get some respect. And even then, you heard the head rigger. "Safe with me," he said and laughed.'

'Only because you are obviously a gentleman,' said Phryne. 'If you don't mind my asking, Mr. Burton, how old are you?'

'I'm thirty,' he said, looking into her face. 'I went grey early. That's good. An old dwarf has more value, because he is obviously not just a child. I'll never be taller than I am and unless I can find a suitable lady dwarf I'll never marry.'

'How about...er...love?' asked Phryne. Mr. Burton laughed.

'A lot of women want to find out about dwarves,' he said primly. 'They are...er...interested in my...er...attributes. But I will not compromise. It is love or nothing. So far, it is nothing. Now, tell me what you are doing in a circus. Is this a whim, Miss Fisher? Are you bored?'

'I was, until I tried falling off a cantering horse every morning. Now I'm bruised. I really don't know what to say, Mr. Burton, except to tell you that I am here for a good purpose and beg you not to expose me.'

'What purpose?'

'First, tell me. Do you think that there is a reason behind the accidents which have befallen Farrell's in the last few months?'

'No. I think that there is a design. The Catalans went to Mama Rosa—they have no prejudice against gypsies—and she said that there was malice, not the evil eye, behind the incidents. Mama Rosa may be a charlatan, I have no opinion on the matter. But she has her finger squarely on the pulse of the circus, perhaps because she is not part of it. Someone has been making mischief. Is that what brings you here?'

'Yes.'

'Why should you care about us? We are only circus folk.'

'I've had enough of this "only rogues and vagabonds" rubbish,' said Phryne angrily. 'I'm here because a close friend asked me to save his livelihood, which will be lost if the circus folds its tents and goes broke. My motives are excellent. I admit I was bored and a little irritated by that person implying I couldn't leave all my luxuries behind. The luxuries were no loss, but being so lowly is hard to bear and putting up with Mr. Jones is harder. But I will find out what is wrong with Farrell's Circus. I gave my word. Even if I continue to fall off Missy every day.'

Mr. Burton heaved a sigh of relief. 'Good. I don't know if I can help you but I will try.'

'Is there anyone else who might be reliable?'

'They're all reliable, Miss Fisher. But as to who might help you...' He thought about it and gave Phryne the reins while he lit a cigarette. The horse paid no attention to the movement of the leather straps across his patient back. He continued the solid heavy four-four clop and Phryne's head nodded.

'Yes, it is hard to stay awake. That's why I usually have one of the Catalans as a companion. Not that my noble steed Balthasar actually needs to be driven, but he likes some company. Have you noticed the time of the hooves? Exact metronome-measurable four beats in a bar. I'm not telling anyone else or they'll want to make him a performer and then he might not like the wagon so much. Yes. Well. We are leaving the suburbs behind. This is Deer Park. Not that I know if they still have any deer. Or if they ever had any. Hmm. Now, what can I tell you? Avoid Amazing Hans and the lions. He is a little unhinged. Most wild animal tamers are. Bernard Wallace and Bruno are safe enough.'

'Yes. Bruno likes me.'

'Does he indeed? A rare mark of trust.' Mr. Burton seemed impressed. 'Mr. Farrell—well, I don't know that you should go anywhere near Farrell. Since this Jones man came he's been looking wearier and greyer every day. Jones has some hold over him. I suggest that it is good old-fashioned money. Rajah is a flighty beast and so is her trainer. Of the flyers, Lynn Bevan is the only one who might even listen to you. Flyers are very self-involved. They are the aristocrats and the rest of us are cast as peasants. Dulcie is a good girl. So, oddly enough, is Mrs. Thompson. Being married to a clown is a sore trial. You might be able to talk to the clowns. Toby is a depressive but Matthias is all right—or so they say. I do a performance with them. The only time you can get a word out of Toby is between bouts of this illness, when he is quite pleasant. When he's down, he is very down and won't talk. Matthias even has to feed him. But he can still perform and make the whole crowd fall down laughing. Clowns are odd. The Catalans will help but they are looked upon with almost as much suspicion as gypsies. If I were you, I'd look at Mr. Jones very closely. And there are three roustabouts who have certainly never done this work before. One has sticking plaster all over his hands.'

'Yes, I've seen him. He gave the head rigger the finger.'

'Did he, indeed?' Mr. Burton chuckled. 'His two offsiders are also incompetent, but that may not mean that they are criminals. Circuses have a strange fascination for unhappy boys. Unhappy men, too. They run away and join us. Then when they find out that it is all hard work, erecting tents in the rain, eating Mrs. Thompson's stew and no orgies with the girls, they run away again. If they are still here in a week I shall be more sure that they don't belong.'

'What about Mr. Christopher?' asked Phryne. 'Did you know him?'

'Alas, not well. His only confidants were Miss Younger, poor girl, and the clown Matthias. He was a nice man who kept his own counsel.'

'And what about the magician? You left him out.'

'Miss Fisher, I strongly advise you not to go near our Mr. Sheridan unless you have company and are wearing armour. He is what was once known as a bounder. There was a scandal with a country girl in Colac and there will be more. He is oily and pleasing and gets his own way far more often than he should.'

Mr. Burton sounded very irritated and Phryne decided to change the subject. 'How far are we going today?'

'Presently we shall stop for lunch. Then we will have a light afternoon's jog to Rockbank. It was the first stopping place for the miners. Half a mile out we stop and dress for the parade.'

'What?'

'We stop,' said Mr. Burton patiently, 'and put on our costumes. All the people who are not needed to rig the tent and set up the camp ride something and toot or bang something and we parade through Rockbank throwing leaflets announcing the circus. We do not do a performance until tomorrow night. But we have to let the populace know that we have arrived. I would advise you, at that time, to go and collect Missy, give her a quick lick and a promise and find yourself a costume. They will be in the wagon with all the lady's gear. Ask Dulcie for something.'

◇◇◇

Phryne lunched with the Catalans on a peppery stew made out of mutton and garlic in roughly equal proportions. She did not need the proverb, '*Val més bona gana que bona vianda*'—'A good appetite is worth more than good meat'—which Àgata quoted, anticipating the Australian disgust for anything gastronomically unusual. The food was solid and spicy. Phryne conversed in her Parisian French about the Catalans' home. They told her that the mountains there were blue and cold, so high that they reached heaven.

Climbing into the back of Mr. Burton's wagon after lunch Phryne drowsed away the rest of the journey, through country which sloped like the limbs of a recumbent animal, furred with short grass dried to the colour of a lion's hide.

Mr. Burton woke her with a cup of tea. 'Here we are,' he said with satisfaction. 'Rockbank just ahead. Drink that, my dear, and then go down to get Missy and give Dulcie my best regards. You will ride with me again?' he asked stiffly. Phryne gulped the tea. She was filled with a rush of gratitude for his company. She had not realized how lonely she was.

'Mr. Burton, I would esteem it an honour.'

Jumping down, she walked along the trail of wagons which carried the tents and gear and the seating. The first ten had branched off to reach the camping ground. She found Missy standing in a line of horses, detached her and fed her a peppermint.

'Missy, my dear, just look at the state of your coat,' she exclaimed. She borrowed a body brush from the next girl and gave the mare a quick wipe down, finishing by removing dust from the horse's eyes with her handkerchief.

Miss Younger swung past, riding with as much comfort as if she were sitting in an armchair.

'Fern! Take Missy and get Dulcie to give you a costume. Red truck,' she called. 'Joan! Can't you see that's not temper, it's a stone in the hoof? Pick up her foot instantly. Well she might kick! So would I!'

Phryne found the red truck and Dulcie in the midst of what looked like complete confusion. Spangled and sequined garments hung from the sides, along with masks and headdresses and hats.

Dulcie, however, seemed calm and organized. 'Here's your costume.' She handed Phryne a red satin tunic, fleshings and a tall feather headdress. 'Take Missy over to the side and don't let her drink yet.'

Phryne managed to get Missy through the stream of camels and wagons but she could not simultaneously hold the beast and change into the costume. Missy was thirsty and could smell water. She could not see why this human was being so obstructive. She ramped on her front feet and threatened to buck.

A figure landed on Missy's back and brought her down onto all four hooves again. It was a clown in full costume, his face painted into sad lines.

'I'll amuse her, Fern, while you get into that feather thing,' said Matthias Shakespeare. His eyes were devouring her. Under this intense regard, Phryne did not feel threatened. Excitement rose up her spine like mercury in a thermometer. She shivered, licked her lips and dropped her feather crown.

'You are so beautiful,' said the clown, controlling Missy's tantrum with hardly any effort. 'You have been appearing in my dreams.'

'Oh?'

'Starring Beautiful Fern,' said Matthias in his dark brown voice. 'And Jo Jo the clown whom no one loves.'

Phryne stripped off the pink dress and pulled on the spangled tunic and the tights. They had holes in the knees. Then she knelt to remove the turban and pull the feathers down over her telltale hair.

'Fern, Fern,' sang the clown. 'Makes my heart burn. Tell me, do you like me, Fern?'

'Yes,' said Phryne, tucking in the last strand of hair. 'Yes, I like you.'

Matthias made a grab at Missy's neck, slid forward, bounced and landed sitting back to front, his hands grasping for the reins.

'Don't be silly,' said a passing girl.

'It's my profession,' said the clown. With the elegance of a cat, he leapt down, retaining Missy's rein. 'Fern,' he said softly. Phryne searched the painted face for an expression but could discern none. Only the gaze of the dark grey eyes affected her, like a caress. 'Makes my heart burn,' he whispered.

Phryne smiled. He tossed her Missy's reins and did a handstand on her back. The upside-down face looked into Phryne's and she laughed.

Detective Inspector Robinson found a report on his desk and summoned both Grossmith and Harris to hear about it.

'This is the lab's report on the notebook. Mr. Christopher's notebook, you remember,' he prompted. 'The little red book. It's been stained and soaked in blood but they managed to get some clearish images. Have a look at this.'

He showed them a photographic sheet, still wet from developer. They stared at it. In small, neat handwriting it read 'Exit'.

At that moment the phone rang.

'Yes. This is Robinson. Miss Williams? Of course I remember you. Miss Fisher? Yes, I saw her...she's done what?' Robinson grabbed for a piece of paper. 'Yes, I've got that...yes. Call for a letter at the post office...and if we want her have her arrested? What's her name? Fern Williams? Yes. Dangerous? Not really. But I'll keep an eye on her, Miss Williams. Yes, I promise. Thanks.' He hung up the receiver.

'Miss Fisher has got a job as a trick rider in Farrell's Circus,' he muttered half to himself. 'I saw her there recently. Well, I suppose she knows what she is doing. Not my problem yet,' he said grimly to his staff. 'Back to the subject. Look at the rest of the plates.'

They spread them out on the overloaded desk and onto the floor. Robinson bent over the last page. Quite clearly, they could read where Mr. Christopher had written:

To Molly,

I have come into some information which proves that Farrell's is being used by a criminal organization called Exit. I am going to see Mr. Farrell about it tonight. I haven't told anyone because he has a right to know first. He has always been good to me. But if I don't see you again, Molly, know that I always loved you. I love you, Molly. You made me into a man.

Chris

'What's on the rest of the pages?' grunted Grossmith, getting down onto his knees. 'Made him into a man, indeed. Someone was writing love letters to his other half. Christopher/Christine! Disgusting.'

'Shut up, Terry!' snapped Robinson. 'Here. Yes. A list of places. Damn. They're the same as Miss Fisher's list. Phryne Fisher is going with the circus, did you hear? And she's going to all the places that Mr. Christopher has listed.'

'Who's Phryne Fisher?' asked Tommy from the floor.

'An interfering woman,' said Robinson. 'A very clever, very beautiful, very rich, interfering woman. And I'm afraid,' he added, 'that this time she might have got herself in too deep.'

The parade entered the main street of Rockbank. Phryne was riding ahead of the chariot, driven by Miss Younger, four-in-hand. Dust rose and swirled and children cheered. A pair of young men with slicked-back hair gutter-crawled their battered old car beside them and called obscene suggestions to any woman they saw.

Asphalt Arabs, Phryne reflected, were not confined only to sealed roads. She pulled Missy a little aside. Beside her danced Jo Jo the clown. For a second, he laid one hand on her thigh and slid his strong fingers along it. Phryne nearly lost her seat. The clown's hands were charged. Then he was gone and the shouting died away. The respectable citizens of Rockbank had been thoroughly informed that the circus was in town.

Chapter Eleven

Thy feet have trod the pathway of my feet
And thy clear sorrow teacheth me mine own

The Trojan Women, Euripides
(translated by Gilbert Murray)

'I reckon we bring Albert Ellis in,' said Sergeant Grossmith.

'On what charge?' Robinson wanted to know.

'Being concerned in an attempt to murder Constable Harris here.'

'We've got nothing on him. Only on Wholesale Louis and the two others. The Mad Pole and Cyclone Freddy.'

'Well, three out of four ain't too bad,' commented Grossmith. 'I say pull 'em in. Scum like that cluttering up my nice clean street.'

'What about the Brunnies, then?' asked Tommy Harris.

'What about 'em?' grunted Grossmith.

'They'll be out looking for the 'Roys, because they killed Reffo. Jack Black Blake won't be pleased. He probably sent Reffo to sneak on them. He really hates the 'Roys.'

'So?' Grossmith was staring at his constable.

'Why don't we go and talk to the Brunnies?'

This was self-evidently a good suggestion. Grossmith nodded. 'All right. I'll go and have a chat with Jack. Usually to be found in the Brunswick Arms this time of day.' He stood up, filling the room.

'Good idea, Terry,' said Robinson. 'I'm going to give your constable the task of writing out all that can be deciphered from these photographs. And I think I'll write a letter to Miss Phryne Fisher, care of Farrell's Circus and Wild Beast Show. She ought to know about Exit.'

The circus settled for the night. The tents had been erected; the head rigger had dressed the king poles with lights and ropes. After a lot of hauling, the canvas sides and top were laced and the whole resembled a large ghostly-grey pancake. Rajah walked amiably backwards and the entire erection rose like a mushroom. The guys were fastened to the trucks and the ring traced out in wooden blocks.

The tired company dined off mutton stew and retired to their various resting places. Animals made sleepy noises. Only the lions roared and complained, unsettled by the thunder in the air or, possibly, the wandering presence of sheep.

Phryne had been allotted a stretcher bed. She unfolded her quilt and got under it. Her diaphragm was in her sponge bag and, in view of what might happen in a circus, she did not intend to be found wandering outside this chaste tent without it. No one seemed to notice what she was doing, or to care.

Twelve women stubbed out cigarettes, stretched, stowed their mending and rubbed a little more ointment into their bruises. Dulcie put out the light.

Phryne could not sleep. She looked up into the canvas ceiling of the tent, feeling as lonely as she had on her first day at boarding school. There she had known no one, had no friends and was not the sort of person who would fit in. Here she had a few allies, but only Mr. Burton, Bruno and Dulcie could be said to be friendly. She was surprised to find herself crying.

'Never mind, Fern,' whispered Dulcie from the next bed. 'You'll do it tomorrow.'

'Do what?' sobbed Phryne.

'Stand up on the horse.'

'Yes,' replied Phryne. 'I'll do it tomorrow.' She had never felt so much like an alien.

Muttering an excuse, she rose and went out into the dark. She could not stay in the tent any longer. She was looking for something, though she did not know what it was.

Ten minutes later, Phryne was standing outside a lighted caravan watching Jo Jo the clown strip.

The darkness was hot and laden with scents: engine oil, horses, burned sugar from the fairy lolly machine, and sun-scorched grass. A hot wind caressed her face and stirred the skirts of her cotton nightgown. Phryne could not tell why she was fixed in her place, unable to move even if she wanted to. She did not want to move.

The ragged fall of ash-coloured hair was real, she observed, as he shook his head free of the ridiculous cap. With careful, automatic movements he peeled off his shirt, his trousers, and began to unfasten padding from around his tubby waist. When it was gone he was revealed as slim and muscular. His hands were big and gnarled with years of hauling lines.

He sat down to take off his boots and ran considering hands down the length of his body, from shoulder to calf, as if to calm and reassure it—as one would stroke a nervous animal. She heard him sigh, but because of the painted mask she could not read his face.

His lines were as elegant as those of the great cats. Could he, like them, see in the dark? He had risen to his feet, naked and beautiful, and walked to the caravan door, leaning out, scanning the night.

Phryne was still rooted to the spot as if she had grown there. She realized that her position was equivocal, to say the least, and also that she was clad only in a thin nightdress.

The clown looked down and she looked up, green eyes into slate-grey eyes.

'Fern,' he said softly, as though he were tasting the name.

'Matthias,' she acknowledged.

'Were you watching me?'

There was an odd undertone to the question but Phryne answered simply, 'Yes.'

'Why?'

'Perhaps I was curious.'

'So am I. Will you come in?'

He made no move to cover his body. It was, Phryne thought as she climbed the stairs into the caravan, a body worth looking at and not one to be ashamed of. She wondered if his nakedness was an invitation or a threat.

She came up over the last step and shut the caravan door behind her. He drew his curtains. The little room was brightly lit by a kerosene lamp and crowded with possessions—posters, a trunk, and a bed covered with a handmade patchwork quilt. On the windowsill stood the trademark eggshell with his clown's face painted on it, proof of Jo Jo's ownership of his mask.

'Sit down,' he said politely. 'I'm afraid there is only the bed. Would you like some wine?'

Phryne nodded, overcome by his closeness and the brightness of the light. He opened a bottle of wine and turned down the lamp as he saw her wince.

'You've been out in the dark for a while,' he observed, his voice low and detached. 'Here we are, Fern, have a drink with me and tell me what you're curious about.'

'I'm curious about everything,' said Phryne with perfect truth, taking a swig from the bottle. It was a sweet, rich port.

'But you are curious about me in particular.'

'Yes.'

She took another gulp of wine. The paint was still on his face, two yellow stars over each eye, the mouth white and his own lips red. Those grey eyes watched her, giving nothing away. He sat easily on the bed next to her, his bare thigh touching her cotton-covered one.

'Perhaps I just find you...attractive,' she added. 'Why else would I prowl in the night?'

'Why else indeed?' he replied. 'But you are no circus-born kid, Fern. Or you'd know.'

'Know what?'

His nearness was unsettling Phryne. She could feel heat radiating off his skin and she noticed a muscle begin to twitch, a tendon pulling from his hip to groin. Other developments were making themselves apparent. There was no doubt that the clown was pleased to see her.

His voice, however, was still cool. 'No one sleeps with clowns,' he said, passing her the bottle. 'It's unlucky, we're unlucky. And we are supposed to be sad.'

'Why?' Phryne laid a hand on the nearest expanse of flesh and heard him draw in his breath.

'Clowns contain sadness. That's why people laugh at us. How can we be sad if we have lovers?' he asked reasonably. 'Ah!'

Phryne had stroked another part of his back. His muscles under her hands were hard, evidence of formidable strength.

'So you think I don't belong to the circus?' she asked, running her fingers lightly down his neck to his chest and finding an erect nipple.

'No, you don't. You're a good rider but that's not why you're here. Why...Ah!...Why are you here?'

'I won't be able to concentrate,' purred Phryne, 'and neither will you, until we have this over with. Therefore, you shall have kisses for answers. One, do you favour Farrell or Jones?'

'Farrell. Jones is a crook,' he said and Phryne kissed the painted mouth. The greasepaint came off on her lips and coloured them alike.

'Good. Two, will you help me find out what is happening?'

'Yes,' he said and red mouth met red mouth in a deeper kiss.

'Third and last...' She breathed into his ear. Then she paused.

'What?' he said, still not touching, and saw her smile, the black hair swinging back from her face.

'Do you want me?'

The clown mask came closer, until he was staring into her eyes, and for the first time that night he touched her. He slid both calloused hands up her calves to her thighs and she caught her breath.

'I might hurt you,' he said. 'It has been a long time.'

'Because clowns are unlucky?'

'Yes.'

His face glowed with sweat and paint; a desperate clown who trembled at her touch, at her nearness and her female scent.

'I will take the risk. What is your answer?'

'Yes.'

She stripped off the nightgown in one movement and then he was above her, kissing her with hard, fast kisses, his strong hands picking her up and laying her on the patchwork quilt. Paint smeared as he rubbed his face across her belly, his mouth seeking the sweet place where all of her sexual nerves twined into a knot.

Her joints loosened, her thighs parted. Over the flat planes of her breast and hip, the clown's face appeared. His hair fell ragged and Phryne bit her hand to still a cry. His mouth was skillful; he had found the right place.

She could not reach him to caress him; he did not seem to want to be touched. His rough fingers found each nipple and squeezed hard; she gasped on the edge of pain and pleasure. There was such pent-up force in this clown that she was as close to fear as she had ever been.

His mouth moved, sliding up to join with her mouth; an engulfing kiss, bitter with paint. She wrapped her legs around his hips and the first thrust was so strong that it nailed her to the bed. The clown mask filled her vision, which was blurring. She grasped him tightly and began to respond, but his hands came down on her shoulders so that she could not move.

'Please. Don't move. I can't...wait...if you move.'

'I won't run away,' she said, wriggling under the imprisoning hands. 'I will stay all night. Let me go! I won't be pinned down!'

He blinked and released her. Phryne, whom force turned cold, began to regain her lust as the movements became slow and considered. He bent to kiss her nipples. The sliding of painted flesh made a sucking sound, curiously loud in the night. His hair fell over his eyes, hiding their strange light.

Phryne seized his shoulders, forcing him closer, deeper. He groaned and stiffened, then fell into her arms and writhed with release.

She had been so surprised by his collapse that she had lain still for five minutes under his weight. Now he was becoming too heavy. She shoved at his chest and he clung to her, the muscular arms encircling her in a fast embrace.

'You said that you would stay all night,' he whispered and there was that odd note in his voice again. Phryne decided to ask. Besides, she was not yet sated and this man had erotic potential which needed to be developed.

'What is it, Matthias? Why are you so…unsure of me?'

He leaned up on one elbow and wiped the sweet-smelling hair out of his eyes.

The paint had largely been transferred to Phryne's body. She saw that he had a face which in Paris would be called *joli laid*; an ugly face, with high cheekbones, long nose, a wide mouth and soft full lips. His eyebrows were winged at the corners.

He bore her inspection bravely and said, 'There are some women who aren't circus folk who like…who like masks. They occasionally…want to try me. But they never want to stay. Just for an experiment, you see.'

'And you thought I was one of them?' Phryne's voice was cold. He stroked her breast, laying his cheek on it gently.

'You said that you were curious.'

'Yes. I am curious. But you are lovely, a good lover. Hasn't anyone told you that? You're the only person in this circus who likes me, if you don't count Mr. Burton and Bruno the bear. And my curiosity isn't so easily satisfied.'

A smile dawned on his face, curving the soft mouth. 'What can I do for your curiosity, Fern?' he breathed into her ear.

She reached for him and drew him close, relishing the sprung line of his backbone and the hard strength of his buttocks.

'Why, satisfy it,' she said lightly.

Lizard Elsie offered her bottle to the woman lying face-down on the other bed.

'Have a bit of good cheer,' she said in her creaking voice. 'Come on, love, it can't be as fucking bad as all that.'

Miss Parkes looked up in astonishment at the strange voice and slid her knife down under her mattress.

'Come on,' encouraged Lizard Elsie. 'What's bloody wrong?'

'I'm a murderer,' said Miss Parkes flatly.

'Oh, are yer? Who says so?'

'They say so.'

'Well, they can be fucking wrong, can't they? Have a sip. Just a sip. It's bloody good brandy.'

Miss Parkes sat up and accepted the bottle. 'Who are you?' she asked.

'I'm Elsie. They calls me Lizard Elsie because of my bloody blue tongue. I learned the habit early and I don't seem to be able to fucking break meself of it. That's better.'

Miss Parkes had taken a deep draught of brandy and was leaning back against the wall. She had not eaten for two days and the spirit rushed straight to her head and disconnected her wits.

'Now,' said Lizard Elsie, repossessing herself of her bottle, 'tell me how you got to be a fucking murderer.'

'A man,' said Miss Parkes. 'He was my husband.'

'Ain't it always the fucking way,' Elsie spat. 'Did yer kill him?'

'Yes.'

'Why?' asked Elsie, settling down for a long chat.

'I...he mistreated me and made me barren and beat me and then told me to be a whore.'

'He was bloody lucky if all yer did to 'im was kill 'im,' observed Elsie. 'When was this?'

'Ten years ago.'

'Ten years ago? They just bloody found out, then?'

'No, they think I killed another person. A circus performer who lived in the same house as me. His name was Mr. Christopher. He was stabbed to death.'

'And did you?' asked Elsie, interested.

'I don't think so. But I got out of prison, see, and they thought that if I'd killed once I'd kill again.'

'Fucking cops,' said Elsie. 'Have another dram.'

Miss Parkes pushed back her cropped hair, which was filthy. She was still wearing the same suit in which she had rescued Constable Harris from the roof. She noticed that she was grimy, and that her fingernails were black and broken. Elsie scanned her with her parrot regard.

'Hey!' yelled Elsie. 'Duty copper!'

'Yes, madam?' asked the duty officer with heavy sarcasm. 'What does madam require? Caviar? Champagne?'

'Madam requires that you give me and this poor bloody woman a bath and some clean fucking clothes. Then we'll see about some lunch,' said Elsie flatly.

'But she doesn't want a bath,' said the policeman. 'And she won't eat, either.'

'You leave it to old Elsie,' she said with deep cunning. 'Just get us a wash and a comb and some lunch and we'll be right as bloody rain. And fucking put some speed on,' she shrieked at his retreating back. 'I ain't had a bath and a feed for a bloody week.'

'I can tell,' muttered the duty officer and went off to arrange the closure of the men's ablutions for the ladies' bath.

Chapter Twelve

There liveth not in my life, any more
The hope that others have. Nor will I tell
The lie to mine own heart, that aught is well
Or shall be well.

The Trojan Women, Euripides
(translated by Gilbert Murray)

The Brunnies were not hard to find. Jack Black Blake held court as usual in the front bar of the Brunswick Arms in Brunswick Street. When the gigantic figure of Sergeant Grossmith appeared at his side, he did not react.

'Pint,' said Grossmith to the barmaid. 'G'day, Doris! What a fine figure of a woman you are.'

Doris giggled. She, like Mary of the Provincial, was evidently unaware that bosoms were not fashionable. Hers were of a light biscuit colour and were trussed so high that they nestled under her chin. Grossmith found her charming. He liked a woman to be a real woman, not an imitation boy.

'Hear you had a little trouble,' remarked Grossmith to the air. The man beside him grunted.

'Trouble? No.'

'Someone shot Reffo,' suggested Grossmith. 'The 'Roy Boys, or so I hear.'

'What of it?'

'Listen, Jack, you got a chance to put the 'Roy Boys where they belong—behind bars. They shot your mate and they're trying to stand over you for your territory. Now, are you a lot of sissies or are you the Brunswick Boys?'

Men gathered behind Grossmith. He could hear them breathing. Doris moved prudently to another part of the bar. Grossmith identified the men in the bar mirror. The Judge, an ex-wharfie, sacked for always sitting on a case, hulking and dumb. Little Georgie, who carried a knife and had liquid black eyes. Billy the Dog, who grinned, showing rotten teeth. The Snake, hefting a bottle thoughtfully. He was a tall man with a thin moustache and the cold flat eyes that gave him his name. Reffo had been his mate. They all exuded menace.

'It's no use crowding me,' remarked Grossmith artlessly. 'I ain't your enemy.'

'You ain't exactly our friend,' said the Snake through a closed mouth.

Grossmith grinned. 'You bet. I ain't never going to be your mate, Snake. But at the moment we could be allies. What have the 'Roys got themselves into? It's too big for them.'

'Then it'd be too big for us,' said Jack Black. 'All right. We can make a deal.'

'Oh, can we?' asked Grossmith. 'What deal is that?'

'You leave us alone and we'll tell you.'

'No,' said Grossmith after a moment's thought. 'I can't do that, Jack. You know I can't do that. My chief is set against gangs and I can't go over his head.'

Jack Black laughed suddenly and called for another beer.

'But,' said Grossmith, 'you want to get rid of the 'Roy Boys and this is the way to do it. Because if you think that you can start a gang war in Melbourne like they have in Chicago, Jack, you got another think coming. You use the police for your revenge, and that's good, I'll put in a good word for you if I can. But you go out and buy a machine-gun and I'll hang you if it's the last thing I ever do. I'm not having it and that's flat. And that's all I've got to say, so I'll be going if you don't want to talk.'

'Fetch Iris,' ordered Jack, and Snake left the bar.

Grossmith ordered another beer and said slowly, 'One of my constables was shot last night.'

'Yair?'

'In Brunswick Street.'

'Oh?' Jack yawned.

'Lizard Elsie was with him.'

A faint interest dawned in Jack's eyes. 'Mad as a coot,' he said. 'That Elsie.'

'Yair. She almost bit Wholesale Louis' ear off.'

Jack Black roared with laughter. So did his men.

'She still playing that trick? She's a mean bitch when she gets going! So where is she?'

'Lizard Elsie?'

'Yair. Lizard Elsie.'

'In the clink,' said Grossmith.

'Best place for her,' decided Jack Black. 'She might dry out. She's been all right, the old Else. Done me a good turn, once. Picked me up outa the gutter and brung me home when I had a difference of opinion with…some people. And I don't reckon she had nothing to do with Reffo. She never joined any mob. She's always been on her own. But since she got on the red biddy she's been going downhill. Poor old Elsie. The terror of publicans.'

Grossmith filed away the information that the Brunnies, at least, did not seem to hold any grudge against Lizard Elsie. He turned to see a girl being ushered in through the swinging doors.

Pretty Iris had been with the Brunnies for three years. Grossmith put her age at about twenty-five. She was slight, fashionably dressed and pale, with light brown hair and blue eyes. Her hand bore one small but very bright diamond. Diamonds also flashed in her ears. Pretty Iris had expensive tastes.

'Jack?' she inquired. Her voice was soft and high. The only things that Grossmith didn't like about her were the rigid line of her thin lips and the baby intonations which she used on susceptible men.

'Iris,' he acknowledged. 'Give the lady a seat, boys.'

Iris perched on the bar stool between Jack and Snake and asked, 'What's going on? I was at a dress fitting. I'm gonna lose my job if you keep dragging me away from the salon. Madam was most upset.' In her spare time, when not assisting the Brunnies in their nefarious schemes, Pretty Iris was a mannequin.

'If you lose your job you'll have more time to devote to us,' said Jack Black irritably. 'This is…'

Iris' fine eyes widened. 'I know who it is.' She laid a cool manicured hand on the policeman's arm and he was washed with a gust of French perfume. Sergeant Grossmith was intensely aware of the pressure of her fingers. 'What does he want here?'

'He wants you to talk to him.'

'And do you want me to?' She cast a coquettish look at Jack and he shifted in his seat.

'Yair. I want you to.'

'All right.' Pretty Iris was supplied with a small sherry by a disapproving Doris. She sipped daintily and then asked, 'And what does Jackie want poor little Iris to talk about?'

'The 'Roys.'

Her expression changed instantly. The smooth forehead creased into a frown and the red lips pouted. 'Ooh, Iris doesn't like rough boys.'

Grossmith, controlling an inward nausea, nevertheless found Pretty Iris effective. So did Jack Black. His face was darkening. He blinked.

'Talk about it, Iris,' he ordered, and Pretty Iris hitched up her skirt to sit more comfortably on the bar stool.

'There was a man…' she began, and giggled. 'He thought I was wonderful.' She drew out the syllables and Grossmith bit his lip. 'He fell in love with me. The fool.' True venom dripped from the words. Grossmith wondered if Pretty Iris had ever loved any man and why she was so set against the species. 'So he took me out to nightclubs and he bought me presents. He said he wanted me to marry him. But he was only after one thing. All men are only after one thing.' Her voice had deepened. She was forgetting her baby-doll affectations. 'So he tried harder. He began to tell me secrets as though his secrets would bring me closer to him, make me love him. One night when he had been drinking he told me all about a woman—he called her his perfect woman. He loved her like billy-o. She lived in the same house and she wouldn't look at him. I wasn't interested. Every bloke has a perfect woman they want to tell you about. A girl could get jealous, I said. A girl didn't wanna listen all night to a drunk mooning about after his lost perfect woman. So he said, "I'll tell you a secret," and I said, "What secret?" And he said, "I'm going to make a lot of money very soon." And I was interested, so I said, "How?" and he leaned real close and he said, "Exit." I said, "I never heard of it," and he smiled and said, "No," so I pressed him.'

Grossmith was listening intently. Pretty Iris bloomed under the attention. She ordered another sherry. When it came Jack Black put his hand over the glass.

'Not until you tell the rest,' he said. Pretty Iris pouted again and wriggled in her chair. 'Beast!' she complained.

'Go on, Iris,' said Jack Black unsteadily. She raked him with her eyes.

'So he said he was going to get a lot of money from Exit. I asked what it was and he laughed again and said it was a funeral parlour. And he said that it was real big. Not just small time, he said. He said he was going to get hundreds of pounds from Exit. I asked him what he was going to do and he wouldn't tell me. I asked him who else was in it. He said three names. Damien Maguire, William Seddon and Ronald Smythe. I asked him who was helping him and he said the 'Roy Boys. No, actually he said that it was Albert Ellis. But Ellis isn't in anything on his own. I made like I didn't know the name and then he got sober all of a sudden and begged me to keep schtum. I said I would,' Pretty Iris ended artlessly. 'Or otherwise he would have got cross.'

'You're a talented woman,' said Grossmith slowly. 'And I can see why they call you Pretty Iris.'

Iris glowed. She patted him on the hand again. Jack removed his palm from her glass.

'You're a good girl,' he told her. 'A very good girl and Jack's going to get you a present.'

'Ooh!' squeaked Pretty Iris. 'A present!'

Grossmith could stand no more. As he got up he said, 'Thanks, Jack. What was the man's name, Iris?'

'Smith,' said Iris with infinite scorn. 'Robert Smith. They're all called Smith, aren't they?'

Grossmith left the pub, thinking hard.

Phryne Fisher crept back into the women's tent in the early morning, noticing that several other beds were empty. She was sated and dreamy. Once the initial frenzy born of long frustration was over, the clown had been an excellent lover. His touch went deep, right through to her bones. His body was strong and smooth and sweet to the mouth. He might well prove addictive.

She burrowed into her quilt and slept like a log for three hours, after which she was woken by Dulcie.

'Up you get, Fern. Breakfast is on and it's time to fall off a horse again.'

Phryne stretched, dragged on the cotton dress and decided to omit washing. She rebound her pink turban and went to the cook-tent for brackish tea and wodges of bread and jam. Not even if she was starving would she consider Mrs. T's porridge. It heaved sullenly in its cauldron and appeared to be semi-sensate.

She walked into strong sunshine, blinked away dust and went to fetch Missy from the horse lines. Her supply of peppermints and carrots was holding out. Missy sidled up to her to be groomed.

Miss Younger was standing in the middle of the ring. The big top looked so permanent that Phryne could not believe it had been disassembled before her eyes the day before. She led Missy into the ring and released the leading rein.

Moving round and round, in a smooth canter, Phryne slid easily up onto her knees and gently into her hands-and-feet bridge. This was the point where she usually fell off. Listening for the command to stand and feeling her tights slide across and squeeze, she was overcome by a vision of the clown. She smelt greasepaint and felt the electric fingers. Sweat dropped from her forehead to spot Missy's grey back. And without remembering that she had fallen off before, she stood up and stayed up.

The ring flew past. Various lookers-on shouted congratulations. Phryne did not hear them. She was standing up on Missy's back, one foot either side of the spine, her arms by her sides. Miss Younger smiled for the first time in Phryne's experience. She directed Missy into another circuit and Phryne stood like a pillar, leaning inwards, wondering why this skill had taken so long to learn.

'Both hands down,' ordered Miss Younger. 'Right at your feet. Now stand on your hands.'

Recalling the clown's face upside down, Phryne laughed and lifted her legs. She stayed upright for three beats, then sat down astride. The muscles in her upper arms trembled with fatigue.

'You ride tonight. Get them to give you a costume and some weights to strengthen your arms. Well done,' said Miss Younger. 'Joan! You're next.'

Phryne allowed Missy to walk out of the ring. Dulcie, sitting casually on a trapeze ten feet above the ground, caught the balls she had been juggling with her partner Tom and called, 'I told you you could do it, Fern!' Phryne, dizzy with achievement, laughed aloud.

She was passed by a running, rolling, tumbling group of dark men. The Catalans shouted a cheerful greeting as they bundled into the space behind the ring not yet occupied with seating.

At the door Phryne met three clowns. Jo Jo in practice dress and with his own face, leading Toby his brother, attended by Mr. Burton in shorts and a paint-stained shirt. Phryne slid down from Missy and bounced as her feet stung.

'It'll get you like that,' said Matthias. 'Jump, rather than get down too gently. Congratulations, Fern! I knew you had it in you.' He grinned, an intimate and challenging grimace, crinkling the corners of his eyes. Something deliquesced in Phryne's middle. 'Fern, Fern, makes my heart burn,' he added, clutching at his chest and turning the corners of his mouth down. 'When will you love me, Fern?'

Phryne mouthed, 'Tonight?' and the clown's eyes glowed. He gave a slight nod. 'Oh Fern,' he yelled, reaching out stiff arms, 'come to me, Fern!'

Phryne felt eyes upon her from knee level. The rapport between herself and Matthias must not be revealed to Mr. Burton's acute gaze. She turned on the clown a look of withering scorn.

'Garn,' she drawled and led Missy out into the light, ignoring Jo Jo, who howled like a dog after her.

'I did it,' Phryne exulted to Bernie, who was leading Bruno into the tent. 'I did it!'

The man smiled at her. Bruno, recognizing a friend of bears, sniffed at her pocket until she gave him a peppermint. He licked her hands rather thoroughly in case any should remain, then got up and waltzed slowly in a circle.

'Good bear,' said Bernie absently. 'Well done, Fern! Dulcie said you'd manage it. Come on, Bruno.'

Missy, who objected to bears, tugged at her rein. Phryne was recalled to the present. She hummed as she brushed Missy, combed out her mane and tail, and left her tethered in the horse lines munching hay.

Having now nothing to do, she went questing for a job. Delight fizzed in her head like champagne. She had stood up on a horse and was now a trick rider in Farrell's Circus.

She threaded her way through the maze of guys and pegs around the big top and found herself in a canvas alley among the flesh eaters. Voices were raised. Amazing Hans was not happy.

'Farrell, I have known you for years. I came to you with only three beasts and no money. I know that. I am under an obligation to you.' The lion tamer was shouting. Phryne decided that she needed a cigarette and stopped, fumbling in her pocket. It took her a long time to separate the cigarettes from her handkerchief and then find her lighter. She listened hard.

'But now what this Jones wants me to do, it is impossible. I used to put my head in old Joe's mouth but he was ancient and tame and had no teeth. My lions are young. They are strong. Lions have a natural instinct to bite anything that is put between their teeth. Do I not know? Was I not trained by the great Hagenbeck? What I am demanding of the beasts is not foreign to their nature. That was Hagenbeck's skill. These creatures are gentled. They love me, they do not fear me.'

'Scared, eh?' said Farrell's slow Australian drawl, scathing to the pride. Phryne heard Amazing Hans draw in a deep breath. The lions moved uneasily in their cages, catching their trainer's mood.

'Yes!' he yelled, loud enough to make Phryne jump. 'Yes, I'm scared. I, the Amazing Hans, am afraid. And I am not ashamed of it. I will not do as this idiot asks. And I will leave your circus. Sole's want another trainer. I shall take my lions and go. Now get out of my tent.'

Farrell had just begun to answer when someone grabbed Phryne by the shoulder. 'Snooping, Fern?' asked Mr. Jones.

She held out the cigarette and the lighter and remembered her accent.

'Just trying to get a light.'

He lit her gasper with a flourish. Up close, Mr. Jones was less attractive than he had seemed, and he had never posed any threat to Valentino. He was tall, running to fat and overdressed in a suit and tie. He had white hair and flat brown eyes. He stank of Californian Poppy, cigar smoke, and mouthwash with an underlying reek of rotten teeth.

'I reckon you were snooping, Fern,' he said slowly, and the hand moved to pinch her breast. 'You be nice to me and I won't tell Mr. Farrell and get you sacked.'

What would Fern do? thought Phryne as the hand took further liberties with her body. Treacherously, it was beginning to react, recalling the touch of Matthias and Alan Lee. Phryne made up her mind that Fern was a good girl.

'Sorry,' she said, refusing to meet his eyes. 'I'm not that kind of girl.'

Mr. Jones had evidently met this response before. He gripped her chin and forced her to look into his face. It was a face that might have been carved out of soap. One gash made the mouth.

'It's your job, Fern,' he said softly. 'You wanna walk home from Rockbank?'

Deprived of the response of Miss Phryne Fisher, which would have been a swift knee in the privates, Phryne was at a loss. She twisted out of the grip.

'Please,' she said reluctantly. 'I need this job.'

Farrell could be heard leaving the lion tamer's tent. Jones was either anxious to accompany him or still a little in awe of him. He released Phryne from his gaze.

'Remember that you owe me a favour,' he said, and Phryne watched him walk cockily away. She noticed that her hands were trembling. The cigarette smoke wavered, tracing blue squiggles on the still, hot air.

'I'll remember,' she said softly, enraged at her helplessness. 'Oh, I'll remember.'

The next person to catch her by the shoulder was Molly Younger, and she stepped back a pace as Phryne turned on her fiercely, fists clenched.

'Oh, sorry, Miss Younger.'

'Who did you think I was?' demanded Molly Younger.

'Mr. Jones,' admitted Phryne. Miss Younger's face grew grimmer.

'Him.' She summed him up comprehensively with one phrase. 'He don't belong. Now, girl, I want a word. Come to my caravan, I've got to change.'

Phryne, wondering what this was all about, followed Miss Younger's straight back as she stalked through the circus to a neat painted wagon with shafts. Miss Younger did not like trucks.

'Come in,' she snapped as Phryne paused. 'Shut the door.'

The caravan was sparsely furnished. Only rows and rows of blue ribbons and rosettes decorated the walls. The bed was flat, hard, and covered only with a thin blanket. Phryne sat down on it and looked at Miss Younger.

She had pulled off her hat and her fair hair was dragged out of its severe plait. With her hair loose she looked more female. Pouring water into a tin dish on the floor, Miss Younger peeled off her shirt and riding breeches. She was wearing a pair of battered silk shorts and the rest of her body was bare. She stepped into the dish.

Phryne watched without comment. Nudity was common in the circus, when it was a matter of changing clothes or washing. The etiquette was not to look, or not appear to be looking. Phryne wondered if this rule applied in a private caravan. Molly's face was set and her lips tight. She did not seem pleased and Phryne wondered what she wanted with Fern.

'I told you when you came,' said Miss Younger, sponging dust off her body, 'that if you behaved like a tart you'd be treated like one.'

Phryne nodded. The fair hair bobbed across Miss Younger's shoulders. She had almost no breasts, and strong muscle was outlined and shadowed by her hair.

'Then you went and did it.'

'Did what?'

'I smelt you. I can smell you now. Greasepaint and lust. You slut!'

Phryne sat back on the hard bed and stared. She had not remembered that one cannot keep secrets in a circus. Miss Younger stepped out of the dish and flung the water out the door. She did not dress but stood, hands on slim hips, glaring.

'You tart!' she yelled suddenly. 'I could smell the polecat stink of you from Missy's back. You haven't even washed.'

Phryne decided to say exactly what she meant.

'I haven't done any harm,' she began.

Miss Younger's chest heaved and she began to breathe in short, painful gasps. 'No harm? No harm? You've only been here a few days and you lie down with a clown!'

'I like him,' said Phryne coldly. 'What business is it of yours?' She decided to attack. 'Haven't you ever had a lover?'

Hands shot out to her throat and began to strangle. Phryne choked, broke the grip with both thumbs biting into the tendons and punched Miss Younger in the stomach. Her fist bounced off muscles like rubber. Miss Younger screamed at Phryne, 'Slut!' and Phryne slapped her across the face with all her force. The woman crumpled to the ground.

'He's dead,' said Miss Younger, flatly. 'He's dead.'

Phryne accepted Miss Younger into her arms. The woman knelt with her face against Phryne's breasts and moaned. 'He's dead. Mr. Christopher is dead. Murdered.' Phryne did not know what to say. She had not realized just how much the man had meant to the horsemaster. Molly Younger was now weeping freely, with her head buried in Phryne's lap, kneeling between her knees. Her tears were soaking the cheap cotton dress. All Phryne could do was embrace Molly close and say nothing.

After ten minutes, bitter lamentations were whispered just above hearing.

'He wanted us to travel together,' she heard the woman say. 'He wanted us to live together, to share a caravan. I said we couldn't because...because we weren't married yet and I wasn't a tart. It hurt his feelings. He went back to his boarding house and...I wanted him,' she sobbed. 'I never wanted a man before. They say I only love horses. I do love them. But...you stink of love,' she snarled suddenly. 'A little slut off the streets, out of the dancehalls, and you've...' She drooped. 'You've got love, even the clown, even though no one sleeps with clowns.' She groaned, then demanded shrilly, 'Did you enjoy him, then, slut? Did he please you, Jo Jo the clown? Did he touch you and kiss you until you were dizzy? And did you lie down and open your legs and...' Her voice choked again.

'Yes,' said Phryne, treading very carefully. 'I lay down with him and he loved me and I loved him.'

'You won't do it again!' Miss Younger clutched at Phryne's hips and sank her fingers in around the bone.

Phryne winced. 'Not again,' she said softly. 'Not if you say not.'

Miss Younger made a convulsive movement, forcing Phryne back onto the bed. She slid upwards, rubbing her body against Phryne's as though she wanted to penetrate it, to be inside her skin and bones. Her rigid lips gaped and she kissed Phryne's mouth with great force.

Phryne held her tight and kissed her back. The mouth was strong, with a muscular jaw, and Molly kissed wildly and clumsily as though she would bite. Phryne was seized with great pity. Mr. Christopher and Miss Younger. Man-woman and woman-man. They were made for each other and no one else would fit. Miss Younger broke off the kiss and shoved Phryne away.

'It's all right,' said Phryne gently. 'It's all right for you to love women. I know two women who live together in the country and they are perfectly happy. No one has even noticed.'

'No!' Miss Younger screamed, mouth still wet from contact. 'No! Not you, not any woman! I'm not a freak, not a pervert! I have done without love, I can forget about love. Only when I smell the stink of sluts on heat, like you, does it come back.' She was panting and the grip on Phryne's arm was bruisingly tight. 'I only ever wanted one person in the world, the only one I could love. I never thought there'd be anyone. I'm a man, you stupid bitch. I'm a man. Cursed with this body, which is wrong and bleeds and betrays me. Formed wrong. Born wrong. And so was he. Born different. Born for me, my only one, my dear love. And he's dead. Gone. I've lost him forever. And I never lay with him, never found out about love while I had the chance. Leave me,' she said harshly.

Phryne stood up and moved away. She stopped at the caravan door as the woman gasped, 'The clown.'

'Yes?'

Miss Younger veiled her eyes in the cloud of her hair. 'Do you really want him?'

'Yes,' said Phryne honestly.

'Then take him,' said Miss Younger. 'Even if he is a clown. Take him while you can get him.'

'Yes.'

'Like I should have taken mine.'

She turned her face to the wall and began to weep, deep shuddering sobs, like a man crying, unwilling. There did not seem to be anything Phryne could do. She left, closing the door behind her. A roustabout, seeing her dishevelled condition, laughed.

'I knew she was one of them sheilas that don't like men,' he jeered.

As Phryne walked past she unthinkingly, and with accuracy and force, slapped him off his feet and into a pile of elephant dung.

Chapter Thirteen

Death cannot be what Life is, Child; the cup
Of Death is empty and Life hath always hope.

The Trojan Women, Euripides
(translated by Gilbert Murray)

'Dear Fern,' began Jack Robinson, then stopped. He always found composition difficult. His pen spluttered and the words just would not put themselves in the right order. 'Hear you're with the circus. Hope you're doing well,' he went on, then wondered how he was going to convey the information about Exit and Mr. Christopher's murder which Phryne needed to know. Years of writing official reports had cramped his style.

'Heard a bit of gossip the other day,' he wrote, getting an idea. 'Bloke that was with your show. A man-woman act. His name was Mr. Christopher. It seems that he was murdered, Fern. Someone stuck a shiv into him. They say there was blood dripping through the ceiling of this boarding house he was living in. Real creepy. Living in the same place as your magician, Mr. Sheridan. I think they got some woman for the murder. I can't understand how she could do it.'

Robinson paused and took a gulp of tea. He was proud of himself. That ought to convey his unease about the case of Miss Parkes. Now for Exit. 'I also hear…' What *was* he going to say?

Aha. '…rumours about a new show. They want dancers, so if you're back soon you can audition for it. It's set in a prison. One of them surrealist things. I don't like the idea much. Seems kind of morbid. I'd be looking for the Exit if I was in the audience. Still, there's no accounting for tastes, as the old woman said when she kissed the cow. I'll tell you more if you want to phone me. And say the word and I'll come and take you away. Much love, Jack.'

Robinson scanned the letter. That ought to alert Miss Fisher to the danger, at least, and warn her to look out for any mention of Exit.

He put the letter into an old envelope and gave it to an attendant constable, ordering that it be taken by car to Rockbank to be collected with the circus' mail. Miss Fisher should have it today. He worried about her.

'Sir?' Tommy Harris put his head around the door. 'I've deciphered all I could and Sergeant Grossmith has just got back and wants to see you.'

'Good. Tell him to come in and bring your notes. Ah, Terry,' he said expansively, 'what news on the Rialto?'

Before his sergeant could tell him that the Rialto was in the city and that he had been to Brunswick Street, Robinson motioned his minions to a seat. 'Well, Terry?'

'I got onto Pretty Iris,' said Grossmith. 'By Jiminy she's pretty, and as hard as nails. Pure vitriol runs in her veins. She told me that someone called Robert Smith told her he was going to make a lot of money from Exit. He said it was a funeral parlour. That's how we lost Seddon, you recall, sir. He said he was going to get hundreds of quids for doing something, though Iris didn't know what, and that Albert Ellis had hired him. That's about all, sir.'

'Very good. What have you got, Constable?' Robinson asked Harris.

'Not all that much more, sir. There's several lists of dates and names attached to them. But I thought you'd be interested in some of them. On plate ten, the last page, it says "Ronald Smythe". He's on the list of Western District places, sir. And so is Damien Maguire.'

'Are they indeed?' Robinson leaned forward and Tommy riffled through his notes.

'I found this on plate three. It's a bit faint but you can just make it out. Next to "Portland", sir, down in that bottom corner.'

He pointed and the detective inspector squinted over the pale scribble. 'It's William...yes.' He looked up with a light in his eyes. 'William Seddon.'

'Well,' said Terry Grossmith. 'Three of 'em. What else is on them plates, Harris?'

'Love letters, Sarge. Never sent. Perhaps drafts. To a lady called Molly that he was going to marry. And one note that I don't understand.'

'Spit it out, son.'

'It says, "Money. Farrell sells Circus? Jones not rich. Who provided cash?"'

'Clear enough,' said Grossmith. 'If that Jones is the Jones I think it is, then he ain't got a pot to piss in. Small-time crim with the 'Roys. Thought he hadn't been infecting the street with his presence lately.'

'Which Jones?' asked Robinson anxiously.

'Killer Jones...oh, Lord,' said Grossmith. 'Your Miss Fisher's there. And Jones likes girls. He likes 'em half-dead.'

'She can look after herself,' said Robinson abruptly. 'You said something important then, Terry. Where did the money to interfere in this circus come from? Not from Jones himself. From the 'Roys?'

'I can't imagine it,' said Grossmith. 'Albert Ellis has more flash than cash.'

'Harris, get onto it. I want you to find out who owns Farrell's Circus and who put up the money for Jones. Then I want you back here by this afternoon with a bag. We're going to Rockbank tonight. I'm going to take you boys to the circus.'

◇◇◇

Phryne Fisher, unable to find an occupation which did not involve sewing, strolled into the girls' tent. It was empty. She opened her suitcase, took out a Coles notepad and a pencil and wrote busily for ten minutes. Then she tore off and folded the papers and stuffed them down her front.

The suitcase seemed even more in disarray than when she had left it. She put it down on her bed and rummaged through its contents. It had certainly been searched. Her little gun and her box of ammunition were gone.

With a great effort she managed to saunter casually through the circus and into the carnival, where Alan Lee was leaning on one pole of his carousel. She took off her cardigan, draped it over her arm and took his hand under cover of it.

'Fern?' he said under his breath, as her hand slipped in his grasp. Her palms were sweating. 'What's gone wrong?'

'They're onto me,' she said, her lips hardly moving. 'Can you send these telegrams for me?'

'Yes.' He took the pages that she slipped him and shoved them down his shirt. 'Can I do something else for you?'

'Call Dot on this number and ask for any news. And try to send the telegrams without anyone seeing you. I'll come back in an hour. You might have to wait for a reply.'

'You frightened, Fern?'

'No,' she lied.

He held her hand in a strong clasp for a moment, then released it.

'Break a leg, Fern.'

Phryne was afraid that she would. Who had searched the suitcase? One of the girls? If so, who? And was this idle curiosity? No. Idle curiosity would not take the gun.

It was time that she took the initiative. But there was not much she could do until she had some answers. Finally she wandered down to where Dulcie was repairing a large box.

'H'lo Fern, come and help me.'

Phryne took one side of the box and tilted it, so that Dulcie could tuck the piece of cloth she was gluing underneath.

'What is this?' Phryne found her voice. It was shaky.

'It's the magician's disappearing-trick box. See,' Dulcie motioned Phryne to set the box down and walked her around it, 'it looks solid.' She tapped it. 'It sounds solid. But this side is just cloth, painted to look like that stained wood. So all the sides match and it ain't too difficult to make Dulcie vanish.'

'How do you vanish, then?'

'I just lift up the side and out I go.' She demonstrated. 'There's a screen between me and the punters.'

The screen was also painted to look like the box and was of canvas. Dulcie fitted neatly between the screen and the outer wall of the box.

'Only thing to do is not to giggle,' said Dulcie. 'What's the matter, Fern? You look pale.'

'Miss Younger…' said Phryne. Dulcie patted her shoulder.

'It's real hard for her,' she said slowly. 'Losing Mr. Christopher like that. But it's not surprising that she went crook. She sorta looks after us girls. And it's my fault too, Fern. I oughta told you about clowns.'

'What about clowns?'

'They're off limits,' said Dulcie slowly. 'I dunno why. It's just always been like that. It's all right for them to marry, like old Thompson, but not to have lovers, not to be happy. Clowns ain't supposed to be happy. You did the wrong thing, Fern.'

'So I did the wrong thing.'

'And you gotta give him up.'

'Do I?' Phryne was bewildered. Just as she had thought that she was understanding the circus, it had turned unaccountable and alien again. 'And if I don't?'

'Then you'll be a tart. They'll all be coming to the tent and asking for you. You'll be pestered to death.'

Phryne thought about it. The clown was too sweet to surrender because of the circus' strange views of morality. He was also the only person who could make her feel loved. She needed him. The affair would have to be secret. Then she remembered that one cannot have secrets in a circus. It was give up the clown or be taken for a tart. The decision was already made. There were worse fates than being pestered. She presumed that they would not go as far as actual rape.

'Then the pesterers are going to get a shock,' she said defiantly. 'I'm not giving him up. He's lovely.'

Dulcie sighed. 'Oh, well, Fern, if that's what you want. But it won't be easy for you. I hope you know what you're doing. You look a bit upset. Come and we'll see if Bernie can give us a cuppa. He might even have some ginger biscuits left if that thieving Bruno ain't scoffed the lot. That's why he keeps 'em in a tin. Bruno ain't got the hang of tins yet. Or, no, we can't. Bernie's washing Bruno today. We'll think of something. Mr. Sheridan,' she called. 'I've fixed the box.'

The magician came out of the large caravan emblazoned with his name and smiled at Dulcie. Even in a dressing-gown he had a morning-suit manner.

'There's my good girl. My two good girls,' he added. 'Hello, who is this?'

'Fern,' said Dulcie. 'We gotta go, Mr. Sheridan.'

Sheridan slathered a lascivious smile all over Phryne, leaving her feeling smirched. He stepped back into his large caravan like a cuckoo into a clock.

'Jeez!' snorted Dulcie, dragging Phryne away. 'Every time he does that I feel like I gotta go and have a wash. It's no jam being a magician's girl. Here, look at the state of your arm. Fingerprints, they are. What did Miss Younger do to you, Fern?'

'Nothing. Nothing really. She was upset.'

'Yair. Well, you can stay out of her way until tonight. I'm going over to see a friend in another camp. You want to come?'

This was a surprising announcement. Phryne nodded and went with Dulcie back to the girls' tent to wash off Mr. Sheridan's smile and change into another once-washed cotton dress. This one was lime green and had a matching scarf.

As they crossed the circus into the carnival, Phryne realized that Dulcie was not going to stop there. They were going to the gypsy camp.

The invisible boundary was crossed. It looked just like the other camps, except for the people. Dark eyes lifted from washtub and lathe and stared with the absent-minded indifference of cats.

'Here,' said Dulcie and stopped outside a tent. It was bigger than the others and striped in red and yellow.

'Come in,' said an old voice. They ducked in under the fringes of many brightly coloured shawls and came face to face with Mama Rosa.

She was massive. Her face was beaky, strong and determined. She had a shawl draped over her mass of white hair and her blunt-fingered hands were folded in her lap. She was wearing what had been someone's grandmother's good black silk dress. On Mama Rosa it looked like a wizard's gown. She had the huge Gothic authority of a mountain.

'Dulcie,' she said. 'And Fern.'

They sat down on cushions at her feet.

'What do you see?' asked Dulcie tensely. Mama Rosa opened her hands and cupped a crystal ball.

'Dark,' she said. 'Danger.'

'For me?' asked Dulcie. Mama Rosa shook her head with a click of earrings. 'Fern. In the darkness there are eyes. And teeth. Pray that you not be devoured. You will receive a message this afternoon. Heed it.'

Her eyes closed. Dulcie and Phryne tiptoed out.

'Whew!' said Phryne. 'She's amazing!'

'Yair,' said Dulcie. They walked across the gypsy camp and into the carnival. Phryne remembered Alan Lee and had to get rid of Dulcie.

'I'll see you later,' she said. 'I've got a friend here.'

'I hope he don't mind about the clown,' said Dulcie. 'Ta ta. You better take a rest this arvo. Show tonight. But no matinees tomorrow.'

'Why?'

'Melbourne Cup,' explained Dulcie and went away.

Phryne had forgotten all about the Melbourne Cup. If she were at home, she thought, she would be having her last fitting for a fashionable dress, in order to go to the Cup the next day and dazzle the eyes of all beholders. She would bathe in scented water and perhaps eat a little chocolate, Hillier's of course, before dressing, her maid waiting on her as she did so. Then she would recline in the back seat of her Hispano-Suiza while Mr. Butler drove her to the racecourse, with Lindsay or some other suitable escort. There she would sniff the roses, look at a race card occasionally, and dine on chicken patties and drink champagne while the horses thundered past.

It seemed like a dream. Fern the trick rider bought herself an ice-cream and paid to see Samson, the Strongest Man in the World.

Fifteen muscle-racking minutes later, Samson finished his act by twisting a poker provided by a local into a knot. The man who had donated the poker exerted all his strength, grimacing, trying to untwist it again. Samson let him struggle until he gave up. The man put the knotted poker back into the offered hand and Samson flexed a few deltoids and straightened it with one smooth motion.

'Show's over, folks,' said the strong man. 'Hello, Fern.'

'Samson, you really are very strong.'

He wiped his forehead on a towel.

'The poker's easy,' he said dismissively. 'That bloke could do it if he knew how. It's a knack. I hear you can stick on a horse good-o, Fern.'

'It's a knack,' said Phryne. 'Samson, if I need you, will you help me?'

'You can count on me. You know that. You got trouble, Fern?'

'Possibly. Might be tonight. I'll…' Someone came into the tent. 'See you soon,' concluded Phryne. She walked out into the sun again.

Alan Lee drew her into the cover of his tent and dropped the flap.

'We can talk if we're quiet,' he said. 'I got your answers and a letter from town, I thought it shouldn't go in the circus mail. What's gone wrong?'

She laid her forehead against his shoulder. 'Nothing but my nerve,' she said. 'I've lost it. Don't let go of me.'

His arms closed around her. She could hear his heart beating. On impulse, she unbuttoned his shirt and laid her cheek against his skin. Her heart began to resume its normal pace and her breathing slowed.

'Funny. That's what frightened animals do,' he said softly. 'Or threatened ones. Huddle together, touching flank to flank.'

Phryne did not speak. She was as close to a frightened animal as she had ever been. She leaned on the diddikoi. They lay down together on the dry and dusty grass, her head on his chest.

After five minutes she sat up. 'All right. Now, what are the answers?'

'I rang the number you gave and Dot says the lawyer told her that the circus is owned half by Farrell and half by a company called Sweet Dreams. They own funeral parlours, Dot says. The lawyer made an offer and Sweet Dreams will not sell. They said their half-share cost them three hundred pounds. There isn't such money in the world. The officers of the company are someone called Sweet, his wife and a Mr. Denny. The capital is ten pounds.'

'You have an excellent memory,' commented Phryne. The arms around her tightened. He stroked a long hand down her face and turned her head into his chest.

'I just hope I got it all. You're important to me, girl. Don't go getting in too deep.'

'Any more messages?'

'Just that she's praying for you and hopes to see you soon. To make sure that you know it's her she says to tell you that Ember has come down off the curtains.'

Phryne laughed. 'And the other?'

'He says he's sent you a letter. He also says he'll be with you soon. I told him about Sweet Dreams. Was that all right?'

'Yes.' Phryne was reluctant to drag herself out of this soothing embrace. He had a quality of deep, disinterested calm which was like hot water on a bruise, or a warm hand on the back of a cold neck. Reluctantly, Phryne got to her feet.

'I can't stay here any longer,' she said. 'I'll be missed. Stand guard while I read this letter.'

Alan Lee stood by the tent flap as she scanned rapidly through Robinson's neat page. He heard her say, 'Well,' before she folded up the letter and gave it to him.

'You'd better keep this for me,' she said, kissing him lightly. 'I'd better not be found with anything strange.'

'Be careful,' said the young man, stroking her arm. 'Call us if you need us.'

'You'll hear me from here,' promised Phryne and peeped out of the tent. No one seemed to be looking. She slipped out into the carnival and was gone, an ordinary-looking circus performer in lime green that did not suit her colouring.

Alan Lee read the letter before he stowed it in his pocket. He wondered where he had heard the term Exit before. Shaking his head, as if he thought that might make memory surface, he went back to his carousel.

◇◇◇

'What's the matter?' Miss Parkes leaned over Lizard Elsie and put a cool hand on her forehead.

The old woman moaned. 'I ain't had much to eat for a fucking week. Then I wash all me bloody grime off and eat a good lunch—for a fucking prison it was a good lunch—and me bloody insides just ain't used to food. I been on the red biddy for a fortnight.'

'What's red biddy?'

Miss Parkes had never met anyone like Lizard Elsie before. Not even in prison.

'Metho and port.' Elsie writhed. 'I gotta gutsache.'

'Do you want me to call a doctor?'

'Nah. I've had it before. I'll be all right. I've lasted fifty years on the street and you couldn't kill me with a bloody axe.'

Miss Parkes was clean, clothed in her own garments from her suitcase, which Constable Harris had personally packed. She was full of steak-and-kidney pie, peas, mashed potatoes and about a spoonful of jam roly-poly. Her despair had left her as though it had never been. She wasn't sure what would take its place. But for now there was this poor tattered creature. Elsie was in pain. Something should be done. It was the first time Miss Parkes had thought about anything but her own inner horror since she had been arrested.

'Constable,' she called timidly, 'I think Elsie's ill.'

The duty officer made a brief inspection of Elsie and commented sagely, 'She's been starving and she's been hitting the metho. She'll be raving fairly soon. Poor old Else. Not that she can't put up a fight. Took three of us to arrest her once. I'll get some brandy off the sergeant when it gets too bad. I'm sorry to leave you in with her but there ain't no other cell I could put ladies in.'

'I don't mind.'

'You yell if she gets obstreperous,' said the young man, 'and I'll get you out.'

'All right.'

For seven hours, until she was relieved by an unsympathetic policewoman, Miss Parkes watched Elsie through delirium tremens. The old woman swore, screamed and twisted in pain. She winced away from snakes and little men who were staring at her. She clung to Miss Parkes so hard that her fingers left bruises and the latter required all her half-forgotten gymnast's skills to hold Elsie down and stop her from tearing herself to bits.

'Oh, Elsie, how could you do this to yourself?' she asked aloud as she was led out. One black eye nailed her to her place. Elsie had returned for a moment.

'Fear,' croaked Lizard Elsie and dropped out of consciousness.

Miss Parkes was given police-issue tea in the sergeant's office, which was entirely against the rules. In the room over her head an argument was going on about her.

'But we can't let her go,' objected Constable Harris. 'She's got nowhere to go.'

'Plenty of places,' said Grossmith. 'The men are complaining about her. Won't wash, won't eat. She's a loony and ought to be in a loony-bin.'

'She isn't loony,' said Robinson. 'We just frightened her out of her wits. You know how it is with ex-prisoners. But I agree with Harris. We can't let her go until we find out who did it, or she might be next. There are things which connect that boarding house with Albert Ellis and with Exit. These are ruthless people. Well, let's go down and talk to her. See what state the poor woman is in.'

He led his companions down the stairs and into the custody sergeant's office. There was a well-dressed woman there, obviously a visitor, drinking tea from a thick white cup. Robinson had to look at her twice to believe his eyes.

'Miss Parkes. You feeling better, then?'

'Yes, thank you.' Miss Parkes rose collectedly to her feet. 'I did knock on the door of Mr. Christopher's room. I lied to you because I was frightened. But I did not kill Mr. Christopher, Detective Inspector.'

'No,' said Tommy Harris. 'You didn't.'

'Do you know who did?' asked Grossmith.

'I'm afraid not, Sergeant.'

'Until we do,' said Robinson, 'I propose to retain you in custody. We've had some shootings. I think you'd be better off in here.'

'Of course,' said Miss Parkes. 'I can't leave. Not until Elsie is through her DTs.'

'She's yelling for you,' said the duty officer, returning. 'I got some brandy. Only a spoonful at a time. Oh, Detective Inspector Robinson, Elsie's creating—'

'Where's 'Melia?' shrieked Elsie. 'Them snakes is afraid of 'Melia. Where is she? Bloody find me 'Melia!'

'Coming, Elsie,' called Miss Parkes and went back unescorted to her cell.

Robinson scratched his head. Tommy Harris beamed. Sergeant Grossmith grunted.

'It's not right. This is a bloody police station, not a recovery ward for aged female inebriates!'

'Language,' chided Detective Inspector Robinson.

Chapter Fourteen

They assumed to be mighty rakish and knowing, they were not very tidy in their private dresses, they were not at all orderly in their domestic arrangements...yet...there was a remarkable gentleness...an untiring readiness to help and pity one another deserving of as much respect...as the everyday virtues of any class of people in the world.

Hard Times, Charles Dickens

Once Phryne had demonstrated that she could stand on Missy's back steadily, despite complaining flyers, tumbling Catalans, roaring lions, two clowns playing a violin in a choice of keys, and a wire walker bashing two saucepans together, she was dismissed for the afternoon and told to get some sleep.

This was not an easy matter, although she was so tired that she could have lain down on a barbed-wire fence. The affair with Matthias the clown was known, so she could not sleep in his bed. Someone had found and removed her gun, so they knew where she slept in the girls' tent, which meant that she couldn't sleep there either. By an association of ideas she crossed the circus grounds and curled up under Bernie's awning, next to Bruno. He was affected by the weather, which was hot and somnolent.

He lay down beside her, laying his formidable head on her hip, and whickered softly through his nose.

It was the first time that Phryne had ever been lulled to sleep by a snoring bear.

She was woken by Bernie. Bruno scrambled onto all fours, hoping for biscuits. Phryne sat up and rubbed her eyes.

'You look like something out of a fairy tale,' commented Bernie. 'Dinner's on. Mr. Thompson must have bought his wife flowers or something. She's had a rush of blood to the head and dished up a quite decent Irish stew. For a change. Don't waste this opportunity, Fern. It may never come again.'

Phryne splashed her face in Bruno's drinking water and felt refreshed.

Mrs. Thompson's Irish stew, though it would not pass at the Ritz, was pleasant and filling. She perched on a bucket near the heat of the cook tent, and various people greeted her as they passed.

'Ah, Fern,' carolled a voice like buttered toffee. 'Fern, Fern, makes my head turn. "For beautiful Fern I groan and...er... girn."' Matthias looked at her severely. 'Don't laugh. It's Scotch. Probably Burns. "Fern will teach and I will learn. I gave my heart to beautiful Fern." There. Can I have some stew, Mrs. T?'

'If you promise not to make any more poems,' said the older woman. Matthias laid his hand on his heart and promised solemnly. Phryne saw that he had his other fingers crossed behind his back. She grinned up at him.

'Help me carry this?' he asked. 'I have to take some back for Toby.'

Phryne slung her tin plate into the washing-up water and accepted the dish. 'What's wrong with Toby?'

'He's gone off again,' said Matthias sadly. 'Poor Toby. Gone funny, you could say. He doesn't see or hear. Come in,' he invited as they reached the caravan. 'Tell me what's wrong, Fern. I have to feed him.'

Toby sat where he had been placed in a comfortable chair in his own caravan. His eyes were open. He seemed to be breathing. That was his only sign of life.

'How do you know something's wrong?' asked Phryne, cutting up the solid bits of the Irish stew. The ugly face with the beautiful grey eyes turned to her.

'You were seen fighting off Jones behind the lions. You were molested by Miss Younger. You flattened a roustabout who said something nasty to you. Then you were found by Dulcie who took you to Mama Rosa. After that you vanished into the carnival, possibly with a diddikoi called Lee, or the strongman, Samson. Then you rode Missy in practice, took her back to the lines and groomed and fed her, then fell asleep with Bruno. Open your mouth, Tobias. It's din-dins time.'

'Do you know everything?' asked Phryne, astonished.

'No. But I want to know about you. I'm worried, Fern. Something is brewing.'

'You bet,' said Phryne. She wanted to say more but Toby's open mouth and expressionless eyes worried her. 'I'll tell you later,' she said uneasily. 'You finish feeding him and then we can go into your caravan.'

'Don't go out,' he said quietly. 'Toby won't tell, will you, eh Tobias? Swallow, now, there's a good fellow. It's kosher. It's mutton and onion and potato. Eat up, Toby.'

He spooned stew into Toby's mouth until he finished his ration. Matthias gobbled his own dinner and turned Toby to face the wall.

'Now,' said the clown, 'if you trust me, tell me.'

Phryne, in a low voice, began to tell him about the murder of Mr. Christopher, the accidents on the road, which could all have been done for a central purpose and were attributable to the three roustabouts, the half-share of the circus owned by Sweet Dreams Pty Ltd, the names of the company's officers, and the strange hint in Jack Robinson's letter.

'Exit,' mused the clown. 'I seem to have heard it before. Then again, it's a word you see a lot. On every theatre wall, for example. But death is an exit too. Could that relate to funeral parlours? Tell me your real name,' he said and Phryne leaned toward him and slid her hand behind his head to catch a handful of the ragged silvery-brown hair. She breathed her name into his ear.

'A name that tickles,' observed Matthias. 'It's clear that those three are responsible and that Jones is their paymaster. He wants to ruin Farrell, for some criminal reason. Why shouldn't we just…er…lose them? Your Samson could tie them into Turk's heads and leave them out in the bush somewhere. No?'

'No,' said Phryne. She was firm on the ethics of assassination as a tool of practical problem solving.

'We could at least tell someone,' said Matthias. 'That Jones has got it in for you, Fern. I don't like the way he looks at you.'

'I don't like the way he looks at me, either. I've got some help and more coming, I suspect.' She looked into the grey eyes. 'And there's time.'

'Time for what?'

'For things to develop,' said Phryne. The clown's mouth curved up into a smile.

He kissed her gently on the shoulder that showed through the boat neck of the lime-green shift.

◇◇◇

The bell announced showtime. Phryne accompanied the clowns to the girls' tent, where Dulcie gave her the scarlet tunic, a feather headdress and a pair of tights, which had been mended. Jo Jo, carrying two violins, a bow, and a heavy bag which clanked, walked his brother into the canvas antechamber and stood him against the wall.

'First act: the Thompson-and-Dog Turn to warm up the crowd,' he commented. 'You can see through here, Fern.'

The ring was brightly lit. Thompson, in baggy trousers and huge shoes, was encouraging his fox terrier to leap through a hoop. It wouldn't. He lowered the hoop. It refused. He laid the hoop on the ground. The dog was impassive. Finally he picked up the hoop and tried to leap through it himself. He stuck. The dog began to dance on its hind legs. It seemed to be amused.

Thompson, with the ring around his knees and elbows, frog jumped out of the ring. The audience laughed and applauded.

'Liberty horses,' said Jo Jo. 'Hold still, Toby.' He was applying white paint to his brother's immobile face.

Into the ring ran ten horses, all perfectly white. Phryne was close enough to see where whitewash concealed the occasional unmatching sock or ear. In response to Farrell's whip, they walked, cantered and ran. Then they all stopped and bowed. A boy ran along the line, attaching a cloth with a number to each back. Farrell selected one horse out of the throng and blindfolded it with a black bandanna. He turned it around tail to nose three times and then let it go.

'Ladies and gentlemen! These horses are so highly trained that number three will find her own way back into order blindfolded.'

He set the horses to cantering again. The blindfolded mare, listening with her ears pricked, hesitated for perhaps ten seconds, then joined in the canter around the ring, slotting herself in neatly between number two and number four. The crowd applauded and the horses left.

'The Catalans,' muttered Jo Jo. 'Third billing, and they are worth it.'

Phryne applied her eye to the peephole again. In ran nine men and a boy, turning somersaults. They rolled and tumbled, encouraging each other with shouts in what was presumably Catalan. One man stood on another's shoulders, who took another on his own. The pile walked calmly across the ring, fell apart and the three rolled safely in the sawdust.

Two boys brought in balancing poles. The Catalans play-fought with them, their voices harsh and mocking. Then four of them lined up, arms linked, and three more leapt to their shoulders and balanced there. The structure wobbled a little, then was still. Two men climbed up, shoulder to foot to shoulder and linked their arms, poles held out. The structure firmed again. Phryne reflected on the weight which the men at the bottom must be carrying. She wondered what else would happen.

With a cry, the boy ran at the pile of men. No hands reached for him. He swarmed up three stories of humans and planted his feet on the two top men's shoulders. Slowly, he stood up.

For a moment he was perfectly still, arms outstretched. He looked like a bronze image of some heroic child from a Greek legend. The electric lights made a halo around his sleek black head. Applause rocked the tent. Then the pyramid fell quietly apart, the boy was lowered from the top, and all ten of the Catalan Human Pyramid were on solid sawdust again.

'High wire,' said Jo Jo the clown. 'Hold this mirror for me, Fern.' Phryne held the mirror over her shoulder, her eyes glued to the peephole. 'One moment,' said the clown. He kissed her on the ear. 'Last chance before I paint my mouth,' he added hopefully. Phryne did not move.

A line had been rigged twelve feet off the ground. A man was walking out along it, sliding his feet, until he was in the middle. He yawned, stretched and sat down. Then he lay down and closed his eyes. Unable to get comfortable, he rolled over onto his stomach, twisted around and then rolled onto his back again. Giving this up, he sat on the rope. A roustabout with a long pole fetched him a chair. He took it, set it on the rope and sat down, fumbling for a cigar, which he lit. Then he leaned back, blowing smoke rings. The chair tipped. The audience held their breath. The chair tipped further and fell.

Just as it seemed that a broken back was inevitable, the high-wire artist twisted, regained his feet and stood on the rope, the chair in one hand and the cigar still in his mouth. The audience sighed with relief. There was something odd about them, Phryne thought. Their eyes were bright, their mouths wet. They licked their lips.

'They want him to fall,' said Jo Jo's voice next to her ear. 'They always do, the crowds. That's why he does that pratfall. Keeps them on the edge of their seats. Now, Toby, are we ready?'

He gave his brother a brisk brush down and produced the violin and bow. Toby took them.

'Ready?' asked Matthias. 'We're on, brother. Time to give them a chance to bring in the lions.'

Tobias' eyes seemed to fill with personality, as though it was being poured into him from a jug. He gulped and said, 'Yes, Matt.'

'Break a leg,' said Phryne, and the brothers Shakespeare entered the ring on the receding wave of the tightrope walker's applause. Dulcie wandered in and looked over Phryne's shoulder.

'Jo Jo and Toby!' announced the ringmaster and cracked his whip. Jo Jo looked hurt. Toby took exception to the ringmaster. He walked up to him and gestured at the whip. The ringmaster cracked it again. Toby bared one thin arm and shook his fist at him. Farrell menaced him with the whip and he went back into the middle of the ring. He produced his violin and put it to his shoulder.

Jo Jo was interested. He tried to take the violin away from Toby and Toby knocked him down. He got up and Toby knocked him down again. He sat in the sawdust and cried. Then he was visited by an idea. He rummaged in the battered bag and found a violin of his own. Toby drew the bow across his instrument and a sweet long note sounded. Jo Jo copied the movement, without a bow. He rummaged in the bag again. In succession, he attempted to play the violin with a cricket bat, a stretched out stocking, a pencil, a sponge and a saw. Toby began to play a Bach air so sweetly that Phryne wondered why he was a clown, not a concert performer. A sawing noise ruined the sound. Jo Jo was finding out that you couldn't play a violin which was cut in half.

He sat down and howled, holding one half of a violin in each hand in a pose that seemed to contain tragedy. The audience screamed with mirth. His brother ignored him and continued to play. Ravishing music poured from the violin. After a while, Jo Jo put the two halves of his instrument together again and plucked the strings with his fingers. The music was sweet beyond belief.

Jo Jo was led sobbing out of the ring, overcome by the music. The crowd laughed and clapped.

While the clowns were performing, the cages of lions had been brought in. Now the iron walls had been built and Amazing Hans summoned his beasts to appear.

As he called them by name, they sat up and snarled. 'Sarah, Sam, Boy, King, Queenie, Prince!'

Phryne had seen lion tamers before. And she really did not like the lions. The clowns paused in the antechamber.

'You're marvellous,' said Phryne. 'Really terrific.'

'Did you hear that, Toby?' asked Jo Jo. He touched his brother's cheek and waved a hand in front of his eyes. 'Oh, dear, he's gone again. Now, Fern, what about you? Can't go on with a naked face, it's indecent. Let me just stand Toby over here and I'll paint you. We might as well match, eh? Tip up your chin. Now stay still.'

Matthias could not have been more professional. He smoothed greasepaint numbers five and nine into Phryne's skin, carefully blending it in the palm of his hand. Then he drew in her eyes, provided red for her cheeks and lips and tucked a stray wisp of black hair under the feathers.

'Pretty bird,' he said. 'Look at yourself.'

Phryne surveyed the face in the mirror and did not know it. The paint abolished features with which she was tolerably familiar and transformed her into a circus rider, born in a trunk and exactly the same as all the others. She smiled, then frowned. She was looking at a stranger.

A whip cracked in the big top. The lions were removed and it was interval. The crowd came streaming out, in search of fairy lollies and saveloys and ice-cream in tubs.

'I'd better put poor old Toby back in his box,' said Matthias. 'Back later, Fern. Don't miss the flyers. They are very good.'

Phryne learnt that she was required to stay within the purlieus of the tent. She obtained a cup of tea and sat down on the grass to consider her situation.

There was too much that she did not know. She could pin down most of the accidents at Farrell's Circus to the abominable Jones and his three henchmen. The tall one, the dark one, and the man with the sticking plaster on his hands. That was clear. What was not clear was why. If Jones wanted his half-share, he now had it, at the cost of three hundred pounds. What if Jones was the appointee of Sweet Dreams Pty Ltd? Phryne presumed that he was. He wielded too much power over Farrell not to have some financial or other very strong stake in the show. Mr.

Burton, a very shrewd person, thought it was money. So Jones, or Sweet Dreams Pty Ltd, had their half. Why should they keep on? And why should they kill Mr. Christopher? If they had?

Phryne felt wrath glow in her insides about Mr. Christopher. Christopher/Christine, he had been billed. Criss/Cross, the man-woman, perfect complement to poor Miss Younger. She would never find another man like him. Phryne was desperately sorry for Molly Younger.

'Heads up, Fern,' warned Dulcie. 'The Bevans are on.'

The trapeze was occupied. Two young men, one at each end of the tent, were stretching and bending on gear slung from the king poles. They were clad in fleshings and tunics and they glittered with spangles. From the ground they seemed to have naked legs, chests and arms. They unslung the trapezes and swung out lazily, sitting on the bar like children on a swing, far over the audience's heads.

One slid down and swung. The other slid as well, with a heart-stopping jerk which Phryne hoped was done for effect. They swung by one hand, by one leg, backwards and forwards.

A young woman in a cloak was climbing a rope as easily as walking up a ramp. She reached the flies, unclasped the cloak and dropped it fluttering to the ground. It seemed to fall very slowly. It was a long way down. The audience's eyes followed it. Two more men swarmed up ropes to the ceiling, just under the hot lights.

'Now,' she heard the biggest man call, hanging upside down by his knees. Some kind of cuff attached his ankle to the trapeze.

Swinging gently, the first man lazily let go of the bar with his knees and flipped himself into space. Just as lazily and with absolute timing, the catcher locked his hands onto his wrists. The crowd screamed. The catcher swung back and deposited the flyer on the perch. The next Bevan performed a somersault. The third did a double somersault. Five people changed places between trapeze and perch, moving with the assurance of birds in their native element. The young woman Lynn flew non-chalantly through the air, her lithe body a streak of blue, glittering as she turned, and was snared by her catcher's safe hands.

'Ladies and Gentlemen!' announced Sam Farrell. 'Silence if you please. Miss Lynn Bevan will now attempt, for your astonishment and delight, the most dangerous feat ever to be done by an aerialist. The triple somersault!'

The audience clapped. Phryne winced away from their hot eyes.

'Called the death trick,' continued the ringmaster, 'thought to be humanly impossible. Now, could I have complete silence please.'

The drum rolled and was still. The blue-clad girl appeared to be impossibly high and impossibly delicate. She could not defy gravity for long enough to roll three times. Phryne held her breath. So did the crowd.

The catcher and the girl, hanging by their knees, began to swing. They were carefully out of phase. One movement seemed to be wrong and ugly because it did not reflect the other. Only when Phryne had begun to gnaw the greasepaint off her lips did the girl leave her perch and spin like a ball in the air. Once, twice, thrice and her hands came out of the last roll. The catcher had her safe, or as safe as she could be hanging by both wrists high above unforgiving sawdust. From up there, Phryne thought, the net must look like a pocket handkerchief. The crowd roared with relief and admiration. Miss Bevan was decanted neatly onto the stand and the Flying Bevans slid down ropes to take their bow.

'While they get the net folded, we have jugglers,' said Dulcie. 'One of which is, come to think of it, me.'

She ran into the ring, catching balls tossed to her by her tall, handsome partner. He smiled at her as she tossed back objects of different sizes and weight. There were balls, a matchbox, a club and an orange. Dulcie managed them without appearing to concentrate. The pair moved around the outside of the ring, tossing objects and quips, as the roustabouts rolled up the safety net and carried it out.

Then they took the centre. A boy ran in with a bundle of lit kerosene flambeaux. Dulcie and Tom took one each and passed them. Then two each and finally three. The flames flared and streamed as they were passed with precision from one hand to the other, so that Phryne was dazzled. She wondered how burned they had got, practising this dangerous trick. Finally, they caught up three each and brandished them.

Bernie entered, with Bruno in tow, passing Dulcie and Tom. The bear took a scooter away from a clown and got on it. He pushed off and scooted around the ring with solemn dignity, then dropped on all fours and was fed a ginger biscuit. He sat down, sat up and rolled over on request. Then the band struck up a waltz and he bowed to Bernie and waltzed him confidently around the ring to the strains of an out-of-tune *Blue Danube*. Bernie fed him another ginger biscuit. Phryne suddenly thought that this was a terrible thing to do to a wild creature.

Sultan and Rajah lumbered in to stand on tubs and awe the audience with their hugeness, and Phryne remembered that she was on soon. She had better go and look for Missy.

She found her standing quietly with the other horses. Feathers nodded between her ears and her harness was glittering with stones. The elephants walked out, and in came Mr. Sheridan the magician. He wore immaculate evening dress and carried only a small wand. Phryne watched him pass, disliking his manner. She pinned down the cause of her distaste. He was a parvenu, an affected social climber. She recalled that his father was reputed to have been a grocer and wished his son had stayed a counter-jumper, where he belonged. Dulcie, in tights and a spangled costume, came behind him, bearing a collapsible table. Behind her were two stagehands carrying the disappearing box.

Phryne patted Missy and gave her a carrot. The dark passage was full of horses and girls. The hot air smelt sweetly of greasepaint and it was stifling. Phryne went back into the tent and looked through the peephole again.

'I conjure,' announced Mr. Sheridan, 'a dagger!'

Out of the air a dagger came floating down toward him. Phryne was close enough to see that it was suspended by nearly invisible fishing line.

How Shakespearean, thought Phryne. Parlour stage craft. She was not interested in Mr. Sheridan. The audience, however, were enthusiastic.

'We're on,' said Miss Younger's voice. 'Mount up.'

Phryne ran her hands over Missy's back and the horse flinched and kicked.

'What's the matter, Missy?' she asked. When she peeled back the tinselled riding blanket, something pricked her finger. She pulled it out. It was a splinter, fully two inches long. If she had leapt onto Missy's back without knowing of it, her weight would have driven it into Missy's flesh, which the mare would have pardonably resented. She put the splinter into the webbing belt, smoothed down her skimpy tunic and got up. Missy did not shift.

'On we go. One circuit, knees. Next circuit, on the signal, stand. Three more circuits, standing. Then down and off and follow the parade. Go,' said Miss Younger and rode Bell up the ramp and into the ring.

Phryne and Missy followed third in line, nose to tail with the next horse, up the incline. The ring was brighter than sunshine. Phryne blinked. The horses began to walk, then canter, at their smooth pace. Miss Younger cracked her whip. Obediently ten girls in feather headdresses rose to their knees. The whip cracked again and Phryne was standing with the others and the ring and the faces were flashing past. Missy was moving without fault, as smooth as cream.

Phryne felt a smile balloon up onto her face. She felt the strange force holding her on and upright. This is how a billy of tea feels when you spin it round your head, she thought as they completed the last circuit and slipped down to ride astride out of the ring and the tent, to turn and follow the tail of the procession.

In the crowd, Constable Tommy Harris picked out the third girl in the rush as Miss Phryne Fisher, only because he had been told that this was Fern Williams. He was dressed in his own clothes, elastic-sided boots, a clean white shirt, moleskins, a waistcoat and a pale wide-brimmed felt hat. He was fascinated. He had always loved circuses.

Detective Inspector Robinson was also somewhere in the crowd. He was difficult to spot in any gathering because he seemed to melt and blend, so that it was hard even for his friends to remember exactly what he looked like. He had no memorable features.

Sergeant Grossmith, under Robinson's orders and profoundly out of place away from his precious Brunswick Street, was in Rockbank waking up the local constable. Jack Robinson meant to make a clean sweep of the circus. He had already spotted one man he knew—the little man with the sticking plaster on his hands, assiduously sweeping up horse droppings.

'Ronald Smythe, or I'm a Dutchman,' he breathed. Since he had definitely been born in Richmond, he was sure of his identification.

The grand parade was just starting when a hand plucked at Constable Harris' clean white sleeve.

'You looking for Fern?' asked a voice behind him, in the gloom above his seat. 'Come down here, then. She wants to talk to you private.'

Constable Harris had only been in the police force for eight months. He jumped softly down into the dark and after a short and painful interval, knew no more.

◇◇◇

Phryne rode Missy out of the tent and allowed a handler to take her away. She looked around for Dulcie or Matthias and could not see them. It was dark after the lights in the big top and she stood still to let her eyes adjust. Soon people would be streaming out of the tent again, to play games in the carnival and eat more ice-cream. They were merely the audience. She was now part of the show. She pulled off the feathers and ran her hands through her hair, hoping to cool her head.

At which point someone flipped a sack over her and scooped her off her feet. She was too astonished to scream. When she started to struggle, someone shoved a sharp blade through the sack. The point was icy on the hot flesh of her back.

'Say one word,' grated a voice, 'and it'll be your last.'

Chapter Fifteen

As a god self-slain on his own strange altar
Death lies dead.

The Forsaken Garden,
Algernon Swinburne

Detective Inspector Robinson, unable to locate Phryne, drifted over to the carnival in search of the person Dot had mentioned as her friend. The carousel music blared, brassy and loud. Jack Robinson jumped aboard and went round with the horses. Poseidon, Artilleryman, Carbine and Spearfelt bobbed and swayed. He sat down on one called Windbag. Alan Lee had a taste, it seemed, for Melbourne Cup winners. Robinson had an affection for Windbag. It had come in first in 1925 over the favourite Manfred, netting a nice return at five to one. Alan Lee was taking tickets from the children. Robinson settled down on Windbag to wait.

Phryne was extracted from her sack, bound and gagged and flung into what felt like a tent. It smelt sweaty and hot and there was dead grass under her, which crackled as she moved.

She tried her bonds; they were tight and expertly applied. She rolled over and sat up. Something shifted in the dark and made a suppressed noise, like a partly strangled oboe. Phryne peered into the gloom. Something humped over the ground and touched her. Then a chest became apparent and a male chin, which scraped over her face until teeth could seize her gag and drag it down, at the risk of dislocating her jaw.

'Ouch,' she commented. 'Who are you?'

The man mumbled again. Phryne got the idea and knelt up, finding the gag in his mouth and pulling it away. She still could not see, but got the general impression of someone quite large and young.

'Who are you?' she asked again. The figure coughed, spat and then whispered, 'I'm Constable Harris. Tommy Harris. Are you Miss Fisher?'

'Yes. But they know me as Fern. Is Jack Robinson here?'

'Yes.'

'Right. Well, he'll find me. Find us. Who scragged you?'

'I couldn't see. It was too dark.'

'Me neither. Can you turn and reach my hands?'

'I'll try.'

He struggled with positioning and at last his fingers found the knots. He scrabbled for a while and then said, 'Can't be done. My fingers have gone numb.'

'Never mind. What we need in these circumstances is calm.' Phryne was not feeling calm. 'We'll have to pass the time. Talk to me,' she said, leaning against his comfortingly broad back.

'What about?'

'Tell me all about Exit and Mr. Christopher.'

Tommy began to feel less outraged. He was still ready and willing to lose his temper if it would help, but dragging against his bonds had only damaged his hands. So he began, in his soft country voice just above the level of hearing, to tell Phryne Fisher all he could remember about both cases. Because he was naturally meticulous he told her everything, including the decor of Mr. Christopher's room, the collapse of Miss Parkes, Lizard Elsie's falling asleep with her head on his shoulder in the custody area, and the shooting which had left a pool of blood on Brunswick Street.

Phryne did not interrupt. When he had got down to the present, she said, 'Interesting. Now I'll tell you what I've been doing.'

Phryne recounted her struggles to stay on Missy's back. She talked about the social organization of the circus, the carnival and the gypsies. She told him about the clown Matthias and his brother Toby. She mentioned the various acts that made up the show, the grace of the flyers, the importance of the rigger, and the unfillable void which Mr. Christopher's death had left in Miss Younger's life. Pieces began to fall like dominoes. The two stories dove-tailed in a way that would have made a Chippendale carpenter swell with pride. At the end of this recital Phryne knew who had killed Mr. Christopher and why. She had discovered who was sabotaging Farrell's Circus and why.

She nudged the young constable. 'Listen!' she said urgently. 'If you get out of here, then you have to tell Jack all about this and make sure that he catches the guilty parties. I expect they'll come for us soon. Stick to your story that you came looking for me because someone told you that I was a tart.' He made a shocked exclamation and Phryne snapped, 'I tell you, that's your best chance. By circus standards I am a tart. They all think so. Now, this is important.'

Carefully she told Constable Harris all that Jack Robinson needed to know to solve the portfolio of problems currently in his possession. Towards the end, she stopped.

'Can you hear something?' she whispered.

'No.'

'I thought I heard a footstep.'

'I didn't hear anything.'

Phryne completed her theory. Harris nodded. Then he remembered that he could not be seen and said, 'All right, but I can't leave you.'

'Yes, you can,' said Phryne acidly. 'If you get away, then you can find Jack and rescue me. Clear?'

'Yes,' the young man said reluctantly.

<><><>

Alan Lee walked around the carousel to the unremarkable man sitting on Windbag and said, 'Tickets, please.'

'I must speak to you,' said Jack Robinson. 'About Fern Williams.'

'Wait till we stop,' said Alan. 'I'll get Bill to take over. Then we can talk.'

The carousel went round again, to the tune of 'A Bicycle Built For Two', a full quarter tone flat.

Grossmith found that the Rockbank constable had been called out on a sheep stealing case. He gritted his teeth.

They came for Phryne a little after midnight. She heard footsteps and she and Tommy Harris struggled to replace their gags.

Phryne was dragged upright by unseen hands. Someone chuckled.

'Leave him,' said an oily voice. 'He's just a bumpkin. Come sniffing after this tart, I bet. But this one...' He slung Phryne over his shoulder. 'Jones wants this one.'

Phryne was taken out of the tent. Left alone, Constable Harris struggled afresh with his bonds. The gag had slipped back into his mouth and he was rendered mute.

Phryne was carried, her mid-section bumping painfully, through darkness which smelt of canvas and cooking. She tried to see where she was but could catch no clue. Most parts of the circus looked the same, viewed from upside down.

She was conveyed up the steps of what was probably a caravan and thrown down into a chair. Light wounded her eyes. She shook her head and squinted.

'Ah,' said Mr. Jones, whom she now knew to be Killer Jones of the Fitzroy Boys, 'you owe me a favour, Fern.' He reached out with hands scarred to the knuckles and grabbed the front of her scarlet tunic and ripped it slowly open.

Phryne stared at him. There were four people in the caravan. The small man with the sticking-plastered hands. Ronald Smythe, she presumed. The tall man must be Damien Maguire.

And the sneering roustabout whom she had slapped across the face. Everybody except Smythe was staring at her, willing her to struggle, wanting to savour her defeat.

Mr. Jones, now kneeling, was engaged in untying her ankles. She shuddered at the reason he might do that.

'I owe you no favours,' she said though the gag. Mr. Jones removed it. He obviously liked screams and he clearly expected that he would not be interrupted.

'You got in the way, Fern,' he said with slow relish, peeling off her tights. 'You been snooping. You even had a gun. Was that a nice thing to bring into the circus? We got to teach you a lesson, Fern.'

Her much washed knickers gave way under his pulling fingers and tore down from their band.

◊◊◊

'I should find Fern,' said Robinson to Alan Lee without urgency. 'Lot of things been going on in this circus.'

'This ain't the circus. This is the carnival. The circus is over there,' Alan Lee corrected him. 'She was in the parade, all of the girls were. She'll be in the girls' tent by now. I'll take you.'

Alan Lee and the detective inspector began to stroll through the carnival, chatting casually, but when Alan called Dulcie out she told him that Phryne was not there.

'She ain't been back,' said Dulcie. 'But I know where she might be. And before I say it, I think she's all right. She don't belong in a circus but she's all right, Fern is.'

With delicacy, she told them about Matthias the clown.

◊◊◊

Phryne was helpless. For a moment she lay in panic. Her fate appeared to be set. Jones dragged the webbing belt from around her waist. She made no sound until he broke the thong which held the holy medal and pocketed it. Phryne gave a pitiful cry. Her last link with her own self had gone.

Ronald Smythe's nerve broke. Phryne was far too old to attract him. His chosen sexual objects were all below puberty. 'I don't like this,' he said. 'Boss just said to dispose of her. He didn't say nothing about rape.'

'Don't you want a turn?' sneered Jones. 'She can't complain. She's a spy. Probably belongs to the Brunnies. Don't you think she's pretty?' He indicated Phryne. Her ankles were now free and her hands were still behind her back. The forced arch of her spine thrust out her breasts. 'She's defenceless,' added Jones. 'She can't fight back.'

'I'll wait outside,' said Ronald Smythe. He went out and Phryne heard a match strike as he lit a soothing cigarette.

Jones had found the fastening of the webbing belt. He took out a wad of notes and riffled them.

'Whacko,' he gloated. 'The girl *and* the money. What was this, eh? Bribe money?'

'Keep looking,' advised Phryne. 'You'll be surprised.'

He found the card case, opened it and read the elegant lettering. 'Miss Phryne Fisher. Well. Private detective, eh? You've been playing with the big boys, ain't you? Little girls oughtn't to play with the boys.'

He approached menacingly. One of the roustabouts seized Phryne's ankle and the other one grabbed for her foot.

She considered the caravan. It was hung with objects which she could not reach. Her hands remained tightly fastened. She had only a second to act before she would be rendered helpless. Mr. Jones reached for the buttons on his trousers.

Phryne let go of her civilization. Years of ladylike behaviour and carefully learned social rules had peeled off along with her clothes. Her rank, wealth and the protection of class had been deliberately abandoned when she joined the circus. She was the ten-year-old ragged girl standing guard over her favourite pig-bin at the Victoria Market, menaced by the bigger boys in the dark behind the stalls. She was the eighteen-year-old Phryne at bay in the black cornices of the Place Pigalle, with the Apache hulking towards her.

A surge of strength went through her like an electric current. They might rape her. But she would not be a victim.

◇◇◇

'No,' said Matthias Shakespeare worriedly, 'she isn't here. And she said she would come,' he added softly. 'But perhaps, since Dulcie told her about the rules, she is no longer interested in clowns.'

'I don't think so,' said Dulcie. 'She seemed interested to me. Said she'd rather be thought a tart than give you up. Where can she be?'

'Perhaps she did not feel it was safe to come to me, or stay in the girls' tent,' said Matthias. 'You can't keep secrets in a circus. Perhaps...Miss Younger?'

Dulcie considered this. 'We'll go and ask,' she said. 'But quietly. Everyone's asleep.'

Samson, Alan Lee, Robinson, and Matthias the clown, still in clown gear and makeup, followed Dulcie through the canvas lanes.

◇◇◇

Phryne jackknifed away from the hands. She pulled her feet free and kicked Jones full in his most threatening part. As he screamed and fell to his knees, Phryne doubled up and brought her bound hands to the front. Damien Maguire aimed a slap at her, which connected with the side of her head. She fell against the caravan wall, dizzy, and was grabbed and shaken. She bit at the passing hands, managed to catch one and shut her jaw with all her force. The hand slid back into her mouth and her back teeth closed on the hand between the thumb and the wrist. She bore down until she felt a bone crack. Blood rushed into her mouth and she had to let go or choke. Jones glared at her as Maguire dragged her off her feet and into a headlock. The sneering roustabout was nursing his hand, holding it between his side and his arm and moaning.

'She's a wild beast,' Jones snarled from his crouch. 'And you know where we put wild beasts. In a cage.'

Phryne, naked and choking, clawed with bound hands at the steely forearm which was crushing her throat. Then she was back in a bag, jogging up and down as she was carried.

Vengefully, she gloated that the blood wasn't hers.

◇◇◇

Miss Younger was not asleep. She stared at Dulcie.

'No, she isn't here,' she said flatly. 'I haven't seen her. Why? Is she missing?'

'She might be,' Dulcie temporized.

'Well, she's a tart. She's probably looking for customers in Rockbank.' Miss Younger slammed the door. The policeman, the carnies and the circus folk looked at each other.

'What now?' asked Dulcie.

'We'd better search,' said Alan. 'I don't like this. Fern's no tart. She wouldn't just go missing. Not when she's got at least two good reasons to stay.' He looked at Matthias and grinned in a brotherly fashion. Jo Jo the clown smiled uncertainly at the carnie. 'I don't like this,' repeated Alan.

'Nor me,' agreed Robinson. 'She's reliable, Phr—Fern is.'

◇◇◇

Mr. Sheridan the magician had packed all his goods away, secured his caravan and started the engine. It purred. He got out and pulled several pegs, unlatching hidden hinges. The decorated sides fell away and he stacked them neatly on the ground. He left the one proclaiming his name, 'Mr. Robert Sheridan, the Great Magician', uppermost. He looked at the resulting neat Bedford van, painted an unobtrusive shade of grey. It was clearly a tradesman's truck, full of tools and odds and ends of plumbing.

He took out a large envelope and laid it on the pile of sidings, putting a stone on top. Then he got into his van and drove toward Melbourne, which was only twenty-five miles away.

◇◇◇

Phryne was shoved into a steel cage. Someone cut the bonds on her wrists. She heard the door clang behind her. A bolt was shot. The darkness was absolute. She could see nothing. Her legs were free and she had no gag. Her mouth still tasted of blood. The reek of the carnivores was all about her. In front of her, something stirred.

Fur brushed iron and claws sounded on the wooden floor. Something stood up and shook itself with a sound like a beaten carpet.

Phryne had been told that the moment before the prey was seized by the predator, it went limp. It ceased to fear or care. An archaeologist friend had talked about the moment when a lion's teeth closed on his shoulder. Dreamy, he had said. The world had ceased to matter. The last mercy, he had said, to creatures destined to be dinner was that they went down sweetly and gently to death, reconciled to their place on the menu.

'I am not reconciled,' muttered Phryne. She tried to think. Screaming would only alarm the lion and she did not want it alarmed. She squeezed herself into as small a compass as she could, drawing in her limbs and making herself into a ball. Fear almost overcame her. The primitive Phryne who had run from lions on the Pleistocene grasslands was taking over what remained of her mind.

'Nice kitty,' said Phryne, afraid that her voice might have devolved along with her courage.

Police Constable Harris had found a rough edge on a tent peg. It had taken him almost an hour and his wrists had not been improved, but he had weakened his ropes enough to break them. He tore with swollen fingers at the other lines and stood up, staggering. He felt at the walls. They were canvas. He could hear the cough and smell the cigarette smoke of the man who was placed at the tent flap to prevent his escape. Tommy felt in his pocket, took out a pen knife and fumbled it open. They had not even bothered to search him. He slashed at the tent wall. It gaped. Constable Harris walked through the rent and into the circus-scented dark.

Ronald Smythe did not notice that he was gone.

Matthias, Robinson, Samson, Dulcie and Alan Lee had covered the horse lines and the jugglers and tumblers. They interrupted Mr. Burton in his study of Shakespeare's sonnets and he was cross.

'No, I don't know where she is. But I do know who she is. Why? Is she lost?'

Jo Jo the clown nodded. His face was already painted into sad lines but now the underlying flesh echoed them.

'She didn't come when she said, Matt?' snapped Mr. Burton. 'This is serious.' He walked out along his caravan's driving seat and stepped onto Samson's shoulders. The huge man accepted the small added weight without comment. Mr. Burton settled himself comfortably. 'Well, come on.' He tweaked Samson's hair as though it were a rein. 'To the rescue.'

Jones, favouring his groin, got to his feet. 'We'd better do something about the hayseed,' he said roughly. The others followed him to the tent. Ronald Smythe was on guard, chain smoking. 'I heard a scream,' he said nervously. 'What...er...happened?'

Damien Maguire laughed. 'She kicked Jones in the balls and fought like an animal. So we put her where she belongs.' He peered into the tent. 'Hey, you there?'

Maguire lit a match. Apart from some shredded ropes, the tent was empty.

'You idiot!' Jones cuffed Smythe. 'You let him escape!'

Tommy Harris was lost. He blundered around in the dark until he came out into a relatively lighted stretch. A grotesque creature was approaching. It was nine feet tall and had two sets of arms. He gulped. Then it passed him and he saw it was a little man sitting on a big man's shoulders. Detective Inspector Robinson said curtly, 'Ah, Harris. Where the blazes have you been? Where is Fern?'

Constable Harris was about to protest that he had done rather well in freeing himself, all things considered, but this was not the time. He said, 'They got her. Jones and the others. They took her toward a caravan.'

'Where?' snapped Mr. Burton.

Constable Harris looked around helplessly. 'I don't know,' he said. 'It all looks the same in the dark.'

Detective Inspector Robinson swore in a way that would have gained Lizard Elsie's admiration.

Darkness blanketed Phryne's eyes. She was not cold. She was considering death. There was not much chance that she would get out of this cage alive. She stank of blood. She was sure that she was oozing terror. She was losing what grip she had on her wits and she could not reach the bolt. Every time she moved, the creature shifted and came a little closer. She looked and smelt like prey.

'I don't want to die,' she mourned softly, hearing her voice as small as a child's. 'I don't want to die yet. There are a lot of things I haven't done.'

Even the reeking dark in the lion's cage seemed precious and infinitely preferable to whatever lay beyond. She would go out like the flame of a candle. Where does the candle flame go when the candle is blown out?

She laid her painted face against the iron bars and bared her teeth at death.

◇◇◇

'What could you see?' asked Robinson urgently. Harris shook his head.

'Feet,' said Dulcie urgently. 'Running.'

'Catch him!' said Robinson to Harris. Ronald Smythe, fleeing in terror from his allies, was tripped and fell flat on his face. Alan Lee was on his back in a moment.

'Tell us where Fern is,' threatened the carnie in his silky voice, 'or I'll kill you.' Alan Lee was seriously worried and did not allow the presence of two policemen to cramp his invective.

'I'll take you to the Boss,' quavered Ronald. 'Don't hurt me!'

Robinson applied issue handcuffs to Smythe's wrists and he led them to the right.

Jones was standing in the place where a caravan had rested, cursing. Damien Maguire and the other roustabout looked blank. There the searchers found them.

It was a short fight but nasty. Jones yelled for Farrell, dived back for his caravan and came up short facing a monster. It reached out two sets of arms. Samson seized Mr. Jones by the waist and tucked him under his arm as neatly as if he had been a fractious child. He struggled. 'Excuse me, Mr. Burton,' said Samson politely, 'could you help?' The dwarf sprang down from Samson's height and twisted his tie around Jones' neck.

'I am very displeased with you,' he told the enpurpling face. 'If you give my colleague here any little difficulty, I shall have to strangle you all dead, instead of half dead.'

Mr. Jones ceased to struggle.

Harris and Alan Lee circled Damien Maguire, who had a knife. Lee feinted one way, Harris another. Maguire turned, threatening, 'Come closer and I'll stick yer. You won't take me again!' Lee went left, Harris right. The man kept turning so that they could not get behind him.

Robinson had secured the roustabout's hands behind his back by dint of knocking him down and kneeling on him. He watched Maguire with concern. And where was the interfering Miss Fisher?

Jo Jo the clown looked into one of the nearby tents and picked up a large iron skillet. Then he stood just outside the circle with it hidden behind his back. Alan Lee looked at him.

'Ringwise,' said Jo Jo calmly, as if he were giving directions in a rehearsal. Alan Lee moved clockwise, Harris lunged forward, and Jo Jo crowned Damien Maguire with the skillet. The blow made a loud, heavy, soggy noise and the bank-robber fell to earth, he knew not where. They handcuffed him. Jo Jo, Alan Lee and Constable Harris shook hands.

'Now,' said Robinson to the half-conscious Jones, 'where is she?'

Jones spat. Mr. Burton hauled on the tie.

◇◇◇

Phryne had tried once more to undo the bolt. She had the advantage of opposable thumbs, but her hands would not answer her orders. The lion's attention was attracted by the movement. It rolled over, stood up and padded towards her. She shut her eyes. A cold nose slid up her arm, a heavy paw held down her knees. Teeth scraped her skin. Phryne felt it at last. Sleepy acceptance weighted her eyelids. Warmth bloomed in her blood. She sighed on a gust of the predator's breath. The teeth took hold of her arm, pulling her into the middle of the cage.

Then Bruno sniffed her all over, looking for ginger biscuits.

The gathering crowd of rescuers, who had managed to extract from the roustabout the secret of Phryne's whereabouts, came running with torches. Amazing Hans had been woken and carried a loaded rifle, weeping but ready to shoot. Jo Jo, Alan and the lion tamer entered the lions' tent carefully, dreading what they might see.

They looked into all the cages, waking the occupants, who snarled and muttered. Phryne Fisher was not there. Then they came to Bruno's cage beyond the tent wall. They stopped and stared, struck dumb.

A naked woman, bruised and streaked with dirt, was lying curled up in the middle of an iron cage. Her face was painted and her black hair fell forward like a cap. Her head was pillowed on the bear's back. Her hands were buried deep in cinnamon fur. To Alan and Jo Jo, she seemed like a forest goddess, tamer of beasts and invulnerable. To Detective Inspector Robinson, she was evidence of a criminal act which he was intending to take out of Mr. Jones' hide. Samson considerately averted his eyes. Mr. Burton was reminded of a print out of the Marquis de Sade.

To the handcuffed Jones she was an erotic memory which would torment him until, after due process of law, they put a bag over his head, strapped his hands and dropped him into eternity.

Phryne opened her eyes and blinked. 'Oh, there you are,' she said dreamily. 'I can't reach the bolt.'

Jo Jo and Lee undid the cage door and she crawled out. Bruno leaned a questing nose after her and grumbled.

'Anyone got a ginger biscuit?' asked Phryne, and collapsed into the waiting arms.

Chapter Sixteen

'I tell you what, Squire. To speak plain to you, my opinion is that you had better cut it short and drop it. They're very good-natur'd people, my people, but they're accustomed to be quick in their movements; and if you don't act on my advice, I'm damned if I don't believe that they'll pitch you out of the window.'

Hard Times, Charles Dickens

An unconscious Phryne was being cleansed and tended in the girl's tent by Dulcie and Joseph the horse doctor.

Outside, Samson threw down an armload of wood and Mr. Burton kindled a small fire. All the participants of the evening's turmoil sat down on the bone-dry grass. Constable Harris, awed by Samson's size, stared up at the big man. By cripes, but he was huge. Then he asked his chief, 'What do we do now, sir?'

Robinson was tired. 'Nothing to be done for the moment, son. Sergeant Grossmith has taken the prisoners to Rockbank and then he'll come back for us. I've sent out a road alert to all stations between here and Melbourne, but I reckon that bastard Sheridan has shot through. I hate to lose him.'

'After what he did to Miss Parkes, trying to frame her for something she didn't do and nearly driving her mad, is he going to get away?' protested Constable Harris. 'Surely not, sir.'

'We'll catch him.' Robinson accepted a mug from Mr. Burton, who had brewed tea over the fire. 'Don't you worry. You've done well, Harris.'

'Thank you, sir.' Tommy Harris was not as pleased as he might once have been at receiving a compliment from a superior officer.

'What has Sheridan done?' Mr. Burton asked Harris. Because he was sitting down and the dwarf was standing up, Constable Harris was looking into Mr. Burton's eyes. They were bright and intelligent.

'He's done a murder—your Mr. Christopher,' said Tommy. 'And he tried to frame Miss Parkes for it.'

'*He* killed Chris?' Miss Younger had come out to see what all the excitement was. Her face knotted with hatred. Tommy Harris shivered at the sight of such implacable fury and pain.

'Yes.'

'Why?' she wailed.

'I don't know. He said he loved her.' Tommy was getting confused.

Miss Younger made a guttural sound that he would have expected from a wounded animal. Then she demanded in a fierce, hard voice, 'Where is he?'

'He's run,' said Robinson. 'No use hoping to catch him, Miss. But we'll get him in Melbourne, if he ain't took ship and gone by now.'

Mr. Burton tugged at Miss Younger's shirt. 'Sit down and have some tea,' he urged. 'You can't get to him, Miss Younger.'

She pulled away from his touch. 'Freak!' she screamed at him and stumbled into the night. Mr. Burton stood quite still. His face showed no expression.

'Poor woman,' said Farrell from the other side of the fire. 'I'd better go after her. If she should find our Mr. Sheridan there wouldn't be nothing left for you to hang.' He walked away into the dark, calling, 'Molly!'

'Tell me what this reprobate of a magician has done,' insisted Mr. Burton.

Tommy sipped his tea, which was heavily laced with rum, and told the story while the dwarf listened with the closest attention.

'But what will his criminal associates think of him deserting them like this?' Mr. Burton asked in his precise, scholar's voice.

Robinson laughed. 'If Albert Ellis knew about it, he'd spit chips and there'd be more blood on Brunswick Street. But they don't know about it. This tea just about hits the spot, Mr. Burton. Any more in the pot?'

'Certainly,' said Mr. Burton, and refilled the detective inspector's cup.

Tommy Harris caught the dwarf's eye and grinned slowly. Mr. Burton made an excuse and trotted out of the firelight, with Tommy following.

'Constable Harris,' said Mr. Burton, speaking with great deliberation, 'it is not very far to Rockbank, where there is a telephone operator who is already awake. All I need is the number. What do you say?'

Harris drew a deep breath. 'I'm risking my career,' he began. Then he remembered Miss Parkes and her courage and her pain. He recalled Reffo dying in his arms. Lizard Elsie's remembered face grinned at him. He made up his mind and opened his notebook at the page where he had written down Albert Ellis' telephone number. The dwarf needed only one look. Then Harris went back to the fire and Mr. Burton faded into the scent-laden circus night.

◇◇◇

Phryne woke abruptly, stifling a scream. Something was breathing close beside her. She put out a hand and touched hair, slid down and found a human face. Eyelashes flickered against her palm.

She saw that she was lying on a canvas swag in a dark tent. The flap was open. Moonlight streamed in. Outside, she could see a man standing with his heels together in the back-saving stance of a soldier. He was a truly large policeman, in low-voiced conversation with a mountain of muscle. Silver light slid over marble contours. Samson and Sergeant Grossmith were keeping guard over Phryne and discussing horse racing.

Sergeant Grossmith had lodged his captives in the Rockbank lock-up, first evicting the chickens that were the usual inmates. The Rockbank policeman, reinforced with three of Grossmith's own men, was guarding them with a gun.

'I favour Strephon,' murmured Grossmith. 'In this weather, over that sort of track.'

'It's a long distance,' commented Samson. 'I'm backing Statesman. More staying power. And he won the Derby, too.'

Phryne moved a little and yelped. All of her body hurt. Alan Lee said softly, 'It's all right, Phryne,' and stroked a gentle hand down her arm.

'Alan?' She touched his face.

'Yes, it's me, and you're all right. Lie down again.'

'And it's me, beautiful Fern,' said the voice on her other side. Greasepaint smeared over his ugly face, Jo Jo smiled anxiously. 'Unless you want me to go away.'

'No!' Phryne clutched at him with weak fingers. 'No. Please stay. Please, both of you, stay. I was so scared,' she said, lying down between them. 'I'm so cold.'

Alan Lee and the clown locked hands across her, folding her in a double embrace.

'How did you both come to be here?' she wondered aloud.

Jo Jo laughed and said in his treacle-toffee voice, 'Someone had to stay with you and we couldn't agree as to which of us. Dulcie washed off your paint and tended your bruises. We thought that you might have been…molested but you hadn't. But you are going to have legs like a tattooed lady in a few days, Fern. Phryne. A name that tickles. Phryne. Hmm. Alan said that you needed warmth. Contact.'

'He was right.' Phryne snuggled closer to sides and flanks, breathing in vitality and concern. Jo Jo stroked back her black hair with his free hand.

'And since we...er...share your regard...'

'Seeing as we love you,' Alan Lee did not mince words, 'we couldn't leave you. You were limp and Dulcie was afraid for you. She said that you were in shock. She wanted to stay but that head cop said that you'd like men better.'

'Cheek,' murmured Phryne.

'Then it seemed silly for me to have a fight with your other bloke, so we lay down together. I like the clown, Phryne,' said Alan Lee. 'I never been this close to any circus folk before.'

Jo Jo chuckled. 'I never thought I'd be holding hands with a carnie, either. You have a profoundly disturbing influence, Fern. But it won't be for long, I suppose.'

'Don't ask her now, Matt. She's worn out,' said Alan Lee. Phryne was falling asleep.

'Ask me what?'

'Not to leave us,' said Alan Lee reluctantly. Phryne reached out both hands. The clown and the carnie took them.

'I can't leave now,' she said drowsily. 'What a silly thing to say. I've got a contract. I'm a rider...in Farrell's...Circus.'

They waited in the dark but she did not speak again. She had leaned her head against Jo Jo and one hand lay curled open on Alan's chest. Phryne Fisher and Fern Williams were both asleep.

◇◇◇

On Tuesday, after an early lunch, most of the performers assembled in the big top. Phryne had dressed in her cotton shift and was redolent of goanna oil. She had been repossessed of her belongings, and Dot's St. Christopher medal hung once more at her throat. Her fear was gone. She felt renewed. She had come close enough to death to smell his breath and she had not died. She was, however, so stiff that Samson had carried her into the ring and placed her in a chair as though he were handling a new-laid egg. She sat between Alan Lee and Jo Jo the clown. Dulcie and her partner Tom were there. Amazing Hans sat beside them. Mr. Burton had perched on a tub on which elephants were wont to stand. The Catalans were gathered into an interested group. Even the Flying Bevans had made an appearance. Bernie, without Bruno, talked racing with Sergeant Grossmith. Sam Farrell sat in the middle of the ring, turning his hat in his hands.

Robinson walked out to join Farrell and clapped his hands. No one paid any attention. Sam Farrell stood up and cracked the ringmaster's whip. Instant silence fell.

'You want to know what has been happening to Farrell's Circus?' he roared. 'Bit of shoosh and we'll find out.' He bowed to the policeman and sat down again.

'This is a long story,' Robinson began. 'You'll have to be patient because I don't know it all, either. We'll start with the furthest event in time. A man called Jones approached Mr. Farrell with an offer to buy half of his circus. January, wasn't it, Mr. Farrell?'

'Yes.'

'Mr. Farrell refused. Then things began to go wrong. Fires were lit. Animals died. The show began to lose money. So, in March, Mr. Farrell had to accept the offer from Sweet Dreams Pty Ltd. They bought half of his circus. With the deal, however, came Mr. Jones. He could not be said to have been an asset. And things continued to go wrong. In April the circus harboured an escaped prisoner called William Seddon. He accompanied you in the guise of a roustabout and took ship at Portland for Rio. Once there, the cocky bu—bloke couldn't help gloating. He sent me a postcard. That's when I found out about Exit. Seddon had escaped by being carried out of Pentridge in a coffin. We think that it had a double shell and Seddon was snugged under a real corpse brought in with the laundry. The prison doctor may not be a terrific practitioner but he can diagnose death all right, when he sees it.'

This got a laugh.

'More things went wrong. Farrell was losing money, even though he had given in and sold half the show. Mr. Jones and others were there to make sure that when Sweet Dreams Pty Ltd offered to buy the other half, keeping Farrell on as manager, he would agree. Exit wanted the circus to be entirely under their control. Where do you hide a leaf? In a forest. Where do you hide a wanted man or an escaped prisoner? In a circus. It has a floating population of runaways and roustabouts. Although they're not performers, some of them wear paint when they move nets and things in the ring. What Jones and Exit didn't know was that you can't keep secrets in a circus.'

Phryne looked to either side, at the dark gypsy profile and the lumpy countenance. She took both hands in her own.

'You identified Jones and the three others as outsiders almost as soon as they stepped onto your site. You began to suspect. And Mr. Christopher knew. He must have had a sight of Jones' papers, or overheard a conversation, because he wrote it all down in a little book. But because he was an honourable man,' Robinson looked sidelong at Grossmith and dared him to snicker, 'he went to tell Farrell first. This is a family circus and Farrell had been his friend. He told Farrell. Jones overheard. And so Mr. Christopher had to die.'

Miss Younger groaned. Phryne looked at her with deep pity and guilt. Here was someone whom she couldn't help. Dulcie moved closer to Molly and took her hand. The horsemaster endured the touch for a moment, then snatched her hand away and wrapped her arms around herself, as though she were in great pain. Sam Farrell hung his head and his fingers bent his hat brim out of shape.

'This murder was done by the man who was the proprietor of Exit,' Robinson went on, 'the Mr. Denny who was the sole active officer of Sweet Dreams. He did it so well that we arrested the wrong person for it.'

This got a laugh as well. Robinson held up a hand.

'We kept her because her safety was endangered. The murderer was using some city criminals for his Exit schemes. There's been a feud between them and when one lot informed to us, a man was shot dead in Brunswick Street in broad daylight. We didn't like the look of things.

'Then, into the equation came an interfering woman.' He purposely did not look at Phryne. 'She had been asked to solve the circus' problems and find the saboteurs. She did that in a few days. But she did not know enough about Exit, until last night. She was captured with my constable, and after they pooled their information we all knew who it was. Then it was a matter of catching the villains and rescuing the innocent.' Phryne chuckled at his application of the term to herself. 'So we did that and here we are.'

'But who is the murderer? That mongrel Jones?' asked Bernie, reflecting that humans were a lot more complex than bears.

'No,' said Phryne, trying to stand and failing as her knees gave under her. Jo Jo and Alan Lee held her up between them. 'It was Mr. Robert Sheridan, the magician.'

'But how?' teased Robinson. 'He had an alibi.'

'Easy. He was an illusionist, remember? The disappearing Dulcie trick? The dagger in the air? The ceilings of the house were holed by water, discoloured. All he had to do was to put a paper patch over the plaster as he removed it, so that it would look the same from the ground. Then he needed a couple of pulleys and a solid, heavy dagger suspended on fishing line. He could poise the dagger, point down, above the paper patch. He knew that Mr. Christopher always slept on his back because of the cream on his face, and he could guess that Mrs. Witherspoon wouldn't like her guests to move the furniture around, so his bed would stay in the same place. The end of the line passed over the pulley, along to the other in a similar hole in his own ceiling, and down into his room. He could release it any time he liked. He could then go down to tea and wait for someone to discover the body. The door was locked and bolted. The only way in was through the window and only Miss Parkes could have got in that way.

'It was a really clever, utterly wicked plan. All that the police would find—did find—was Mr. Christopher dead, transfixed by the missing knife, and a few sheets of paper, broken when Sheridan pulled the knife back up again. There's enough space in the roof for him to crawl along, I'll bet. He just pasted another prepared patch over the hole, removed his apparatus and smiled at the cops. The police arrested Miss Parkes. He set her up. He stashed the weapon in her room. Locks don't even slow him down. He tried to get rid of me last night by putting a splinter into Missy's blanket. I found it. That must have irritated him. But Jones says that he got his orders from Mr. Sheridan the magician.'

'Where is he, then?' demanded Miss Younger, really wanting to know.

'He's gone,' said Robinson. 'We'll get him. Roadblocks went up last night. But he was the mastermind. Jones'll hang for the murder of poor bloody Reffo in Brunswick Street. The rest of the 'Roy Boys won't be walking pavements for a good few years. Smythe'll go to trial for his original offences. Maguire'll go back to jail for life, for armed robbery and escaping lawful custody and for attempted rape and attempted murder of Fern here.'

Phryne swayed on her feet, tasting a backwash of terror. Her escorts bore her up, clown's arm and carnie's arm crossing at her back.

'Steady, Fern,' murmured the clown. 'The show must go on, you know.'

As she grinned weakly, Mr. Farrell stood up.

'What of the show?' he asked. 'What about Farrell's Circus?'

'Ah. Now, there's a letter.' Robinson groped in his pocket. 'Yes. This was found on the pile of decorated panels from Mr. Sheridan's truck. It's addressed to you,' he told the astonished Phryne. 'Shall I read it?' Phryne nodded and Robinson began to read. '"Dear Fern (for I will preserve your pseudonym), *Vicisti, Galilaee!* You have conquered. I have just been privileged to listen to your admirably detailed exposition of all my little plots from behind the wall of a certain tent. I don't know to whom you were talking but if that fair young man is indeed Constable Harris then I am sunk. You seem to have found the splinter in Missy's blanket. You are a very dangerous woman.

'"This, then, is my *Apologia pro sua vita.*"' Phryne snorted. Mr. Sheridan couldn't even get his Latin right. '"It was so easy,

Fern. The skills which I have laboured so long to learn were not being valued as they deserved. Wirth's let me go and Sole Brothers did not appreciate me. So when I obtained employment (at a derisory salary) with Farrell's Circus, I decided to increase my income and to show the world what magic can do.

'"You are aware how easily the human eye is deceived. It was simplicity itself to smuggle in a suitable corpse, a pauper from the morgue. Then it was just as easy to smuggle William Seddon out in a trick coffin. He was a little cramped but he was very grateful. He paid me a hundred pounds, having come into several inheritances. Likewise, I instructed Damien Maguire in some elementary sleights of hand and provided him with chloroform and a hacksaw by distracting the guard. And Ronald Smythe left his house as a policeman. Among other policemen he blended until he could slip away and join the circus. He had made an attempt to remove his fingerprints with acid. This, as you are aware, cannot be done. However the consequent pain seems to have soured his temper. I was sorry that he had to escape. A detestable little man.

'"Even more revolting was Killer Jones, the person I borrowed from the Fitzroy Boys, led by Albert Ellis. I do trust that he comes to a bad end. I'm sure that you will do your best to attain this much wished for result. I told Pretty Iris about Exit, once, when I was drunk. I fear that she told the Brunswick Boys and they told the police. I had to order Reffo, who was Pretty Iris' messenger, to be shot. This was regrettable. But I doubt if he will be much missed. I wanted Jones because I needed someone who was in a position of authority to ruin the circus. That stubborn fellow, Farrell, would not deal on ordinary commercial lines. He had to be forced and Jones was the man to do it.

'"I do hope,"' the letter continued blandly, '"that he has not done you too much damage, Fern. I ordered him to subdue you and keep you out of the way for the night. But Jones is terribly prone to exceed his orders."'

Phryne flinched. Alan Lee hissed a curse through his teeth and Jo Jo hugged Phryne tighter. Samson pounded a stony fist on a massive knee.

'"But if you are reading this you are still alive and that is the main thing."' Robinson's flat voice did not rob the writer of any of his offensiveness. '"Now, I am not coming back, so I have given you my half of the circus. The deed is all drawn up and signed. I hope that this might be some recompense for whatever it was that Jones did to you, Fern. I have made my money and my mark and can now retire. I doubt that you will see me again.

'"Think of me kindly,"' the letter went on. Incredulity blossomed in Robinson's voice and he began the paragraph again. '"Think of me kindly. I have killed the only person I have ever loved. I had a brief fling with Miss Minton and tried to forget Christine with Pretty Iris, who had something of the same cool aloofness. But it was no good. When it came to a matter of money, of course, I had no choice. I killed her because she knew about me and I could not risk disclosure then. All I can say is that she died instantly and in her sleep. I had drugged her and Miss Parkes, who struck me as a very good candidate for the scapegoat. The knife was a twin of the one used in my act. If you examine the ceiling in Christine's room, you will be able to poke your finger through the hole. Illusion. It is all illusion." It's signed "Robert Sheridan, the Great Magician".'

Immediately, every person within hearing distance yelled their opinion of the writer. Miss Younger screamed, 'He was a man! Chris was a man. I'll kill him. I'll kill him, the bastard!' Dulcie was trying to calm her and seething with fury. Phryne went cold, then flushed red. She was trembling uncontrollably. The Catalans, who had received a French translation of the letter from Mr. Burton, scowled in perfect unison. '*Mare de Déu! Monstruos*!' Dogs barked. Toby the clown stirred from his trance to comment, 'Judas.' His neighbour stared at him. 'Bastard,' added Toby, just to prove that it had not been a fluke.

'Shut up!' yelled Robinson, his voice lost in the babble. Amazing Hans asked, 'Could we just catch him and put him in with the lions? That's what Jones wanted to do to Fern. I wonder which lion? Prince, maybe. He'd bite off his head.' Samson rose to his feet, took an iron stanchion and bent it between his teeth.

Farrell cracked his whip again and the voices died down.

'Well, that's the end of a horrible story. When they catch him we can leave him to the law. He's confessed he's a murderer and he'll swing for it.'

The ringmaster had inbred authority. They were quiet now. 'You have to decide,' he said quietly, 'whether Farrell's Circus is to go on. I have let you down. I shouldn't have sold to Sweet Dreams. I should've run that cur Jones out of my show the moment he laid a hand on the first girl. You relied on me to protect you. I didn't. I even allowed an innocent rider to be badly mistreated, then nearly murdered. Half of the show now belongs to her and the way things stand she'll never want to see a circus again. What do you want me to do?'

'Question is,' said Dulcie simply. 'What does she want to do?'

Phryne had conquered her fear. She looked at the deed in her hands, which Detective Inspector Robinson had passed to her.

'I'll give it to you, Mr. Farrell,' she said. 'If you want me to. Then you can keep it or sell it. But the financial circumstances being what they must be, I can come to an arrangement with a wealthy friend of mine. She can fund you for another year. Then, if the show starts making money, you can pay her back and she'll give you your circus again.'

'Would she do that?' he asked suspiciously.

'Oh, yes.' Phryne smiled sunnily. 'She loves circuses. That's the offer. Which do you want?'

'Do we go on?' asked Sam Farrell, looking around the ring.

There was a short silence. Then Mr. Burton said crisply, 'Of course.' The Bevans conferred and nodded. So did the Catalans. Amazing Hans said, 'I'll stay and see how it goes.' Bernie yelled, 'Yes!' Miss Younger looked up from her folded hands and whispered, 'Please. It's all I've got left.'

'We go on,' said Farrell, taking off his hat and mopping his face. He looked at his watch and grinned. 'And now,' he added, raising his whip, 'just in time and for your especial delectation and delight, Farrell's Circus and Wild Beast Show presents...'

The drummer found his drum and played a roll. 'The Melbourne Cup!'

Two tumblers brought in his bakelite radio, trailing a cable from the generator truck. Mr. Farrell turned the dial and the announcer said blithely through crackling interference, 'And it's a beautiful day for the races.'

You could have heard a pin drop. Robinson reflected that circus people were all mad.

'See?' said Samson to Sergeant Grossmith ten minutes later. 'I told you. Statesman had the staying power.'

Dulcie, who had put a bet on Demost for a place, collected from Mr. Burton and gloated over ten shillings.

'I think that I'll go back to bed,' said Phryne. 'I'm not as well as I thought I was.'

Unmarked by anyone but Miss Younger, the carnie and the clown escorted Phryne out of the big top.

Chapter Seventeen

'Squire, shake hands, first and last! Don't be cross with us poor vagabonds. People must be amused. They can't always be a-learning, nor yet they can't always be a-working, they ain't made for it. You must have us, Squire. Do the wise thing and the kind thing too and make the best of us, not the worst!'

Hard Times, Charles Dickens*

That same Tuesday morning Mr. Sheridan drove his unobtrusive van into the docks. It was six o'clock and there was no gang working. He had bought a passage to Bolivia on a small cargo tramp called *Legerdemain*. He thought the name a charming coincidence. His Oxford tweed suit was immaculate and his manner as smooth as ever. He hummed as he stopped the van by the first shed.

A flurry of many-coloured pigeons sprang suddenly into the dawn sky. Mr. Sheridan was puzzled. There must be someone about and he had seen no one.

A cold metal tube touched his cheek. He turned his head slowly. It was the barrel of a shotgun. Behind it was a sneer.

'Going somewhere, Boss?'

* lisp omitted in the interests of clarity

'Oh, it's you, Louis. You gave me quite a start. Take that gun out of my ear.'

'You're trying to shoot through, Boss.' Behind Louis was Albert Ellis with all his rat's teeth showing. 'You've left Killer in quod. He'll hang. And you were running out on the rest of us. That's not friendly, is it, boys?'

'Not very friendly at all,' agreed Cyclone Freddy.

'If you think you can just leave us in the lurch, you're wrong. Where's the money?' demanded Ellis.

Terrified, Mr. Sheridan went the colour of a tallow candle. They meant it. The world was going out of his control. His voice shook, losing its affected unctuousness. He dragged out his wallet.

'You can have it. You can have it all! Just don't kill me. You can't kill me, Ellis!'

Albert Ellis took the wad of bank notes and smiled gently. 'Wrong again,' he said. He flicked his finger at Wholesale Louis, who tripped both triggers. The twelve-gauge shotgun roared.

They watched with interest as the remains of Mr. Sheridan twitched, spouting gouts of blood.

'He's dead, Boss,' said Louis, turning away and breaking the gun open. He stowed it inside the Gladstone bag in which he had smuggled it past the gate. Then he took a last look at the mess which had been Robert Sheridan, the Great Magician. 'Christ have mercy,' he gasped, backing away and crossing himself. The others crowded to look. Something that could recall his childhood Catholicism to Wholesale Louis must be dreadful indeed.

In the blood-soaked chest, something stirred. Bloody white and red fragments were all that remained of Mr. Sheridan's head. He could not have been alive. Albert Ellis and Cyclone Freddy followed a terrified Wholesale Louis out of the vicinity as fast as they could. Whatever it was that was happening with that corpse, they did not want to know. Besides, someone must have heard the gun and soon there would be inconvenient questions asked of bystanders.

The lump in the tweed coat moved again. It struggled forward. A white dove, spattered with blood, poked its head out from the ruin of its master's natty suit. Seeing no predator, it fluttered groggily up onto the truck window, gripping the ledge with its claws. It preened shakily, distilling red drops from its beak, shook itself, then flew upward. There was a flourish of snowy wings, fanning out as it wheeled, puzzled. Then the magician's last dove settled on the grain-shed roof, where the pigeons pecked companionably in the red and gold sunrise.

Three weeks later, Lizard Elsie and Miss Parkes were sitting together in a room in Mrs. Witherspoon's refined house for paying gentlefolk. Miss Minton was gone. Her producer had come up trumps. She had landed a dancing part in a travelling show and was in Sydney.

Constable Harris had paid a visit and demonstrated the trick ceiling, finding that the magician had left his two pulleys and the fishing line in place. Tommy had operated the weighted line and the force of the fall had driven the knife six inches into the mattress.

'Houdini's trick,' Tommy had explained to Mrs. Witherspoon. 'He couldn't even make up his own trap.'

Mrs. Witherspoon was mortified. She had trusted Mr. Sheridan and mistrusted Miss Parkes and she felt terrible. That was the only reason why Lizard Elsie the sailor's friend was dwelling under her genteel roof.

'Well, Elsie?' asked Miss Parkes. 'What are you going to do now?'

'Look for another sailor, I reckon.' Elsie grinned. With her hair combed and with clean clothes, she had gained a certain gypsy beauty. She bore her fifty years very well. Miss Parkes took her hand.

'You could stay here,' she suggested. Elsie squeezed the hand for a moment, then released it.

'I'm too bloody old a dog to learn new tricks,' she said gruffly. 'I'll get a room and find a man. Don't you fucking worry about me.'

Miss Parkes reached into her handbag and laid something in Elsie's lap. It was a police-issue dinner knife, sharpened to a razor point.

'What's this?' asked Elsie.

'It's a present. I won't need it any more.'

Elsie shoved the knife into her old black handbag and rose to go.

'Stay one more night,' begged Miss Parkes. 'Have dinner with me. We'll invite Tommy Harris. What do you say, Elsie?'

'Yair.' Elsie smiled her wickedest smile. 'He owes us a favour, I reckon. Pity he ain't a sailor. I always had a fancy for sailors.'

◇◇◇

At the same time, approaching Sebastopol, Phryne Fisher was discovering that making love in a moving caravan, with the windows open, the air moving sweetly over naked skin and the horse walking at a steady pace, was both delicious and soothing to the bruises.

Miss Younger, who had seemed more settled since the news of Mr. Sheridan's death had come to the circus via a week-old newspaper, had seen Phryne climb into the clown's caravan and had not snarled. A packet of photographic plates of Mr. Christopher's book had been delivered to her by a sympathetic Robinson. She would read them every night until she died. She looked at the caravan with a perfectly blank face, then wheeled Bell and galloped off in a cloud of snuffy dust.

◇◇◇

On the road to Hamilton Phryne walked toward Skipton Church. It seemed like an ordinary bluestone building; she wondered why Mr. Burton had insisted, chuckling, that she see it.

She paused with her hand on the wrought-iron gates. White things poked out of the tower. Gargoyles, if she was not mistaken.

Phryne stared. Four gargoyles grinned demoniacally from the church tower. There was something odd about them. They were not pigs or dogs or dragons, like the standard received gargoyle of Notre Dame. She edged closer. What were they based on? Curly decorations, horns. Phryne began to laugh helplessly, clinging to the church gate. Skipton Church was guarded from evil spirits by four gargoyles in the shape of fanged, feral sheep.

She had almost recovered from Skipton Church when she was watching a team of sweating yokels in a tug of war with Rajah at Lake Bolac. Rajah allowed them to drag with their utmost force, without moving a muscle. Then she reached out with her trunk and gave a sharp tug and fifty men flew off their feet and into Lake Bolac with a mighty splash.

◇◇◇

Detective Inspector Robinson attended the committal of Albert Ellis and his gang for various offences, including the murder of Robert Sheridan, stage magician. He sat through the whole lengthy, complicated brief of evidence with a broad smile on his face.

◇◇◇

Farrell's Circus and Wild Beast Show was nearing Hamilton. Jo Jo the clown kissed Phryne awake.

'Almost at Hamilton,' he observed. 'You're going home from here, aren't you, Fern?'

'Yes.'

'Will we see you again?'

She sat up abruptly and dragged on her cotton dress. 'Do you think I'm going to waste a skill that cost me so many bruises to learn?' she demanded. 'I'm a circus rider now, and don't you forget it. And I found you, too.' Her voice softened. 'I won't forget you, Matt dear. I'll see you again.'

Hamilton was a prosperous town, clean and windswept. The circus trucks turned off Ballarat Road for the camping place down by the railway line. The parade, Phryne's last, proceeded along Cox Street and into Gray Street, attended by running children.

Down Gray Street went Phryne, mounted this time on Rajah the elephant, high up and elated. Jo Jo the clown was encircled by Rajah's trunk, swept up and dropped unceremoniously beside her. Drums banged and trumpets tooted. Miss Younger led her liberty horses past the Argyle Arms, where the drinkers cheered. Phryne tossed her head and her crown of feathers danced.

'Oh, this is lovely,' she sighed. The clown laid a hand on her thigh.

'So lovely that I don't know how you can bear to leave us,' he said. He flung an armload of bright pink leaflets to the crowd. Shearers and stockmen and graziers stood and gaped. Phryne caught a paper as it flew past.

'FARRELL'S CIRCUS AND WILD BEAST SHOW,' it read. 'THE BEST SHOW ON EARTH. LIONS! TIGHTROPE WALKERS! BRUNO THE BEAR! TUMBLERS! TRAPEZE ARTISTES! COME ONE, COME ALL!'

'I don't know either,' she told the clown. 'But I have to go. My dear Matt,' she said, pulling his hair, 'you won't forget Fern?'

'Never while I have wits,' declared the clown, sliding sideways. Rajah caught him and replaced him neatly. The screaming that ensued if she allowed someone to fall off hurt her ears.

The Victoria Hotel emptied, and men waved hats from the men's outfitters across the road.

'There's the doom of the circus,' said Jo Jo, pointing. Phryne looked and saw a grand building. Emblazoned on its high plastered front was 'The Prince Regent Cinema'.

'Will you give me a home, Fern, when the circus is all gone and no one laughs at clowns any more? When the road is only a path that leads to the movies?' There were real tears in Jo Jo's grey eyes.

Phryne embraced him, careless of greasepaint, and the gentlemen looking through the window of the Hamilton Club made coarse remarks about circus ways.

'Of course,' said Phryne. 'But I don't believe it will happen.'

She looked back on the procession. Spangles and tinsel sparkled in the hot sunlight and the drums beat and the cymbals clashed. Hooves pounded and camels bubbled and Miss Younger's horses shone like snow. Clowns ran tumbling along the pavement. Dulcie and Tom tossed an assortment of odd articles from one to the other. The crowd laughed and jostled.

'No,' said Phryne. 'The circus is too strong. It can't die.'

Chapter Eighteen

Mid pleasures and palaces,
Though we may roam,
Be it ever so humble,
There's no place like home.

'Home Sweet Home', John Payne

After the grand parade Phryne walked out of the big top leaving Missy with a final handful of carrots, and met Dot her maid under the canvas awning. The ring was blindingly bright with lights. Trapeze artists hung from the flies. Tumblers and jugglers bowed. The crowd roared.

'Hello, Miss,' said Dot uncertainly. 'Miss Phryne?'

'Yes,' said Phryne. 'Come on, Dot, I can't bear goodbyes. Where's the car?'

'Just over there, Miss. I've brought a hamper and some clothes for you.'

'What?'

'Well, Miss, you can't travel like that.'

Phryne became aware of Dot's immaculate stockings and polished shoes, her small dark-brown straw hat and the quiet good taste of her ochre linen dress. She felt suddenly dishevelled and garish in scarlet tunic, none too clean, and mended tights. She pulled off her feather crown.

'No, I suppose I can't,' she said regretfully.

Phryne collected her suitcase, changed her clothes and left her costume on her bed.

The applause and music broke out again behind her. She hurried Dot across the circus and into the carnival.

'You didn't think that you could run away from us all?' asked a voice as rich as treacle toffee.

Jo Jo, Dulcie, Samson with Mr. Burton on his shoulders, and Alan Lee were standing by the car. Dulcie got up from her seat on the running board.

'Goodbye,' she said. 'Come again. You'll make a good rider.' She kissed Phryne and faded back into the darkness. Samson shook her hand and Mr. Burton leaned down to allow her to kiss him. 'Don't forget that you're part owner,' Mr. Burton reminded her. 'You must come and see how your investment is going.' Alan Lee stroked her gently on the cheek and smiled. 'You won't forget me,' he stated.

Bruno appeared, on a chain. Phryne reached into the big car and gave Bernie a whole tin of imported English gingerbread. She awarded the bear a handful. He licked her and stood up for a last waltz.

Jo Jo stepped forward and they gave him room. 'Fern, Fern, for you I shall yearn,' he sang. 'I'll never forget you Fern, my Fern.'

'I won't forget you,' she said, blinking back tears. 'Jo Jo my dear.'

She got into the car with Dot, who wrapped a rug around her. Mr. Butler started the Hispano-Suiza and the engine roared like a lion. The others backed away. But Jo Jo jumped on the running board and brought something out from under his shirt with a flourish. He dropped it into her hands, then tumbled away.

The Hispano-Suiza took the empty country road from Hamilton. Powerful headlights lit up trees and sheep.

'Miss?' asked Dot, worried by her silence. 'How are you?'

Phryne took stock. She was stronger. Her muscles had firmed and developed. Her hands were hard and calloused and her fingernails were broken. Her once-white skin was tanned.

The silkiness of the carriage-rug lining made her realize all of a sudden how tired she was of rough cloth next to her skin, of eating Mrs. Thompson's skilly for lunch and sleeping in a tent. The clean scent of Dot's soap and the leather-polish smell of the car made her aware that she, by contrast, stank of sweat and unwashed hair and greasepaint and horses. She felt how much she had missed silk and hot water and service and sleeping in a soft bed. How much, too, she had missed belonging. She had no place in the circus. She belonged to the comfortable world of telephones and eggs for breakfast, of coffee brewed in a pot and library subscriptions and handmade shoes.

But she had been stripped of all her helpers and her luxuries and she had survived. She had triumphed. Phryne, all by herself, had conquered terror and violence and death. She had even learned a new skill. If all else failed, she thought as the great car rushed through the hot night, she could be a trick rider in a circus.

She looked down to see what she had been cradling in her hands since she had left Farrell's. Jo Jo's last gift. She held it up to the light. It was a red satin heart with 'Matthias' embroidered on it. Jo Jo the clown had given her his heart. She pressed it to her breast, over her own heart.

Lightning flashed directly overhead. Mr. Butler stopped the car and got out to put up the hood. Thunder cracked and rumbled.

'The weather's breaking at last,' commented Phryne and patted her maid's hand. 'I'm all right, Dot, just a bit dazed. But I'm glad to see you,' she added. 'And I'm glad to be going home.'

To receive a free catalog of Poisoned Pen Press titles, please contact us in one of the following ways:

Phone: 1-800-421-3976
Facsimile: 1-480-949-1707
Email: info@poisonedpenpress.com
Website: www.poisonedpenpress.com

Poisoned Pen Press
6962 E. First Ave. Ste. 103
Scottsdale, AZ 85251